D1015745

murder alfresco

Also by Nadia Gordon

Sharpshooter

Death by the Glass

nadia gordon

murder alfresco

a sunny mccoskey napa valley mystery

CHRONICLE BOOKS
SAN FRANCISCO

Though Napa Valley and the adjacent regions are full of characters, none of them are in this book. This is a work of fiction. Names, places, persons, and incidents are products of the author's imagination or are used fictionally. Any resemblance to actual people, places, or events is entirely coincidental.

Library of Congress Cataloging-in-Publication Data:

Gordon, Nadia.
Murder alfresco : a Sunny McCoskey Napa Valley mystery / Nadia Gordon.
p. cm.
ISBN 0-8118-4630-X
1. Women—Crimes against—Fiction. 2. Napa Valley (Calif.)—Fiction.
3. Wine and wine making—Fiction. 4. Sausalito (Calif.)—Fiction.
5. Restaurants—Fiction. 6. Women cooks—Fiction. 7. Houseboats—Fiction.
8. Cookery—Fiction. I. Title.
PS3607.0594M87 2005
813'.6—dc22

2004029778

Manufactured in Canada

Book and jacket design by Benjamin Shaykin
Composition by Kristen Wurz
Typeset in Miller and Bodoni 6

Distributed in Canada by Raincoast Books
9050 Shaughnessy Street
Vancouver, British Columbia V6P 6E5

10 9 8 7 6 5 4 3 2 1

Chronicle Books LLC
85 Second Street
San Francisco, California 94105
www.chroniclebooks.com

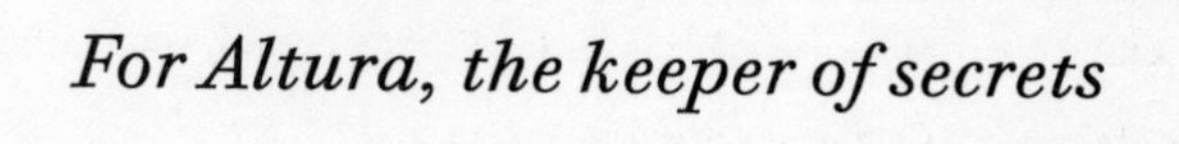

For Altura, the keeper of secrets

The thread of consequence cannot be broken.

Ted Hughes
Tales from Ovid

I

Gray. For more than a month, the sky over St. Helena had explored the theme. Billowing gray clouds were followed by flat gray clouds, which were followed by gauzy gray clouds, granite-gray clouds, and steely gray clouds. A steady rain fell on the sodden earth, and thick gusts of wind whipped the hilltops, sending showers of sickle-shaped eucalyptus leaves twirling groundward. Vineyard workers layered rain gear over wool and fleece and slogged through the wet to examine the vines, sinking to their rubber-booted ankles in mud. And yet, there were those who did not object. In a town overrun by tourists much of the year, in a region with no shortage of hot days and blue skies, a rainy March was not necessarily unwelcome and many took secret pleasure in it. They stayed home, lit fires, read books, and listened to the gusts of temperamental winds and the patter of drops thrown against windows.

The wet weather broke suddenly. One morning a tender, head-high breeze glided down Main Street. The handful of early pedestrians out patrolling the sidewalks and lingering at corners turned to face it, letting it lift and toss their hair. Moments later, the sun emerged warm and bright. The Napa Valley basked in the first sunshine of spring. Within a week, the landscape was transformed. Tufts of canary-yellow oxalis blooms sprang up in all but the most disciplined yards, daffodils and tulips emerged from bare soil, and white blossoms popped out of the darkly naked branches of fruit trees. Fresh calla lilies stretched their slender torsos from between great green leaves and uncurled spirals of creamy white flesh.

On the night that Heidi Romero was murdered, Sunny McCoskey went to bed early. She had left the window open and a cold, wet breeze came in, lightly scented with apple blossoms from the tree in the backyard. Tiny white petals drifted in the bedroom window and settled on the hardwood floor.

Hours later the telephone woke her from a deep sleep. It was Andre Morales, the dark-haired, golden-eyed, supple-skinned local chef she'd recently begun to think of as her boyfriend, even if she hadn't actually called him that yet. He asked her to come out for a late, after-work drink with him and some of the others from the restaurant, and she said yes before she was really awake. After she hung up, she had no choice but to get out of bed and get dressed. It was no good introducing disappointment to a relationship so early on.

In the bathroom, she did her best to put a fresh face on an essentially exhausted head after a long day at work. Luckily the night would lend some cover. She ran her fingers through her short auburn hair, then brushed on eye shadow and mascara. Her green eyes were looking more lively. There was nothing she could do about her hands and arms, which were nicked and scarred with scrapes, cuts, and burns all the way to the elbows from years in the kitchen. Her nails were as short and plain as her palms were callused.

Half an hour later she was standing in the crowded front room of the Dusty Vine, staring at Andre Morales's shoulder blades as he pushed his way ahead of her to the bar. The Dusty Vine had endured a remodel in the last months. A former honky-tonk full of regulars and grit, it now boasted Italian furniture and Parisian lounge music. The regulars stubbornly persisted alongside the crowd of would-be and actual hipsters. Andre handed her a beer and led the way to a fresh-looking group gathered in a far corner that greeted them with loud enthusiasm.

After last call, they left her truck in the lot at the Dusty Vine and took Andre's old Porsche back to his place. An entourage followed.

When they arrived, he set the mood quickly. He put on music, lit candles, opened several bottles of wine, and assembled a station for making gin martinis. He emptied his cabinets of glasses as a stream of guests arrived, mostly members of the young, hardworking, and harder-playing crowd that kept the local gourmet establishments operating. These were the cooks, servers, maître d's, and bartenders who worked in the business because the tips were good, the job physical, and the hours conducive to days free for school, sports, and artistic pursuits. They were in possession of their freedom, in concept if not reality, and there was an air of confidence about them. They had dreams and futures, and they knew the secrets behind the privileged experiences they sold. That eighteen-dollar salad was made from thirty-cents-worth of arugula and fennel, and the sixty-dollar bottle of wine could be had for twelve dollars at Safeway. They might not own the houses or drive the cars, but they drank better wine and ate better food than the people they served, and they did it without selling their souls. It was this sensation, Sunny suspected, that gave them the stamina to work all night and then go out.

Andre joked that he liked the way his friends looked next to his furniture. It was true that they were generally young and well-dressed and beautiful. They took up their places beside his modern lamps and on his minimalist, rectangular couches and ottomans as though they had been cast for the roles. A slender girl lay on his shaggy white rug with her Lucite heels and candy-colored toes in the air behind her. He looked around the conversation-filled room with satisfaction. "What a night. Sometimes it all comes together." He gave Sunny a kiss and headed for a group that hailed him.

Sunny filled her glass with a nameless white wine and carried it around. Andre was talking to a couple that had recently taken over the woman's parents' winery and were in the process of revamping its branding and image. Sunny mingled. A woman she knew slightly from various food-related events introduced her to the man she was with. The three of them spoke for several minutes, then were separated by another friend's arrival. Sunny killed some time with a guy who handled PR at a big winery where the wine was not as good as it used to be. He went to refill his glass and she lingered, wondering what next. Across the room, Andre was engaged in an animated discussion with two slick-looking guys she'd never met. The clock on the kitchen wall said two-twenty. Her social buzz was waning. It had, in fact, bottomed out and come to a complete standstill. She scanned the room for a familiar face. The only person she recognized was a girl from Andre's restaurant who waited tables. She was being chatted up by a guy with a goatee and a thick chain hanging from his belt loop. Sunny put her glass on the kitchen counter and walked down the hall to the room where everyone had left their bags and jackets. She moved swiftly, without thinking, collecting her wrap and purse and letting herself out the backdoor almost before she decided to do so. She trotted down the driveway like a fugitive slipping away from a guard.

Outside, a fine mist chilled the air. Shivering in the cold, she walked to the end of the driveway and sat down on the low stone wall that ran up to it. Muffled music and laughter came from the house. St. Helena was not exactly Manhattan. It was not going to be easy to find a cab. She rummaged in her purse for her cell phone, which returned her button pushing with an oblivious blank gaze. She had forgotten to recharge it again. She looked back at the house and its rich cache of functional telephones. Ahead lay a cold night and a dark country road. A lone streetlight cast a fuzzy dome of light in the distance.

Even if she went back inside and called, she would be lucky to reach anyone. There were two cab companies in St. Helena. At this hour, she would be lucky if there was a car on duty. It would take forever to get here. She could walk home faster. Yes, it was dark and she was dressed for a booty call not a hike, but unless she wanted to go back to the party and wait for Andre to extricate himself from his guests, the quickest route home and into her soft bed was a brief, bracing journey on foot. Sunny started to walk.

It could have been worse. She had almost worn the pointy alligator heels, until she remembered the stiletto-eating gaps in the rustic plank floor at the Dusty Vine. Instead, she'd chosen a wispy pair of ballet flats. The rest of the outfit was equally insubstantial. There was a shirt consisting of two puny layers of colored mesh, a pair of light jeans, and a pashmina scarf. Still, she might have been wearing a skirt, for example, or a skimpy dress. She pulled the scarf around her shoulders, tucked the ends into the top of her jeans, and dug her hands into her pockets.

The important part was she could breathe again. To walk out into the darkness alone like a social outcast made her want to leap with joy. There were night people and there were day people, and she was a day person. If she sometimes stayed up all night, it was not in order to be in the darkness or with the party people but because sleep was taking second place to some project or concern. Her favorite time of day was sunrise, and what she liked best about the night was the quiet, not the nightlife.

Her eyes grew accustomed to the darkness. The party mumble receded and all she heard were her shoes scuffing softly on the pavement and the buzz and click of night bugs. She saw only vineyard and trees, the road's white line, and above, hazy stars. The road ran straight as a surveyor's line in either direction with vineyard on both sides. No cars passed. A sliver moon sat halfway up the sky with Venus like a beauty mark below it.

In the darkness, the landscape seemed to expand. The span of road that could be driven in a few seconds without attracting any special notice stretched out on foot and filled the senses. Roadside plants gave off their fragrances. She passed through each of them like scenery. A wild rose, a musky oak, the lush grasses near a drainage ditch. It was hard to believe downtown St. Helena was only a few miles away.

It seemed to take a very long time to reach the streetlight. Eventually she resorted to counting her footsteps to make the distance pass more quickly. The road was so straight she could close her eyes and count to one hundred without straying far from the white line, and she did so several times before she reached the light at last. As she passed underneath it, it went out with a faint pop. She looked up at the shrinking glow of filament. There were various theories to explain this sort of phenomenon. Catelina Alvarez, the Portuguese grandmother who lived down the street from Sunny throughout her childhood and who taught her most of what she knew about cooking, claimed it was a person's aural glow that did it. Whatever the cause, the loss of the solitary light infused the darkness with more power and it pulled at her, as if she would be sucked into its mystery.

Feeling suddenly alone and more than a little timid, she began to wonder whether walking home was really such a good idea after all. There had been more reasonable options. Andre's mountain bike was in the garage, for example. If she had really wanted her predawn exercise, she could have borrowed it and been home by now. Or she could have borrowed his car, asked one of his friends for a ride, or gone to sleep in one of the bedrooms. There was no excuse for her present predicament, she thought, feeling foolish. She stopped to consider turning around. What was she doing wandering around in the middle of the night? It would take too long to go back now. She would do just as well to finish what she'd started. Her mood soured. She went on, feeling both afraid of the ominous darkness and ridiculous for being afraid. For a thirty-two-year-old woman to be intimidated by a short walk at night in a familiar place was simply ridiculous. She mused on the darkness, which was a natural part of existence and served to liberate humans from the controlled productivity of daylight. Darkness meant freedom from work, obligation, decorum. Her spirits rose with the thought that humans, herself included, had grown excessively attached to the light, and had lost some wilder part of themselves because of it, and that in venturing out into the night she was recapturing part of this lost magic.

She walked on and her thoughts turned to Andre Morales, a recent and welcome addition to her life. She would call him when she got home. Maybe he wouldn't have noticed she was gone yet. They were still in the very early stages of their romance, and he was no doubt still evaluating her character, as she was his. Tonight's performance would do little to inspire him. There would be a deduction from her account, that was certain. The only question was how much. He would probably assume it was part of a breezy streak in her personality. That would be a mistake. Sunny was anything but breezy. She'd always been accused of being too serious. Neurotic, possibly, by some people's standards, but not breezy.

She stepped around the flattened carcass of a snake, long dead. Andre may as well know the truth sooner than later, which was that she did not always give social gatherings with new, interesting people priority over a solid night's sleep. The idea was deeply subversive in Andre's world, where solitude and sleep held about as much appeal as sit-ups and vitamins. To reject a party in order to go to bed was the act of a demented mind, or worse, a dullard. For Sunny, sleep made the difference between the joyful execution of the next day's duties and a pained, amnesiac slog through them. For Andre, sleep foreshadowed death, and was the last recourse for a night, to be indulged only if nothing better was in the offing.

He and his staff could work until midnight, close the restaurant, drink and smoke until dawn, and still get up at eight. How did they do it? It was the same at other restaurants. The staff would close the door on the last customer and the night would begin. They possessed a social stamina Sunny could only admire. She wondered how late they would stay tonight. Even the most hearty among them had to go home to bed eventually. With that thought, she began to feel conspicuous. Anyone headed to Highway 29 from Andre's house, and that would be almost everyone, would have to drive right past her. They would certainly wonder what she was doing out there alone. To walk beside the road, especially at night, and particularly alone, was practically a criminal act. Only motorists in distress and deviants walked on roads at night. All decent, sensible, prosperous people drove cars, or at least rode bicycles. It was part of the modern tyranny of efficiency. Anything faster had to be better, and to choose a slower method of doing almost anything was tantamount to a declaration of mental instability. No one would appreciate the truth, that she simply wanted to be alone in the quiet on her way home, and even liked being outside in the open air. She tried to concoct a more convincing explanation in case a carload of Andre's friends pulled up beside her and asked if she needed a ride. It would be embarrassing. The simplest solution was to jog. The less time she spent inviting the scrutiny of passing cars, the better.

Jogging turned out to be a good idea. It banished the night chill and pushed the shadow fears to the edges of her mind. She settled into the new pace. Soon she could make out the white lettering of the stop sign in the distance where the road ended at Fir Hill Drive. From there it wasn't far to Madrona, then Hudson, then Adams, and finally the cottage on Adelaide with its plump white duvet and clean white sheets. Ah, bed. Bed! Soon she would be home and neatly tucked in.

Madrona ran as arrow-straight as Fir Hill, like most of the valley roads between the checkerboard of vineyards. From Madrona, the outline of far ridges of the Coast Range were visible to the east and west. Nearer were more vineyards, their vines lined up like ghost soldiers. She counted her steps in sets of twenty until she lost track of the number of sets. The white line lay thickly on the pavement like a satisfying glaze of sugar on gingerbread.

She'd been jogging down Madrona for some time when she heard a faint new sound. She stopped to listen, holding her breath so she could hear. She heard the rumble of an engine, and a moment later the crunch of tires moving slowly across gravel. A hundred yards behind her lay the turnoff to Vedana Vineyards, marked by a mailbox and fieldstone pillars. The winery stood back the same distance or more from the main road. She searched the darkness. The outline of the cluster of stone buildings was just visible. From behind them, a light-colored vehicle emerged and turned onto the gravel lane coming toward her. The driver didn't have his lights on. She watched. Why didn't they have their lights on? Didn't they notice? Should she wave them down and tell them? They would figure it out eventually. Besides, what if the driver was not the sort of person she wanted to meet in the middle of nowhere in the middle of the night? She looked around. A leafy shrub stood next to the fence a few feet away.

There would have been plenty of time to move behind the shrub gracefully if she had not stepped halfway on a rock and stumbled when she jumped across the drainage ditch. As she got up, the vehicle, a white pickup truck, pulled out of the driveway and turned toward her. She was standing in plain view when the driver switched on his lights, blinding her as the truck accelerated past. She turned and stared after it. All she could see was its taillights, one more orange than the other, probably a replacement. They shrank away with the sound of the engine and silence took hold of the night again.

She stood in the road, staring after the truck. Something about it struck her as odd. Why had the driver waited so long to turn on his headlights? And what was he doing at the winery at this hour? Except for a pair of flood lights illuminating a few sections of landscaping, the winery stood in darkness. The stone buildings looked as stoic and somber as always, and the massive oak in the courtyard stood with its usual air of permanence, its great spread of limbs forming a wide canopy. Except that it was not exactly the same. Something out of place swayed from its lowest limb. At this distance, the length of a football field, it was hard to discern the shape. All she could make out was a pale form twisting from the limb like a punching bag. The sight gave her a chill. It reminded her of a deer hung up for cleaning. She thought of what it could be. It was difficult to make out more than a rough outline from so far away. It could be a swing caught at a strange angle, or a piñata hung up for a party, or a kite. It could be any number of harmless objects caught or hung up in the tree.

She walked back to the driveway leading to Vedana Vineyards. A sign next to one of the stone pillars read, "No public tastings. Tours by appointment only." She stared at the distant shape hanging from the tree and thought of the white truck. Vineyard surrounded the winery with its bare vines like uniform markers in a vast graveyard. She pulled her scarf closer and started down the gravel road.

2

The winery and its outbuildings huddled in the mist at the end of the lane. Her steps crunched on the gravel. She thought of the mobile phone in her bag and wished she had remembered to charge it. Staring at the ground in front of her, she walked quickly. Her heart beat faster with each step and her ears strained to hear the slightest sound. Soon she was close enough.

Wisteria covered the front of the winery. It twisted thickly up posts and tumbled over the eave that shaded the front deck, where a pair of wooden doors were flanked by two large windows. Off to the side of the winery was a small grove of mature olive trees, which Sunny had admired from the road on a number of occasions. The buildings in back were newer and larger, and presumably housed the fermentation tanks, oak barrels, and storage facilities. In between the outbuildings was an open space for parking and maneuvering equipment. Sunny studied these elements while carefully avoiding the oak tree and its strange addition. She had decided to face it, but she had also decided to do so only when she was thoroughly ready. She already knew what it had to be, and if she was right, she wanted to look all at once, not catch sight of it out of the corner of her eye.

The form had been instantly recognizable from the main road, but her mind had resisted the obvious. It could not be that. Now she was close enough to see the climbing rose trained in espalier along the side wall of the winery and the tractor parked in the middle of the compound. She was close enough. It was time to look. She turned toward the oak tree and saw what she knew would be there, what she had desperately hoped she would not see.

Time stopped. Standing frozen in place, immobilized by fear, she listened too intently and heard too much. Where she knew there to be silence and ordinary night sounds, she now heard footsteps, the ominous creak of boards, shallow breathing, the rumble of a distant engine approaching. Whoever did this could still be here. She fought the impulse to run, instead holding her eyes on the vision before her. Hanging from the gnarled old tree, gently rocked by an imperceptible breeze, was a young woman.

She had been tied. Rope ran under her armpits, presenting her almost as if she were standing. Her slender bare feet tipped downward, her delicate toes nearly brushing the ground. A sweep of dark hair fell over her shoulder and onto her breast. She was naked except for the rope that bound her.

Sunny hardly breathed as she walked closer. The girl's head had rocked forward onto her chest, her face slightly turned. Forcing herself to look, Sunny took in the large eyes, shapely eyebrows, and petite nose. She was young, maybe in her early twenties. A deep gash opened the flesh over her eye and a rose of color marred her cheek where she'd been struck. Even so, it was clear she had been pretty. Her delicately shaped features reposed gracefully even in the slackness of death. A blue, swollen tongue protruded from full lips. Sunny looked away.

The girl's hands were bound behind her back and her slender body had been cruelly trussed. Bands of rough hemp rope pressed into her flesh, circling her torso at neat intervals sectioned by knots. The rope passed twice between her legs, pressing her sex between taut strands. A separate rope had been used to hang her from the branch, tied with expertise in an elaborate knot.

Sunny reached up two fingers and pressed them to the girl's neck. The flesh was cold and lifeless, the veins still. Sunny stood before her, helpless. She wanted to take her down, but to do so she would need a ladder, and to hold her up to release the tension while she undid the knot around the branch. The girl would probably have to be cut down. The question was what to do now. It would take too long to go back to Andre's house. She could go out to the main road and wait for a car, but there was no way to know how long that could take. No cars had passed since she'd set out. She checked her mobile phone in case it had miraculously recharged itself. Nothing. Next she tried the winery door and found it locked, of course. The window on the side of the winery was too high to reach and probably locked anyway. Frantically, feeling the onset of panic, she took up one of the hand-sized stones used to line the path to the winery door. The front windows were divided into panes about the size of a magazine. Starting in the lowermost corner, she smashed several, then knocked out the wooden bracing in between until there was a hole big enough to climb through. With any luck, an alarm was going off somewhere. Inside, she found a phone behind the front desk.

Sergeant Steve Harvey did not appreciate being woken up at something past three in the morning. He muttered a profanity when he heard who it was.

"This had better be important, McCoskey," he said, his tone betraying the fact that he could already tell it was.

They seemed to run across each other on a regular basis. The last time Sunny had spoken to Sergeant Harvey was at the firefighters' barbecue fund-raiser a week ago. The time before that, it was when she discovered wine fraud was the motive for the murder of a local restaurateur. Now Sergeant Harvey listened to what she had to tell him, interrupting once to ask her to hold on while he got the officer on duty headed over there, pronto. After a moment he came back on the line.

"Sunny? I'm leaving now. A patrol car is on the way. You can tell me the rest when I get there." He paused. "You want to stay on the line while I drive over?"

"No, I'm okay."

"Good. Stay put and I'll be there in fifteen, twenty minutes, tops. Don't do anything, touch anything, or go anywhere. Stay by the phone and call me if anything happens, and I mean anything."

"Right."

Sunny hung up. Her hands were shaking and her face was wet, with perspiration or tears she wasn't sure which. As much as she wanted to stay inside huddled against the wall behind the desk, the girl outside was alone and she couldn't leave her there. There had to be a chance, an impossibly small chance, but a chance nevertheless, that she was still alive. Sunny wiped her face on her sleeve and climbed back out the window onto the porch.

She noted with surprise that it felt better to be outside. The terror of being watched in the open was preferable to the terror of being trapped inside. And Steve had pointed out that whoever was responsible was unlikely to linger at the scene, waiting to get caught.

She went back to the girl. Nothing about her suggested life. Sunny took off her scarf and draped it around the girl's shoulders, covering her body as best she could, then sat down at her feet and waited for the police to arrive. The breeze agitated the body slightly, and her feet, toes neatly painted, each nail a pink oval gem, stirred the air in tiny circles. Her vigil lasted twelve minutes. It was the longest twelve minutes she had ever experienced.

"Why don't you start with why the hell you were out wandering around on private property at three o'clock in the morning," said Sergeant Harvey.

"It's a long story," said Sunny, shivering despite the jacket he had pulled out of the trunk of the squad car for her.

"Bore me," he said, looking hard into her eyes.

Sergeant Harvey was a solid brick of a man with muscular arms that he folded across his chest when he was asking questions, like he was now. Sunny had woken him up, she was sure of that, but his short blond hair was as meticulously groomed as ever, a tiny army standing uniformly at attention. He had a fundamentally gentle nature, but that didn't mean he couldn't be intimidating. At the moment, his manner was anything but soothing.

"Hang on," he said, looking around. "Let's do this right the first time."

Sunny followed him over to a teak lawn bench. They sat down and she waited while he set up a pocket tape recorder between them, then recited the facts of the situation into it.

Sunny stared at the police team swarming around the girl's body. Two police cars and an ambulance had their headlights trained on the oak tree, casting a confusion of shadows. The area had been cordoned off and officers were scouring the scene, gathering evidence. The photographer's flash illuminated the girl's face unexpectedly, burning the image of her purple lips and tongue, the black gash above her eye, and the tableau of gray and yellow bruised flesh into Sunny's mind. She turned away, fighting the urge to be sick. Sergeant Harvey looked at her, silently asking if she was ready. She nodded.

"I want you to tell me how you came to discover the deceased tonight," he said, "starting at the very beginning, using as much detail as you can remember, and not leaving anything out, even if it seems inconsequential."

She looked away and drew a slow breath. Beginning with Andre's phone call asking her to join him at the Dusty Vine, she described everything that had happened that evening. When she was done, he asked her to repeat certain parts to be sure he had them right, then turned the tape recorder off.

"One more question, McCoskey. Off the record." Sergeant Harvey studied her face. "Why you?"

"What do you mean?"

"In your opinion, why are you the one who found her?"

Sunny looked at him uncertainly. "I don't know. I don't think there is a reason. It just happened."

"Wrong. I'll tell you why," he said. "You know who finds most of the dead bodies in this world?"

"The police?"

"Farm workers. The guys who get up before dawn, drive to remote places where the only thing for miles is grapes or sorghum or sugar beets, and go to work looking at the ground. Those guys find the dead bodies."

Sunny nodded, not sure she followed his point.

"Those guys have no choice," he said. "They have to get up before dawn and wander around in the middle of nowhere in the dark. That's how they make their miserable living. But you, you do it for fun." He shook his head and looked away to the east, where the sky had turned teal blue. "Every time I turn around you're crashing through the bushes before the sun comes up, getting yourself in trouble. That's the part I have trouble understanding."

He was talking about an incident that had occurred the previous fall. She'd pulled over on the way to work to check a certain intriguing slope for chanterelles, when the owner drove by and called the cops on her. She'd nearly been cited for trespassing, but managed to buy her way out of it by inviting the officer and the property owner to have lunch at her restaurant on the house. They'd since worked out a mutually satisfactory agreement. She could gather mushrooms on his property, he had a standing invitation for lunch at Wildside when chanterelles were in season.

"Coincidence," said Sunny. "I happened to be mushrooming before work, when it happens to be very early in the morning. Tonight is different. Tonight I wasn't thinking straight. I was tired, and I just wanted to get out of there. Then I saw the truck, and then I saw the body. I know that truck is part of it. Whoever was driving it has to be the murderer. Who else could it have been?"

Steve sighed. "Anything else? Detail about the truck?"

"No, that's it."

Steve nodded. "You've had a tough time. Don't think about it anymore for the night, okay? Try to get some sleep and forget about all this. Something may come back to you once you've had a chance to rest. Maybe you'll remember part of the license plate. Some little detail you forgot."

"I don't think so. I never looked at the license plate. I don't think it was lit. And I didn't see the driver. I'm not even sure what make the truck was. All I know is it was white."

"But you referred to the driver as *he* several times."

"That's just a guess, or intuition, or habit. I don't think I even saw the driver before he hit the lights. If I did, it was just for a second."

"Maybe you saw more than you realize. That's what intuition is. Subconscious data trying to make itself known."

Sergeant Harvey took a long moment to scrutinize her face, going over it for evidence the way she imagined he would go over a car or a hotel room or an object found at the scene of the crime, searching it for clues as if the way she held her mouth or the stray eyelash on her cheek would reveal where to find the white truck.

He nodded to himself. "We'll talk again soon. Until then, don't drive yourself nuts thinking about it. You did all you could." He looked up at an officer who had been trying to get his attention for some time and signaled he'd be right there.

"McCoskey, since I know where to find you, and I trust you can keep your mouth shut, I'm going to send you home to get what sleep you can before work. However, I will ask you not to discuss what happened tonight with anyone until we've had a chance to talk again, and I mean anyone."

"I have to pretend it didn't happen?"

"You don't have to lie. If it comes up, just tell people you can't talk about it until later. The less you say the better. And under no circumstances talk to anyone from the press. I don't want any more information out there than is absolutely necessary. Your little hike has gained us a few hours and I want to make the most of them."

"The killer will assume the girl won't be found until morning."

"Correct. I assume this show was not put on for your entertainment. I'd say you spoiled somebody's surprise."

Sunny looked away. "What do you do now? I mean, where do you start?"

"First we gather as much evidence as we can, assuming we can find anything left under your footprints. Then we go to work trying to figure out who she was, what happened to her, and who knows about it."

"What about the people who own the winery?"

"I'll handle that. You take it easy. I'll be in touch this afternoon. Meanwhile, all you know is you discovered a woman who was an apparent victim of homicide. End of story. No details."

"One more thing," said Sunny. "I think he saw me when I was standing by the side of the road and he turned on his headlights."

Sergeant Harvey made a fist and bounced the thumb side against his lips, thinking. "Anything make you think he came back to check on you?"

"I didn't notice anything."

Sergeant Harvey frowned and gestured for her to wait a moment. He walked back toward the others and was immediately surrounded. Sunny watched the proceedings around the girl. The forensics group had moved farther out, scouring the ground for evidence, and the ambulance team was cutting the girl down at last. Enough daylight had come to show the marks on her face and body in a rainbow of sickening hues. Sergeant Harvey extracted himself from the group vying for his attention and motioned to a somber-faced officer drinking coffee from a Styrofoam cup.

"Jute, drive Ms. McCoskey home, will you? Go inside with her and secure the place before you leave."

3

Rivka Chavez had both the ovens on and the music cranked up in the kitchen when Sunny arrived at Wildside later that morning. Rivka was standing at the cutting block, wearing a white tank top and jeans and singing loudly to a Lenny Kravitz song. The blue and red swallows tattooed on the backs of her arms glistened with perspiration.

Sunny carried her bicycle into her office. It was days like this that made her glad she'd taken a risk on a kid whose sum total experience in a kitchen was the year she spent in cooking school. She couldn't imagine Wildside running smoothly without Rivka Chavez to pick up the slack.

Rivka turned around and eyed the bicycle. "You're feeling ambitious this morning."

"You could say that."

Or you could say that she forgot she had left her truck at the Dusty Vine until about three seconds after Officer Jute pulled away from her house. It was bike to work or walk, and this time she chose to bike. Sunny changed into her work clothes and tied a fresh white apron around her hips, then stood in front of the mirror. Today would be a game. How long can she pretend to be coherent, and that nothing bad has happened. She smoothed her bangs to the side and caught them in a tiny green barrette.

Rivka turned down the music. "Andre called," she said loudly from the kitchen.

"When?"

"About an hour ago. He wants you to call him."

Sunny opened the window and sat on the edge of her desk staring outside. A bumblebee the size of a thimble was nuzzling lavender blossoms one by one. She watched it embrace each flower with its long, hairy legs, then move to the next.

"Also, the fan over the grill is making that sound again, there is some kind of milky pink funk in the water out at Pt. Reyes so there are no local oysters until they figure out what it is, and we really have to do something about the Speedy Gonzalez factor." This last sentence was said close up. Sunny turned to see Rivka standing in the doorway, watching her.

"Did you see one?"

"I saw his calling cards."

"Shit."

"Exactly."

"Where?"

"On the zinc."

Sunny frowned. "That's bad. That's very bad. We're going to have to get more aggressive, I guess. Anything in the traps?"

"Nothing."

Sunny exhaled loudly. "I can't figure out what they're eating. They can't get in the walk-in, and everything else is sealed up tight."

Rivka nodded. She had her black hair braided and twisted up in two tight buns. She was turning the silver post in her ear, the way she did when she was considering something, and staring at Sunny with dark eyes heavily lined with dark lashes. She'd recently started wearing a thick silver cross that dangled between her breasts, just above the double layer of black bra and white tank top. "Maybe they're just doing recon."

"Recon implies an invasion. I'd better call the pest guy today and find out what the options are." Sunny turned back to the bumblebee, who was still ravishing the lavender blossoms outside the window. Mice. That was all she needed.

Rivka lingered in the doorway. "You okay?"

"I'm fine."

"You don't look fine."

"I guess it shows." Sunny rubbed her eyes, fighting the seduction of sleep. "I had a very strange night."

"Do tell."

"I'll tell you all about it later. If I go into it now, we'll never be ready for lunch."

"Intriguing," said Rivka. "Now I'm really curious. Let me make you one of my famous healing lattes. Maybe then you'll be ready to talk."

They went out to the front counter and Rivka fired a shot while Sunny rummaged under the bar.

"Could you make it a famous healing Americano instead?"

Rivka scowled. "There is nothing healing about watered-down espresso."

"There is when you put a splash of this in it," said Sunny, holding up a bottle of house red.

Rivka shook her head. "I don't know how you can drink coffee like that."

"Hair of the dog."

"Dog hair would be preferable."

"You mock my traditions, but someday you will know the truth and be forced to admit the wisdom of my ways. This recipe is an ancient Portuguese panacea straight from Catelina Alvarez's kitchen. One shot of good, strong espresso, one spoonful of honey, one splash of red wine, a little hot water to thin things out, and suddenly the world is a beautiful place. It's better than Prozac."

"Why not crumble some Prozac on top? You've got the caffeine, sugar, and alcohol covered. All that's missing is the hard stuff."

"Don't tempt me." Sunny finished stirring the concoction and swallowed it, then went over to the oven and let the hot air warm her arms and face. It was good to be in her kitchen, in her restaurant. The world may not be an entirely beautiful place, she thought, but at least Wildside was still here with its warmth and good smells and friendly noises to fill up the day. After a night like last night, the heat of the kitchen was the best medicine she could imagine. What would be ideal now would be to bake. She wanted to put her hands into a bowl of dough and knead it, feel the soft, floury mixture crumble under her fingertips and gradually coalesce into a smooth, compact ball. The smell of baking bread would fill the kitchen and banish any bad juju from the night before. With a pang, Sunny remembered the girl's face. She had seen those eyes and would never forget them. The image flashed in her mind against her will.

"You really do look beat," said Rivka. "Did you go out last night?"

"Very."

"Let me guess. Andre Morales the Mexican Bacchus kept you out late partying again, then took you home and ravished you until the cocks crowed."

"You're half right, but the cock never even got close to crowing."

"Oh, really," said Rivka, raising her eyebrows. "No wonder you're all ruffled."

It wasn't a bad job to do the day's butchering, but it wasn't the best job either, and neither Sunny nor Rivka particularly liked it. It was hard work that required both strength and skill with a sharp knife. Some tasks were easier than others. Slicing strips of bacon from the slab of cured pork was no big deal. On the other hand, Sunny had never enjoyed preparing chickens for roasting. The smell of rosemary and lemon chicken roasting in the oven was pure heaven, but the smell of raw chicken on the cutting board, with its sallow skin and pockets of jaundiced fat, was enough to put her off poultry altogether no matter how many times she faced it. A hectic morning was no time to be squeamish, and as a cook, Sunny was very rarely that. She liked to get her hands dirty, liked the texture of all kinds of ingredients, including the slip and slide of raw meat.

Rivka was already working on ravioli with broccoli rabe filling, a time-consuming dish that was a challenge to get just right so they didn't come apart. Sunny reviewed the list of meats that needed prepping. If they did more business, they could order whole sides of beef and pork and make their own cuts. Since Wildside was so small, Sunny worked with the local butcher, who delivered the specific cuts she wanted each morning. All she had to do was trim and shape them. The fish and fowl were another story. When she bought trout or dorado, it came gutted but otherwise whole, as did most of the poultry and game birds. Tuna, salmon, and halibut arrived in heavy slabs to be filleted. Squid, grass shrimp, oysters, and lobster were delivered whole and, in the case of lobsters, oysters, and grass shrimp, alive. Depending on the menu, the day's butchering could take two hours or more.

In the walk-in, Sunny picked up a rainbow trout and admired its compact little body and the spray of dots across its silken belly. They would be panfried more or less as is. Next to them was a tub of baby quail ready to be stuffed with a mixture of wild mushrooms, prosciutto, and herbed bread crumbs and tied up in pretty bundles. Sunny took the tub to a workstation. She picked up a quail, turned it over in her palm, examined the translucent white skin dotted with purple, then put it back in the tub and carried it back to the walk-in, where she chose instead a shallow tray of squid that had arrived earlier that morning, according to the label written on masking tape.

The squid went better because she refused to acknowledge anything remotely animated about them, and because these particular squid, normally a bargain, had been unexpectedly expensive. Any squid with the nerve to command the price she'd apparently paid deserved to be gutted and stuffed with lobster meat. At nine dollars a plate, the upper limit of what she could charge for a calamari appetizer, the restaurant was practically taking a loss on one of her favorite spring dishes. It was almost as bad as the live grass shrimp that she bought from a guy in China Camp and used in the outrageously delicious fritto misto that was the new star of the appetizers. There was nothing more succulent than fried grass shrimp with fried slices of lemon and herbs and aioli to dip in, and almost nothing she made less profit on. The shrimp always sold out, but if Heather and Soren, Wildside's waitstaff, didn't sell all of the calamari by tomorrow afternoon, these little squid would be a foolishly pricey donation to Friday night's dinner, since she still refused to open Wildside on the weekends. The thought gave her a headache. The calamari would simply have to sell.

She selected a worthy specimen, removed the feather bone, pulled the head free, and drew out the viscera. Separating the ink sac from the mess of entrails, she punctured it and squeezed its oily contents into a tiny bowl out of habit since it wasn't enough to do anything with, thinking at the same time how she needed to find a delicate way to persuade Rivka not to overcook the squid. There had been an incident, admittedly after reheating during a Friday night dinner, when the calamari had had the consistency and durability of surgical tubing. Monty suffered through a serving, looking like a dog trying to chew bubblegum. Getting calamari just right was an art that required constant vigilance. She'd mentioned it once already, but apparently it hadn't sunk in because the last batch she'd tasted had been slightly rubbery. She would have to be more convincing in her lesson, without of course raising the Chavez pride and ire. The woman did not like to be told what to do.

One quick slice separated the head from the tentacles. She popped the beak out, rinsed the tentacles, and put them in a bowl. The remaining mantle was rinsed and deposited in a separate dish. Then she took up the next volunteer.

When all of the squid had been cleaned, she stowed them in the walk-in and, moving with detached efficiency, picked up a large section of tuna. She took a moment to hone the razor-sharp fish knife, drawing it across the stone with long, smooth strokes. A sharp knife made all the difference. Slicing tuna was a walk in the park compared to her first cooking job at a busy seafood restaurant in San Francisco. The specialty of the house was blackened catfish. Every morning she would spend the first half-hour of the day cutting the heads off live catfish, which live longer out of water than other fish. A knife was simply too gruesome, and their bones too resilient, so she started using the bone cutter. Overkill, literally, but nothing could be faster. Their glazed eyes watched the approach of the bone cutter with dull resignation. She took to draping a white napkin over their faces before the saw came down. The sound of that bone cutter stuck with her even now.

Tuna was different. The slab of tender, rosy flesh in front of her bore little resemblance to a fish. It was a substance, not a dead thing. She arranged it on the fish board, stroked the cool flesh, and chose a place to make her first cut. The feel of that cool, firm flesh reminded her of the girl hanging from the tree. Her mouth felt dry and sticky. She took a deep breath and pressed the blade into the flesh.

The sound of the knife clattering to the floor surprised her as much as the fact that she was no longer holding it. She saw the silver of the stainless countertop and the black rubber floor mats, then darkness.

Rivka's face was staring down at her when she came to. Her head felt heavy. The thoughts came slowly. Rivka was saying something, it didn't matter what. Translating the sounds into meaning seemed to take tremendous effort. Finally she sat up, staring dully at the holes in the rubber mat between her outstretched legs. The facts emerged gradually. She was sitting on the floor at Wildside. A moment before, she had been standing. Interesting.

Sergeant Steve Harvey called at two o'clock, just as the lunch rush was beginning to peak and slow down.

"Hi, Sunny. Sorry to interrupt you," he said. "Can you come by the station this afternoon around four? I'd like to review everything one more time, just to be sure we didn't miss anything. Does that give you enough time to clear out of work?"

Sunny cradled the phone to her ear while she plated a line of desserts. "Four o'clock should be fine. I'll be there."

She'd been going over the night's events all day in her head, not that she wanted to. She couldn't help it. Throughout their interview last night on the bench while the patrol cars' headlights illuminated the girl's body, Steve kept asking her if she remembered anything else about the truck, any detail or impression she might have forgotten to mention.

"Sometimes things come back to you after the shock wears off," he said.

She couldn't think of anything, but maybe the shock hadn't entirely worn off yet. To say she was tired was not adequate. She had gone beyond tired to some kind of altered state of consciousness, like being drugged or feverish. And then there was that nasty thump on the head from her fall this morning. Nevertheless, the day had gone smoothly enough. The restaurant was full, the waitstaff had all shown up and were busily doing their jobs, the guests ordered lots of wine and left well fed and happy. The most difficult part was the way Rivka kept looking at her.

"You sure you don't want to talk?" she said for the fifth time that day. "It seems like there's something on your mind."

"Later. Can't talk now. Must conserve limited energy resources in order to survive lunch service."

More than Steve's admonition to keep silent, she avoided Rivka out of fear. She knew once she started talking about last night she wouldn't be able to stop until she told the whole story, and she certainly wouldn't be able to run a restaurant with anything like her full attention. In fact, she wasn't sure what would happen at all. Maybe she would tell her story and go to sleep and not wake up for two days. She was beyond the realm of predictability and self-control.

For now it was easier to pretend none of it had happened. She hardly said a word to Rivka or anyone else, and couldn't bring herself to call Andre and explain her mysterious departure. Finally she left him a message at his house, knowing he was at work, saying that she'd walked out on the party because she didn't feel well and didn't want to bother him. What nonsense. Leaving a message, especially a bogus message, was the coward's way out, but there was no alternative. If she was going to continue to function for the rest of the day, the only choice was to repress everything and bludgeon her way through the hours. Just before four, she told Rivka she had an appointment and left the restaurant, pedaling her bike the few blocks up the back road to the St. Helena police station.

4

The coffee table in the waiting room at the police station offered one *Redbook,* thoroughly dog-eared, circa 2002, one *Reader's Digest,* and the classified section of the *San Francisco Chronicle*. Sunny went for the *Redbook,* half hoping for a feature on layered Jello parfaits, for which she had a secret passion thanks to growing up in California in the seventies. Back then, the big dinner in the summertime, eaten outdoors of course, was barbecued chicken, potato salad, sourdough bread, and a rainbow parfait with whipped cream on top. Instead, there were articles on how to please your man in bed, embarrassing moments revealed, and how to turn your man on. She tossed the magazine back on the table and picked up the classified section. She read all the pet ads, then all the garage sale ads, then the used car ads. Still no Sergeant Harvey. Staring dully ahead, she watched employees saunter up and down the hallway behind the bulletproof glass.

It was more than an hour before a uniformed cop waved her in and showed her to Steve Harvey's office. Steve was making some notes at a gray metal desk. Sunny took a seat on the folding chair in front of him and waited, feeling like a job applicant at an interview.

"Sonya," he said after several minutes. "Thanks for coming down."

Sunny noted the formality. She couldn't remember the last time Steve called her by her real name. "No problem."

There was a knock at the door and Officer Jute, the one who'd driven her home from Vedana, came in. Steve introduced him, saying he was helping out with the case.

"We met this morning."

"I didn't realize you're the one who owns Wildside," said Jute. "I ate there about a year ago. Nice place."

Sunny thanked him and waited. The room was very quiet. She could hear kids playing in the distance.

"You want something to drink?" said Steve, ticking his finger against the can of Diet Coke on his desk. "Soda, coffee, water?"

Sunny declined.

"We'll get started then." He punched a button on the tape recorder on his desk and cleared his throat. "Second interview with Sonya McCoskey regarding Vedana Vineyards homicide." He recited the basics of the case, staring through the office window at the hallway as he did so.

Sunny studied his profile. He had grown a scrappy blond mustache that wrapped around the corners of his mouth Village People–style, something which had escaped her notice last night. As always, his short hair was combed vertically and frozen in place with hair gel. With his rigid posture and muscular physique, he might have looked intimidating, if it weren't for the baby face complete with bewildered brown eyes that no amount of official police business seemed to harden. He finished his summary of the facts and turned to Sunny.

"Let's take it from the top. Tell us everything you can remember about last night, starting with when you left the Dusty Vine with Andre Morales. Walk us through it like we're hearing it for the first time."

Sunny went over everything that had happened. Steve and the other officer listened, nodding occasionally. When she got to the part where she heard the truck by Vedana Vineyards, Steve held up his hand.

"Hold right there. Go back a little," he said. "How long had you been walking by then?"

"It's hard to say exactly. Twenty minutes, maybe more?"

"And you left the party at what time?"

"Around two-twenty. I looked at the clock."

"So it's around two-forty, maybe two-forty-five at this point."

"That's probably about right."

"Had you seen or heard any other cars since you left the party?"

"Nothing."

She went on. They listened for a moment, then stopped her again with questions, going over every angle of the truck she'd seen. Could she tell what make it was? Was it new or old? Was there a tool box, rack, or anything else in the back? Did it have a company logo? All she could be sure of was that it was white, didn't have a shell, and had some kind of logo on the door.

"That's all I took in," said Sunny. "I couldn't say for sure what make or year it was. It wasn't a Toyota, I know that. It had an American body. You know, boxier and wider looking."

"What about the logo?" said Officer Jute. "You didn't mention that before."

"I remembered because I was wondering what gave me the impression it was a work truck. I think it was something circular, and printed in a dark color. I just caught an impression as it went by."

"You say you nearly waved the truck down," said Steve. "Why?"

"For a second, I thought I would try to let them know their lights weren't on. You know, like when you flash your lights at somebody. Then I changed my mind."

"Why?"

"I didn't want them to see me. I was out there in the middle of the night with no one around. It didn't seem safe. I didn't want to invite the interaction. Also, I think I decided that maybe their lights were off on purpose. I've done that before on a country road. Turned off the lights and driven in the dark for a little while, just for fun."

Steve and Jute exchanged a look, whether disapproving or conspiratorial, Sunny couldn't say which.

"You didn't want the driver to see you," said Steve, "but they did see you, correct?"

"I'm not sure," said Sunny, rubbing the knot on her head from when she had passed out that morning. "It seems likely. The driver turned his lights on right as he passed me. That's why I didn't get much more than an impression of the truck. I was blinded for a second."

"And then?"

"It accelerated away down Madrona, headed east toward twenty-nine. I watched the taillights for a while. That's when I noticed they were mismatched. One was darker red than the other."

"Which one?" asked Steve.

Sunny thought for a moment. "The way I remember it, the one on the left was cherry red, the one on the right a more orangey-red."

"What about a license plate?"

"I didn't notice it. All I noticed was the taillights."

Steve gestured for her to go on.

"I started wondering what they were doing out there at that time of night," said Sunny, "and I looked back toward the winery. That's when I saw the girl."

"You could see her from the main road?" asked Jute.

"I could see that there was something pale hanging from the tree. Technically, I couldn't see that it was a person, but the silhouette was instantly recognizable. I knew right away that's what it had to be. I was hoping I was wrong, of course. I thought maybe it could be a swing or a piñata or a punching bag. Anything."

It was after six when Steve finally turned the tape recorder off, satisfied, for the moment, with the information they'd gathered.

"Sun, I may want to get you back in here and go over this stuff again once we've had a chance to do a little more research," he said. "I also think it might be a good idea to go out there together, maybe retrace your steps. I'll give you a jingle about that later if we decide it's necessary." Steve looked at the other officer. "Anything else?"

"Just one more." Jute turned to Sunny. "I'm having trouble understanding why you walked home in the middle of the night from the party. Did you have a fight with your boyfriend?"

"No."

"But he wouldn't drive you home."

"I didn't ask him to."

"Why not?"

"He was enjoying himself with his friends, and he was the host. I didn't want to bother him."

"And why didn't you ask one of the other people at the party? It's a short drive. It wouldn't have been much of an inconvenience."

"I can't explain. I just wanted to be away. It was nice to be outside, where it was quiet. I didn't plan to walk home. It was an impulse when my phone was dead and I couldn't call a cab."

"Wasn't it cold outside?"

"It was cold enough to need a jacket."

"But you didn't have a jacket."

"No."

He wrote something on his notepad and looked at Steve. "That's it for me."

Steve looked at his watch. "I'm meeting with a couple of reporters right after this, so you'll be at liberty to discuss the case with whoever you want starting tomorrow. However," he paused to exaggerate his eye contact with Sunny, "you will continue to have much more information about this crime than the general public. I would prefer that you keep it that way. We don't want to start up the rumor mill on this one."

"I understand," said Sunny. "Have you found out anything about who she was?"

"We're starting to piece things together. There's nothing definite yet. Once we have a positive ID and the family has been notified, we'll release what information we have to the media at that time."

They've ID'd her already, thought Sunny, he just doesn't want to say so. "What about leads? Anything?"

"We're still gathering evidence." Steve stood up. "Trust me, we're going to do everything in our power to find those responsible."

Officer Jute excused himself, shaking hands with Sunny and raising his chin to Steve on his way out. "I'll check in later," he said at the door.

"Thanks," said Steve.

Sunny sat back down, hoping Steve would do the same. "Do you know yet how she died?"

Steve stayed standing. "Probably strangled, though there was evidence of some head trauma as well. The coroner is working on it now. We'll know a lot more once the report comes back."

"And what about the people who own the winery?"

"What about them?"

"Did they have any idea why the girl might have been left there? Did they know her?"

"I've spoken with them, and I'll be speaking with them again, I'm sure. Once again, I will point out that, as a material witness, you possess far more information about this crime than those who were not at the scene, including the winery owners. I urge you not to share that information with anyone, just as I will not be sharing information unnecessarily with you, the owners of the winery, or anyone else. We're playing poker, McCoskey, and the stakes are high. Somebody out there knows everything about this crime, but they're holding their cards close. If we go around showing everything we have, it makes it that much harder to bluff."

"So, for example, you won't tell the owners of the winery—"

"Anything more than is absolutely necessary. Exactly."

"And you won't tell anyone I found the body."

"I see no advantage to advertising your involvement. However, with the perpetrator at large, there is certainly a potential disadvantage to doing so."

"You mean he could see me as a threat."

"You would only pose a threat if you had proprietary information, such as the ability to identify a suspect. In your case, you may have seen the perpetrator's vehicle, but that information has already been passed on. Harming you at this point would serve no purpose."

"But if that was the killer leaving Vedana, and if he did see me when he clicked on his lights, he might wonder if I saw him."

"It's possible, but that's a lot of ifs." Steve rapped his knuckles on the edge of the desk decisively. "I think our guy has more to worry about than a witness whose testimony would be of extremely negligible value. A good defense lawyer could discredit that kind of ID—a glimpse of a speeding car at night with headlights blinding you—in about ten seconds. No, if I were him, I'd be either watching or running. Let's just try to keep a low profile and not invite problems."

"Right." Sunny imagined the murderer somewhere, remembering her face in a flash of headlights. He wouldn't know who she was, or where to find her. The link between them was safely severed. "Who are these Vedanas anyway?" she asked. "Why don't they have a gate on their driveway or any security? I smashed the front window of their winery without so much as a dog barking."

"Vedana isn't their name, it's a Pali term meaning sensation."

"I thought it was Spanish for window."

"That's *ventana*," said Steve. "As I understand it, *vedana* is related to the Buddhist concept of *samsara*. Sensation is one of the things that makes us want to be alive, thus triggering desire and attachment, which keeps the wheel of consequence and suffering turning. That's *samsara*. Speaking of windows, the owners were nice about the window you broke, by the way. Their insurance is covering it."

"That's big of them, since I had to sit with the dead body and wait for the police, not them. Since when are you an expert in Pali terminology, by the way?"

Steve looked away, trying to hide a smile. He coughed. "I'm not, but Sarah Winfield is."

"Pretzel-girl Sarah? I thought I saw you hanging around the yoga studio more than usual."

"Just pursuing my practice," said Steve.

"I'll bet."

Steve grinned for a second before he caught himself and assumed a more serious expression. He looked at his watch. "I need to wrap this up. I've got reporters waiting."

"Okay, but just tell me what the next step is."

He made a matter-of-fact face. "Well, the next step is I do my job and hopefully find the perpetrator or perpetrators. You go home, get some rest, and try to forget any of this happened."

"Unless I remember something important."

"Bingo."

5

Coming home never felt so good. Long shadows darkened the street when she hoisted her bike out of the back of the truck and walked it down the overgrown path to the front door. She locked it up next to the ginkgo tree by the fence and went inside, shedding clothes on the way to the shower. Passing the phone, she stopped to turn off the ringer.

The alarm went off at five the next morning, waking her from a dream that was quickly becoming a nightmare. She was having dinner at a restaurant with white tablecloths. For her main dish, the waiter brought a whole, grilled fish. Fork and knife raised, she was just about to cut into it, when the fish looked up at her with one searching, terrified eye.

She lumbered out of bed, thoroughly possessed by the shock of the dream. In the bathroom, she stood under a hot shower, washing away the weight of the heavy sleep. She ran through the dream again and again, as if the impact of the experience was not enough and her mind needed to reinforce it by repetition, or perhaps the opposite, that the impact was too much and could only be worn away by familiarity, facing it again and again until she could get used to that eye upon her and the knife in her hand.

The early-morning mix of denim-clad farmers, construction workers, and commuters in suits sat over mugs of coffee at Bismark's. Everyone seemed to be either reading or talking about the body that had been found at Vedana Vineyards, not ten minutes away. A reverential hush at the uniqueness of the event had fallen over the room, and the patrons lowered their voices to exchange views on the homicide. Sunny carried her latte to a table by the window, happy to be surrounded by daylight and humanity, even if murder was the topic on everyone's lips. The shock had finally sunk in, and she had felt jittery in the dark of the early morning, with a too-thorough knowledge that a murderer might still be nearby and hunting her face.

One of the surly, pierced youths working the counter brought over her bagel and orange juice a moment later. Dreams aside, of which she had had several disturbing ones leading up to the eye of the fish, ten hours of sleep had worked its magic and she felt almost coherent again. Now a bite to eat, and maybe the world would go back to the way she liked it.

She had hardly lifted her cup when Wade Skord appeared beside the table bearing coffee and croissant.

"*Buenos días, amiga!*" he said loudly, turning heads. "You have room for a vagrant winemaker from south of the border?"

Wade Skord had been back less than a week from Mexico, where he had been sailing the Baja peninsula for the last three months. He'd left his winery in the care of a former employee and taken his dream trip. His lined and weathered face was tanner than usual, and his blue eyes sparkled even more fiercely. He sat down and laid his callused hands on the table like artifacts.

"How's life back on the mountain?" said Sunny, delighted to see him.

"The cat doesn't recognize me, but the grapes are glad I'm back. Never trust a creature without roots."

Wade got up and rummaged through the stack of castoff newspapers in a basket by the door and came back with several sections under his arm. He kept the *Napa Register* and handed Sunny the front page of the *Santa Rosa Press Democrat.* In the upper left was a story about the girl, under the headline GRISLY FIND AT LOCAL WINERY. The accompanying photograph showed the winery and oak tree cordoned off with yellow police tape. Steve, true to his word, had supplied few details. The text said only that an unidentified woman was discovered at Vedana Vineyards late Wednesday night in an apparent homicide. Anyone who had seen or heard anything suspicious in the area was urged to contact the police department right away.

Sunny folded the paper. "You ever think about living anywhere else?"

"You mean move? Not me. I'm anchored to the mountain. I may go walkabout now and then, but this scrap of paradise is home. Why? You're not thinking of moving?"

"No, I guess not seriously. It's just this valley starts to feel about as big as a canoe sometimes."

Sunny looked at her watch. She wrapped the waxed paper around her bagel, swallowed the last of her orange juice, and picked up her latte. Wade put down his paper. "Are you leaving already?"

"Afraid so. It's that time. Raviolis wait for no woman."

"Is that the menace du jour?"

"We could FedEx fresh ravioli from Tuscany faster than I can make them myself. I don't know why I put them on the menu. I'm a masochist."

"At least the rest of us are safe. What are you doing tonight?"

"Nothing. Want to come over?"

"I was planning on it. Seven?"

"Seven." Sunny pulled on her jacket and buttoned it up. She stuffed her hands in her pockets, lingering over the vision of Wade Skord.

He looked up. "Seven sounds good. You want me to bring anything special?"

"No, I'll get everything from the restaurant."

"Great. I'll see you tonight."

Sunny didn't move. Wade looked at her again. "Hey?" she said. "You know that story about the girl somebody killed yesterday?"

"I saw that. Terrible news. That's not that far from here. Just around the corner."

"Well, the strange thing is, just between you and me . . . I have to tell somebody." She stared at him. She knew she must have a maniacal look on her face and she tried to control it. "The strange thing about it is, I was the one who found her. I'll tell you about it tonight."

Wade stared up at her. "You set my hair on end, McCoskey."

The truck skimmed across the yellow morning like a boat on a rippling sea. It was a morning like the first morning on earth with a blue sky and fresh, cool air. Sunny rolled down the window and wished she had farther to drive. Instead, she pulled into the parking lot at Wildside and killed the engine.

She sat in the truck listening to a red-winged blackbird trill from the edge of the vineyard that ran up to the back of the restaurant. Perhaps things would go back to normal now. She was rested, washed, fed, and caffeinated. Moreover, she'd been freed of the burden of secrecy. The beautiful young woman's tragic death was known to the world at large. It was no longer her burden. Everyone carried the girl's death now, everyone shared the grief and horror of it. Steve Harvey and his team were working on the case. There was order. Sunny's only task was to come to terms with the memory of the white shape hanging in the tree, tied like a macabre gift.

There was no longer any way to avoid the next order of business, which was to telephone Andre Morales and attempt to explain why she had left his house without saying good-bye two nights ago, and had avoided his calls since then. If he was upset, she couldn't blame him, he had a right to be. She claimed genetic weakness as her defense. The McCoskeys were a disciplined and talented clan stricken with several consistent flaws, among them the inability to articulate their feelings, especially under pressure. Sunny was a typical McCoskey. At least she knew herself well enough to admit that she would do almost anything to avoid having to explain an incident of precocious behavior, including, it seemed, jeopardize the peace of mind of the person she was most interested in pleasing. This, she resolved, was a moment that would require courage and frank language, as well as considerable eloquence. If she did not possess these qualities in adequate supply, she would simply have to fake it. The truth—that she had left because she was annoyed at being kept up all night when her work day started at five every morning—was likely to provoke more bad feelings. On the other hand, there was always the chance Andre would understand completely, and even empathize.

She walked around the back of the restaurant and through the kitchen garden, feeling better with each step. The darkness of Wednesday night was behind her and a new day ahead. The girl's death was a tragedy and a nightmare. It may have been Sunny's nightmare, but it was not her tragedy. She did not have to carry it around forever, and in fact she refused to do so. Encouraged by the sight of the tender green sprouts that had popped up seemingly overnight along the raised rows of black soil in the garden, she bounded up the back stairs, almost crashing into Andre Morales sitting at the top of them.

6

Not that she wasn't glad to see him. It was just that she was not expecting Andre Morales or anyone else to be sitting on the back stoop of the restaurant at this hour. He basked in an air of joie de vivre. The early sun warming his pretty face, his white shirt crisp with enthusiasm, he looked every bit the rising star chef that he was. Even the heavy steel watch fastened around his wrist, a Breitling he fondled affectionately whenever he was bored, seemed to foretell an inevitable, swift rise to fame and fortune.

"Did I startle you?" he said.

"You nearly gave me a heart attack," she gasped.

She leaned down and gave him a kiss. Among Andre Morales's many attractive attributes were full, sensuous lips like a Brazilian beach beauty. Sunny squeezed in beside him on the stoop and they stared at the back garden. The winter crop of lettuces were producing nicely and the spring onions, carrots, and potatoes showed solid ambition above ground. Howell Mountain struck a stoic pose in the distance, and beyond it, the craggy face of Mount St. Helena.

"Mind telling me what's going on, or do I have to guess?" he said.

"I was going to call you this morning."

"I would have been honored."

He was angry. Andre had the very practical habit of becoming calmer, more polite, and even charming when he was upset. She was just about to begin the whole story when Rivka Chavez opened the garden gate and walked up the path toward them. This, at least, would save her having to repeat herself. They were still outside when Sunny heard the familiar sound of Wade Skord's old Volvo purring into the parking lot. She looked at Rivka. "Are we having a party I don't know about?"

Wade Skord opened the garden gate. "Ladies. Gentleman."

"Déjà vu," said Sunny.

"You can't just drop a bomb like that and take off."

They went inside and Sunny steamed a pot of milk and fired shots of espresso. She layered cold milk, then warm milk, then creamy foam into glasses and poured a shot into each. Rivka loaded up a tray with the lattes, orange juice, and a plate of biscotti while Andre opened the French doors to the patio and wiped the dew off one of the tables and four chairs.

Besides Sunny's mania for perfection and the fresh pastas to rival anything served in Rome, Wildside's best feature was its patio. The patio stopped time. It was an intimate space where no evidence of a busier world intruded. At one end stood a massive cedar tree, which littered the patio with amber-colored needles and freshened the air. In the corner across from it, the low adobe wall that circled most of the perimeter rose up to form an outdoor fireplace. In the spring and fall, the maitre d', who was also the sommelier and gardener, kept a fire going, burning vine trimmings and, for the holiday week, piñon logs brought from Santa Fe. Night-blooming jasmine tumbled over the awning that protected the French doors.

Andre pulled up a chair and spooned sugar into his latte. "In the big office buildings in Italy," he said, "they employ a girl barista in a miniskirt on each floor with a little espresso cart."

"Sounds like an urban legend to me," said Rivka.

Andre stirred his coffee and looked up at Sunny, who saw for the first time how tired he was.

"Have you even been to bed yet?" she asked.

He licked the spoon. "I closed my eyes in the shower. Does that count?"

"You stayed out all night?"

"I would have gladly spent it sleeping in the arms of a good woman, but she wouldn't return my calls. I had to turn to my friends for support and distraction."

"Time," said Rivka, making the T gesture. "You guys can hash out the romance later. I want to know why McCoskey's truck was parked out front of the Dusty Vine all day yesterday while she rode her bicycle to work."

"Who told you that?" said Sunny.

"Take a wild guess. I'll give you a hint: He has beady little all-knowing eyes, a shiny dome, and gossips like a teenage girl."

"Lenstrom?"

Rivka nodded. "Who else? With friends like us, you don't need government surveillance."

Sunny shook her head. "How do you know I wasn't involved in some cheap barroom hookup? That is exactly the sort of information a friend does not drag to the surface."

"And?"

"Let me start at the beginning."

"Does the beginning eventually get us to the part I want to know about?" said Wade. "I'm sure the truck story is solid material, but I've got grapes to tend to."

"It all takes us to the same place. I'll move quickly."

She described leaving the party, walking toward home, seeing the truck at Vedana Vineyards, and finding the woman's body, though in less detail than when she told Steve.

"Until the cops get this guy, this story does not leave this table," said Sunny. "None of it, not even that I found her or was involved at all. Monty Lenstrom excepted."

"Heavy," said Rivka.

"Does the person who did this know who you are?" asked Wade. "That's not exactly the kind of folks you want dropping by the house."

"That's why it's better if we don't talk about it," said Sunny. "So I can stay anonymous. Until I told you, only the cops knew I found her. Whoever was driving the truck might have seen me, but they won't know my name or where to find me."

"What kind of rope did they use?" asked Andre.

"Nothing special. Plain brown hemp."

"Tied around her how?"

Sunny explained.

"It sounds like shibari," he said. "Japanese rope tying. A bondage fetish. They always use hemp rope, and the pattern sounds shibari-style."

The table went silent. Andre looking around at the three faces staring at him. "Am I the only one who's ever seen Japanese porn?"

"I've heard of it," said Rivka. "Animated, right?"

"Right. Stylized bondage is stock in trade in Japanese anime porn and manga. Manga are like comic books with very simple illustrations and more pages. The ones for adults are usually pornographic and almost always include rope bondage. Shibari is the Japanese equivalent of the plumber coming by to fix the leaky sink. A porn motif, if you will."

"Do you have any of this stuff?" asked Sunny.

"Uh, I know where I can get some. Why?"

"I'd like to see it. It might help explain what that whole scene was about."

"Do you think that's a good idea? It seems like it would make it worse."

"I know, but it might help explain what happened to her. When can you get it?"

"I'll see what I can do."

"I remember when pornography was something to be ashamed of, unless you were Swedish," said Wade. "Being Swedish, those were the days."

They finished their coffee and went inside, led by Rivka, who froze in her tracks. "Gonzalez!" she hissed.

"Where?" said Andre.

"By the front door, headed toward the kitchen."

Andre stepped over and blocked the entrance to the kitchen. "Come on, mouse, let's see what you've got," he said, acting point guard.

A blip of fur with a strand of tail and enormous round ears darted right and left and dashed past Andre into the kitchen, raced across the floor, and disappeared into a cupboard.

"Now I have you, Señor Gonzalez."

Andre opened the cupboard slowly and jiggled a cardboard box on the floor, leaping back. The mouse ran from behind it, directly toward him.

"Death from above!" he shouted, smashing the mouse with a leather driving moccasin, to devastating effect.

"You didn't," said Sunny, running into the kitchen.

"No more mouse," said Andre, making a fierce chopping motion.

"At least it was quick," said Wade.

"It's better than the trap," said Rivka. "Instant death."

"I'm so glad it's Friday," said Sunny.

Andre cleaned up the remains as an act of chivalry and stood at the back sink scrubbing his hands. "Try to forget about all this morbid stuff, okay?" he said. "It's a beautiful day and you have all morning to cook." He wiped off his hands and rolled down his sleeves. "I've gotta go. Special prep today. We're doing a delicacy from Cambodia for Easter. Deep-fried whole baby chicks. They're so tender, you eat the bones and all. See you tonight."

She listened until she heard the gate open and close behind him, then went to work.

Fridays were always busy and this one was no exception. Spring fever had put the town in the mood to leave work early and settle down over a late lunch with a glass of something cool and bright. Berton, Wildside's sommelier and Renaissance man, spent the afternoon dashing down to the wine cage in the basement to replenish supplies of floral Champagnes, crisp Sauvignon Blancs and Chardonnays, Bandol pink, and marvelously sweet, delicate dessert Sauternes. Sunny and Rivka hardly spoke. With just two of them in the kitchen and a full house up front, it was all they could do to keep up with the waitstaff.

Work was more challenging than usual thanks to a persistent, unusual mood of ennui on Sunny's part. Not in the sense of boredom, but ennui in the sense of a marked lack of enthusiasm. She arranged spears of grilled asparagus without her usual mania for aligning the grill marks. She poured green pepper sauce over the filet mignon with a lackadaisical nonchalance, and even with a feeling of, if she were to name it honestly, despair. She hardly exulted when Soren put in an order for the last plate of calamari. Her mind drooped and lagged, and required a steady stream of boot camp–style encouragement in order to continue. *Buck up, soldier, you're going to dress those greens and plate that rosy slab of king salmon, and you're going to like it!* As the afternoon progressed, her *joie de cuisiner* faltered, staggered, and finally collapsed, leaving her perspiring in a cramped and sweltering kitchen with a seemingly hopeless number of tasks to accomplish.

Rivka caught the mood and grew sullen. When the last customer left, they wiped down the work stations and boxed up everything that would not survive the weekend with a grim efficiency that betrayed their mutual desires to be gone as swiftly as possible. Even the dishwasher worked more quickly than usual. He had finished the pots and pans and was already pulling up the rubber mats in the kitchen to power wash the concrete floors. Heather and Soren divvied up the day's tips, cashed out Berton and the only busser who'd shown up, and left without the usual closing idle.

On Friday afternoons, Sunny's habit was to linger, flipping through the stacks of cookbooks in her office for ideas for the next week's menu, paying bills, and taking care of odds and ends. It was the time her employees dropped in to discuss any concerns they might have, or to ask for time off. Today she couldn't wait to go home. She took the cherry blossoms, pale pink tulips, and lilies from a tall vase on the counter and wrapped them in newspaper for the drive home. Rivka helped her load the food in the truck. Swiftly, wordlessly, feeling as if they were tapping the very dregs of their capacities, they made their last checks that everything was in order, and, exchanging exhausted looks, removed their aprons and headed home.

Sunny took the towel from around her waist and wiped the steam off the bathroom mirror. Two little nose hairs, strays from their rightful territory within the nostrils, grew with stubborn regularity directly underneath, like tiny tusks. She imagined the cell-foremen examining the floor plans to her face and deciding where to put the nose hairs. They'd already installed two of them when the architect arrived and raised hell. They were off by at least a quarter of an inch!

She leaned in and plucked, wincing. Just as the tweezers gripped the second offender, she noticed the window behind her reflected in the mirror, and in the bottom portion of it, a man's face watching her. The scream was already ringing in her ears when she realized she was staring at an equally startled Monty Lenstrom.

7

"What the heck were you doing creeping around the side of the house?" said Sunny, still puffing from the fright he'd given her.

Monty Lenstrom took off his spectacles and polished them on his shirt nervously. "I wasn't creeping around, I was just trying to see if anybody was home."

"What's wrong with knocking?"

"I did knock, but you didn't answer. As I see now, you were in the shower. Nice tan lines."

Sunny punched him in the arm, hard enough to feel the thump of knuckle on bone.

"Ow."

"Why didn't you just hang around on the front stoop until you could hear me moving around inside like a normal Peeping Tom?"

Monty ran his fingers over his scalp, as if checking to see if any hair had suddenly appeared there. "If you must know, I wanted to make sure nobody had you bound and gagged in here. I was a *concerned friend.* I saw your truck out front and the cruiser locked up. I knew you were here. When you didn't answer . . ." He registered Sunny's surprise. "Rivka told me."

"That was fast."

"Is there any wine in this joint, or do I have to open what I brought?"

"There's a bottle of Truchard Chard in the fridge."

"You're Tru Chard Chard, hush hush, eye to eye," he sang, foraging. Sunny finished getting dressed. She came back to find him digging in cartons from the restaurant with a fork.

"No picking. I have a really nice bread and olives and a few slabs of stinky cheeses that will blow your mind," said Sunny. "Just give me ten seconds."

"I'm starving. I was out at the airport all day."

"Why?"

"Auction. Some failed dot-com wine site was liquidating its stock. Unbelievable bargains. I think I paid at least forty percent under cost for a few lots. Good juice, too. Those guys must have had some serious funding. They had an inventory to keep the best wine shop on the Champs-Elysées stocked for a year and no customers."

"Why didn't you tell me?" said Sunny. "That sounds like quality scavenging."

"I didn't want the competition. You know how I am when it comes to business. I'd squeeze out my own mother if it meant I could score some inventory on the cheap."

"At least you admit it."

"Does that make it better?"

Monty found the wine opener and pulled the cork on the bottle of Chardonnay Sunny handed him. "Listen to that," he said. "Music to my wine-besotted ears. Someday we'll tell the youngsters about that sound. It's nothing but the crack of the lowly screw cap from here on out."

"It won't happen that soon, will it?"

"More operations are switching all the time. Nobody can afford the risk of cork anymore, especially at the high end. You know how it is. If a bottle of two hundred–dollar Cab comes up corked, it's a problem. And if ten percent of your inventory is corked, you have a big problem. Nobody used to notice. Ignorance was bliss. Now people know what corked wine tastes like and they bring it back."

"Call me old-fashioned, but I still think there may be something important about a natural stopper," said Sunny. "We might not know what it is for a decade or so. Whatever it is that's lost may not be evident until a wine is ten or fifteen years old. It might be subtle, but I'm sure there will be a difference. A cork is porous, an aluminum cap is not. A corked bottle is still interacting with the environment. A capped bottle is not. The two wines are going to age differently."

"I agree," said Monty, "but the capped wine might age better."

"Better being a subjective term. People think CDs sound better than vinyl."

"And everybody agrees cassettes sound terrible. Quality is only subjective after the base values everyone agrees upon are met. I don't know anyone who loves drinking wine that smells like wet newspaper. Beyond that, you're absolutely right, it's a matter of taste."

Sunny started taking restaurant leftovers out of the refrigerator, piling white takeout boxes on the butcher block in the middle of the kitchen. There were four different main courses, half a dozen vegetable sides, mixed greens, a tub of soup, and several desserts. She turned on the oven and took down an assortment of saucepans. "No one will go hungry tonight."

"If they do, it won't be me."

"So, spill it. What'd you buy at the auction anyway?" said Sunny.

"Loads of stuff. French, Chilean, Australian. I went on a Côtes-du-Rhône spree. I bought some great Châteauneuf-du-Pape and a bunch of Gigondas. Pretty well aged, too. There was nobody there to bid against me. If you're from out of town, you couldn't find the Napa airport without GPS and a police escort. The guys running the thing said—"

Monty was interrupted by the decisive jangle of the string of bells attached to the front door. Wade Skord and Rivka Chavez appeared. Greetings, coat removal, and wine pouring followed.

"By the way, I don't know why I bother asking anymore," said Sunny, turning to Monty Lenstrom, "but is the lovely Annabelle joining us tonight?"

"Negative. Annabelle has stopped eating dinner as part of her attempt to dramatically reduce her caloric intake and live to be two hundred years old."

"She's not seriously doing CR?" said Rivka.

"Dabbling, I'd say," said Monty.

"What's CR?" asked Wade.

"Calorie restriction," said Rivka. "I read an article about it. You eat almost nothing and live forever."

"What's the advantage?" said Wade. He poured himself a glass of wine, added a splash to Sunny's, and chimed his glass against hers. "To protection from evil spirits," he said, meeting her eyes.

"And Peeping Toms. *Santé*."

Sunny handed Monty a stack of plates and followed him with bowls and silverware into the living room, where the plank table took up too much space. The arrangement of pink tulips and cherry blossoms salvaged from the restaurant stood in the middle of the table, together with a rusty Moorish candelabra loaded with flesh-colored tapers. Monty arranged the plates, then took matches from his pocket and lit the candles.

"What's this about Peeping Toms?" said Wade.

"I saw McCoskey in her birthday suit tonight," he said. "The back half, at least."

"Racy!" said Rivka. "Let's hear it."

"He was spying in the window like a pervert," said Sunny.

"Excuse me, I was checking up on a dear friend's safety," said Monty. "What were you doing in there, anyway? Squeezing a pimple?"

"None of your business."

Rivka looked thoughtful. "So you might say that Sunny puts the bare ass in embarrassment."

"Nice," said Wade.

When they at last sat down, it was to a feast of leftovers, beginning with a winter gazpacho of Seville oranges, pine nuts, and paprika, and a platter of grilled asparagus with chopped hardboiled eggs in a marjoram vinaigrette, followed by lemon-rosemary chicken, a small portion of braised oxtail with leeks and carrots that had been unexpectedly popular that week, and, as the pièce de résistance, roasted spring lamb shoulder with potatoes au gratin, of which there was an ample supply since it had been unexpectedly unpopular all week. They opened a bottle of Skord Zinfandel to go with it.

Monty held up his glass. "Inky. Ninety-eight?"

"Ninety-four," corrected Wade. "Nearly the last of it."

"Holding up nicely."

Platters heavy with food went around the table.

"There's nothing like a spring lamb," said Monty. "So tender, so succulent. A wee babe hardly weaned from his mama's milk." He held up a forkful admiringly before devouring it.

Sunny put down her silver. She was divided between feeling ridiculous for her new squeamishness about meat and feeling genuinely squeamish about meat. This was not a sensitivity she could afford to develop. She took a sip of the potent red wine and loaded her plate with a second helping of mixed greens.

"I've been thinking about your murder," said Monty. "In my opinion, it had to be somebody who worked at the winery."

"It's not *my* murder," said Sunny.

"Otherwise there's no way they would have risked being seen going there."

"Anybody would have looked suspicious at two-thirty in the morning hanging a dead girl from a tree," said Sunny, "whether they worked there or not. It's not exactly part of the typical job description. But you can't see much from the road anyway. It wouldn't take much research to observe that you would have darkness and solitude at that hour. And it was a particularly dark night. There was just a sliver of a moon."

"You think they planned it that way?" said Rivka.

"I think everything about this crime was planned," said Sunny. She drank more wine. The astringent alcohol seemed to purify her mouth of the unpleasant topic. She didn't want to talk about the girl, especially not in the middle of dinner, and yet, it was the topic on everyone's mind, even her own.

"So what's the connection to the winery, then?" said Monty.

"It has to be sexual," said Sunny. "The message being sent was blatantly erotic. I would guess some kind of love triangle, but I can't think of how that would lead to the girl's death."

"I've met the winemaker at Vedana several times," said Monty. "A guy named Ové Obermeier. A clansman of Skord's, I think."

"Ové sounds Norwegian to me, not Swedish," said Wade.

"Whatever. Viking type. Gives off a player vibe. Probably he was having an affair with the girl."

"Why would that make somebody want to kill her?" asked Rivka.

"Maybe his wife killed her," said Wade.

"I don't think he's married," said Monty.

"You guys are missing the point. This was not a crime of passion. Nobody got angry, killed a girl on impulse, panicked, and decided to dump her at Vedana. This was a planned, calculated murder done by somebody with a serious screw loose. There may not even be a motive. What I saw was an act of evil." Sunny picked up a spear of asparagus and ate it. "I just wonder if they can catch him."

"What do they have to go on?" asked Rivka.

"I don't know. They paid a lot of attention to the road, trying to get tracks from the truck I saw. Other than that, I don't know what they found. Steve isn't talking. The ground under the tree was moist but grassy, so I doubt they found much in the way of footprints, and rope and trees aren't known for holding fingerprints. The most likely place for physical evidence will be the girl herself, I suppose, and I won't know what they find there until they print it in the paper."

"They'll get him," said Wade. "A guy like that wants to get caught. Somebody who sets up a scene like he set up is looking for attention."

"I agree," said Sunny. "And following that line of thinking, a guy like that will kill again, looking for another chance to make headlines. That's what has me worried." She bit the head off another spear of asparagus. "All I needed to do was look at the license plate and they'd have him by now."

"Hindsight's twenty-twenty," said Wade. "You had no reason to believe you'd need to identify that truck later."

After dinner, Rivka rifled through the CDs for Lester Young and the Oscar Peterson Trio. "This is a job for the President."

Sunny took down a bottle of twenty-three-year-old Bas-Armagnac and four snifters from a cabinet in the living room.

They settled into the couch and comfortable chairs and listened to the perfect sounds: short, concise notes on the piano, guitar warm and sweet, bass like an easy heartbeat, the swirl of the wire brush, and Pres on tenor sax.

"The sound of New York City," said Monty.

"In a hot club on a cold night," said Wade. "Upper West Side."

"In a silk dress and fishnet stockings," said Sunny.

"With a bad man in a good suit," said Rivka.

The kettle whistled and Rivka got up. She came back with a pot of mint tea sweetened Moroccan style and poured it into the colorful, intricately painted glasses Sunny kept for that purpose. She added a few pine nuts to each and handed them around. On the coffee table, she opened an assortment of white containers from the restaurant. There was a slice of Mama McCoskey's Rum Cake, two bread puddings with caramel sauce, and a box of assorted tea cookies.

"Dessert is a little on the heavy side," said Sunny. "I didn't have time to get any fruit. The customers mowed through all the Meyer lemon sorbet. There was one panna cotta with a Riesling-poached pear left, but I sent it home with Heather."

"Damn her," said Monty. "I love the panna cotta and I love the Riesling-poached pear."

"It was pretty good," said Sunny. "The pears came out perfect. They were the color of that Armagnac."

"Stop, I'm in agony," said Monty.

"You know, it wouldn't kill you to eat a meal at the restaurant once in a while," said Rivka. "Then you could order whatever you want."

"You mean pay? My god."

Wade quaffed the last of the brandy in his glass like it was so much bargain-bin schnapps and leaned back in the old leather armchair. He put his feet up on the wooden stool that served as an ottoman. "I don't like it, McCoskey," he said. "I don't like you being here alone. I don't think you should be alone at night until they nab this guy. In fact, it might be a good idea for you to come stay up at Skord Mountain until all this blows over."

"That's the problem," said Sunny. "They may never nab him. I might know everything I'm ever going to know about that girl and whoever did that to her. I have to get used to that idea. I have to forget about the whole business and move on or I'll lose my mind. It's over, at least as far as I'm concerned. Now I just have to get back to normal."

Rivka Chavez, who stayed the longest, had been gone for hours when Sunny heard the rumble of Andre Morales's motorcycle pulling up outside the cottage. The first night they'd spent together started with a ride on that motorcycle, an old BMW with a cream-colored tank. The sound of it still gave her butterflies. He stomped up the front stairs in his boots, rapped his knuckles on the door, and came in without waiting for an answer. She put down the cookbook she'd been reading and watched him. He was wearing the biking leathers that smelled like pinesap and campfire smoke. He put his helmet and gloves on the table and held his hand out to her.

"Come with me, please."

"Why did I have to find her?" said Sunny, tugging the tangles from strands of Andre's hair. "I'm a magnet for death."

"You're not a magnet for death," he said, turning over to face her. "You are just unusually observant. Anybody else would have noticed a truck went by and thought nothing of it. You noticed its lights were off, wondered what it was doing at the winery at that hour, and spotted something different about the tree. I'm sure that that acute attention to detail leads you to many more good things than it does bad. It's a positive trait that happened to get you into a bad place this time around."

"Like chanterelles."

"What do you mean?"

"I always spot chanterelles when nobody else sees them."

"Exactly. Sometimes your eagle eye leads you to a mushroom, sometimes to a dead body. You have to take the good with the bad." Andre stared at the ceiling. "Why don't you take some time off? You haven't had a vacation in a while."

"I have to close the restaurant if I leave town, and I can't afford to do that. We're barely making ends meet as it is," said Sunny.

"That's because your business model is not economically viable. You need more revenue streams. You need to find ways to make money that are scalable and that can keep happening whether you show up or not."

"I'm not selling Wildside T-shirts and coffee mugs."

"They could be nice T-shirts and handmade coffee mugs. You could open for dinner service and weekend brunch. You could do a stand at the farmers' market, branded gourmet products, a cookbook. All the stuff people do to make money. You need to grow. Your costs go up when you expand, but so does your income. And your profit margin expands with volume. Then you hire some people so you're not a slave to the kitchen."

"You're singing Rivka's song. She wants to open for weekends and dinner. She needs to make more money, and I can't afford to pay her any more unless we scale up."

Andre propped himself up on his elbow and rested his tiger eyes on her. "Both of you need to make more money. You can't go on just scraping by forever, and you can't keep doing everything yourself. You'll burn out. With Wildside the way it is, even as a resounding success, it's still a failure because you're not really making a living. You're just getting by."

"I make a living. I like my lifestyle."

"Savings?"

"Later."

"Investments?"

"Not in the monetary sense."

"You can't live hand to mouth forever."

"Do we have to talk about this right now?"

"Is there ever a good time? I hate watching you work this hard."

"You work harder than I do."

"But I know it's temporary. I have an exit strategy. I'm out one way or another inside of five years. And I make more money. You need a plan."

"Let's go back to talking about whether or not I'm a magnet for death. That was more relaxing."

8

Andre got up at six-thirty to play soccer. Sunny paced the house. Finally she called Wade Skord, thinking a trip up to the vineyard would clear her head.

"Coffee brewing," said Wade. "And we've got bud break."

She couldn't get out of the house fast enough, pulling on jeans and grabbing a sweater on the way out. The drive up Howell Mountain did half the job, and the sight of the vineyard surrounded by forest did the rest. By the time she got out of the truck, the breathless, nerve-jangling feeling she'd woken up to was gone.

Farber, Wade's cat, materialized to rub against her legs. He led the way up the stairs and onto the porch, where he had arrayed what was left of the night's prey on the doormat.

"Present for you," she said, when Wade answered the door.

Wade examined the unpleasant deposit. The head remained, and an assortment of red and blue entrails. "Wood rat, from the looks of it."

He praised the cat and tossed the remains into the woods off the western edge of the deck, then led the way inside.

"You're up early for a day off."

She poured herself a cup of coffee. "Do you think the killer is like Farber?"

"The cat? How do you mean?"

"Farber leaves the evidence for you to find so that you will know he is a good hunter."

"He wants me to know he's doing his job."

"Right. He knows, or assumes, that you want the wood rats of the world to be torn to bits, so by letting you know he's out doing your bidding, he builds favor with you."

"And feels important. He likes to feel like a big shot."

"Okay, but what if you were a wood rat yourself, or were simpatico with the wood rats? It would be a very different message."

"Definitely," said Wade. "No cream, by the way. I haven't been to the market lately. No sugar either, but I have syrup."

"For my coffee?"

"It's just like honey, but maple flavor." Wade twisted the top of the maple syrup, scowling at its stubbornness.

"Here." Sunny twisted the top off easily and poured some syrup in her coffee.

"The McCoskey brute strength."

"Anything red open?"

Wade took a bottle of Zin from the counter and she added a splash to her coffee. "It would become a message of intimidation."

They pulled chairs up to the old wooden table. A new three-legged ceramic pot, a souvenir from his recent trip to Mexico, stood in the middle of it.

"Right," said Wade. "If Farber left a human head and entrails on my doormat, I would be worried about my next trip out to the woodshed."

"Exactly. And why would he want you to feel that way? What is to be gained by making someone afraid of you?"

"They do what you want," said Wade. "You can control them."

"My thinking exactly. I think somebody at the winery knows that message was for them," said Sunny. "Somebody over there is very, very nervous right now. We'll find out who it is eventually, because they'll crack under the pressure. That is going to be the cops' biggest lead." She tasted the coffee. "Odd, but not bad."

"Except that the message didn't get delivered as it was intended," said Wade. "You intercepted it. All that got through was that a girl was killed. What if that's not enough? What if they don't know it was for them? Nobody saw her but you."

"Right again. The police haven't identified her yet. That's when the fur is going to fly, when the name is released. If I heard a man was killed and left in a tree at Wildside, I'd be upset. But if I learned it was a guy named Monty Lenstrom, for example, I'd freak out."

Wade went to the kitchen and came back with a slab of cheddar cheese and a couple of apples. He cut both into wedges and added dishes of walnuts and raisins to the spread.

"You eat like a hunter-gatherer," said Sunny.

"If cheese grew wild, I'd never go to the grocery store again." He walked into his office and returned with a newspaper. He put the front page down in front of Sunny. "I wasn't going to show you this. I thought you might want a break from all this business. But since you brought it up."

The entire top half of the front page of the *Santa Rosa Press Democrat* was dedicated to the girl with the long black hair. Sunny read the article three times, wringing each sentence for every nuance of meaning. She had been identified as Heidi Romero. Her family had reported her missing on Thursday night after she never showed up for work that day. She was twenty-six, grew up in Rohnert Park, and lived in Sausalito, a little fishing village turned tourist destination right across the Golden Gate from San Francisco. She worked at the REI in Corte Madera. Her coworkers said she loved being outside, mountain biking, and surfing. Her mother said they knew something was wrong when they found her car in the parking lot and her purse inside her house. Sergeant Harvey was identified as the investigating officer and quoted as saying his team was pursuing a number of leads and awaiting the coroner's report.

Next to the article was a photograph of Heidi Romero at the beach. She had just come out of the water and was standing with her arm around her surfboard and an ecstatic smile on her face. Sunny studied her. Was there any chance this sporty, wholesome-looking girl was into serious bondage? Can you tell who has that kind of kink just by looking? People have their secrets.

"How do you get from this picture to what I saw Wednesday night?" asked Sunny. "Those two worlds aren't supposed to meet. Not ever."

"If I knew," said Wade, "I'd be knocking down somebody's door right now."

They spent the morning hiking the hillside vineyard, examining bud break and pulling weeds. Wade cursed like a pirate whenever he spotted a growth of thistle, pulling it up with passionate hatred. His vitriol continued between offenses. "Thorny bastards," he muttered. "How dare they open up shop in my vineyard. I'd sooner burn the place down than let the thistle have it."

At lunchtime, they visited the garden for greens, baby carrots, and green onion. Sunny made an omelet and salad and rubbed toasted slices of peasant bread with garlic. After lunch, they opened a bottle of Wade's experimental Sangiovese and sat down to stick labels on the Zinfandel harvested four years earlier that was finally ready to be released. When the sun went down, Wade followed her home and they watched his DVD of *The Adventures of Robin Hood* with Errol Flynn and Olivia de Havilland, a film they could both recite.

Andre came in late and left early. Sunny stayed in bed. She wanted the forgetfulness of sleep.

9

It was a garden party like any other. Sunny held a paper plate loaded with food and chatted with people she seemed to know. The afternoon sun warmed the patio pleasantly. Through the trees, she could see a green slope. Beyond it was the pale blue of the open sea. Just inside the trees stood Heidi Romero. She was wearing a skirt and blouse and her hair was pulled back in a ponytail. She beckoned to Sunny with a smile, inviting her to come over so she could tell her something. Sunny stared, her heart racing.

"You can't be here," she said. "You're . . . You're . . . " The word would not come out. She tried to say it, but her throat would permit no air, no sound to pass.

Heidi smiled, encouraging her to walk over so they could talk.

Sunny shook her head. "You can't be here. You've been . . . You've been . . . " It was as though the words lodged in her throat. She woke gasping for air.

"This was one of those super-realistic, vivid dreams, exactly like it was really happening," said Sunny, huddled over a cup of tea.

It was still early on Sunday morning, but she had decided to call Rivka anyway. If Rivka was seeing someone, it would be different. She wouldn't call and wake up two people. But since Rivka had ended her romance with Alex Campaglia, she'd been in a dry spell. "What do you think it means?"

"It's more important to know what you think it means," said Rivka, yawning. "It's a message from your subconscious, not mine. Tell me again what happened in the dream. Give me the high-level summary."

"Heidi wanted to talk with me, but I refused to go over to her. I was afraid of her because she's dead. I tried to say so, but I couldn't."

"And what about when you woke up? How did you feel?"

"I was sorry that I hadn't allowed her to speak to me. I wished I hadn't been afraid. I wanted to know what she was trying to tell me."

"Well," said Rivka, "that seems pretty clear. You couldn't say the word *dead* because she's not dead in your mind. She is still very much alive in your subconscious. There is still something Heidi Romero needs to tell you, and you're going to have to overcome your fear in order to find out what it is."

"Fear of what?" said Sunny.

"Well, in a murder there are plenty of things to fear, but this is probably something more elemental, less rational. Death itself, maybe. You couldn't say the word and you avoided her because she'd dead. Maybe you have to overcome your fear of death in order to find out what she is trying to tell you. Or maybe, as far as your subconscious is concerned, she's not dead. Her spirit is still with you. Maybe you picked her up like a hitchhiker by being the first one to discover the body."

"Where did you get that idea?"

"Nowhere in particular."

Sunny thought that if Heidi's spirit was lingering anywhere, it was more likely at Vedana Vineyards. That was what was bothering her. Endings were important. To end up hanging in a tree, caught up literally and figuratively in somebody else's nightmare, was not a fate she was willing to allow Heidi Romero to endure for all eternity. Something so ugly could not be the end of what sounded like a very pretty life. Maybe the best thing she could do was try to help her make a transition from the hell of her last hours back to someplace she felt at home. "I think I need to see the water," said Sunny.

"Like maybe where she liked to surf?" said Rivka.

"She lived in Sausalito. Where would you surf if you lived in Sausalito?"

"I have no idea. But I know someone who'll know. I'll call while you drive over."

"See you in fifteen."

They drove down Highway 29 and turned west at the 120 split, heading into the Carneros hills. A delicate light touched the vineyard-covered hillsides and turned the sky exuberant blue. At 101, they went south, passing the rolling green hills of San Rafael, the Space Age civic center building famously designed by Frank Lloyd Wright, and finally the downhill stretch to Mill Valley. It was still early enough for the freeway to be empty. Rivka looked toward the upcoming exit.

"Coffee at the Depot?"

"I was thinking Caffe Trieste," said Sunny.

"Sounds good," said Rivka.

They topped the final rise and the truck gathered speed down the other side, rounding a turn at the bottom that opened up a view of the bay, from the mansions of Tiburon to the eucalyptus-covered slopes of Angel Island, the concrete edifice of Alcatraz, and beyond, the distant high-rises of San Francisco crowding the water's edge. To the east, the ridge line of the Oakland Hills ran the length of the horizon. Sunny turned off and cruised into the seaside town of Sausalito.

"If we talk to anyone, we're friends of Heidi Romero," she said. "Nothing more. I don't want to get into anything about finding the body."

"Right."

They parked on the main street in front of the Sausalito marina. The café was peppered with locals, up early to beat the tourists. The guy behind the bar had a grizzled look, with unshaved whiskers and a wide, red face. His fingers were fat as sausages. Sunny ordered a latte and watched him under-tamp the grounds and over-heat a pot of milk. Rivka sighed.

"Would you mind if I gave that a try?" she said.

"You wanna make your own coffee?" the barista joked, his face breaking into a gaping smile. He poured the scorched milk on top of the watery shot, turning it a uniform, ashen gray. "Be my guest."

Rivka came around behind the counter. "That thing you just made? That's not a latte, that's a laxative. Let me show you how to make a real latte. First you warm the milk, gently. Then you need a shot with a nice, golden layer of crema on top."

The barista took Sunny's money, looking amused, while Rivka pounded the old puck out of the portafilter and whipped the espresso station into shape.

Sunny carried a glass of water out to the terrace to watch the boats while Rivka conducted coffee school. A few minutes later, she and the barista arrived at the table, bearing perfectly layered Chavez-style lattes.

"Your friend knows what she's doing, I'll give her that," he said, standing in front of them with his hands on his hips, shielding the view of the marina like a partition.

"And she's not afraid to say so," said Sunny, putting down the paper she'd been reading. She tapped the front page. "Sad story. This was a local girl, right?"

"That's right. She lived over on one of the houseboats docked at the end of town. A real shame. She came into the café sometimes." He looked around at the tables and picked up a dirty plate and napkin.

"In the mornings?" asked Sunny.

"Sometimes. Sometimes at night for a glass of wine. We got music in the evenings and the people come in to relax after work." He walked away and came back a second later without the plate and napkin. "Hey, you girls come back anytime. Ask for Jason. I'll make you a perfect latte or it's on me." He shook their hands and urged them to have a great day. After he left, they sat drinking their coffee in silence and letting the sun warm their faces. Rivka shed a layer, down to her perennial tank top. Sunny followed suit. It had been a long winter.

"You certainly made a friend," said Sunny. "And by viciously criticizing his craft."

"People love you when you bust them out," said Rivka. "He knew that was a terrible latte. Most people don't know the difference, so why should he bother doing it right? It's easier to feed people garbage. Guys like that love to get busted trying to put one over on the general public. It's secretly gratifying to them to know that somebody can tell the difference."

They soaked up the sun and the view of the marina with its forest of masts. A seagull approached them with wary arrogance. Rivka swallowed the last of her latte. "*On y va?*"

"*Allons-y.*"

IO

Nothing, not a cloud or wisp of fog, impeded the view from the top of the hill overlooking Fort Cronkhite. Sunny parked the truck and they walked through the concrete bunker punched through the hillside, then hiked up to the top, where a concrete pad had been laid down for a lookout station. The installation, like many dug into the hills facing the Pacific, had been built in the late thirties as a last defense against invasion from the west. Now defunct, they served as observation points for tourists and weekenders, covert make-out and quickie spots for the amorous, and nighttime venues for rituals involving spray paint, beer, and bonfires.

From the peak, they looked down on the massive orange Art Deco towers of the Golden Gate Bridge and the narrow channel of surging water that separated the two hillsides. Beyond, San Francisco spread out like a scale model of itself. The day was so clear, lines of whitewater could be seen from waves breaking at Ocean Beach, the straight strip of unprotected beach at the city's western edge. To the east, beyond the Oakland Hills, was the perfect pyramid of Mount Diablo in the distance. Immediately to the north, Rodeo Canyon plunged down to a cluster of red-roofed military buildings beside an estuary that ended in a half-moon beach. Beyond the canyon, the forested ridges of Mount Tamalpais rose up. West of everything, the vast blue of the Pacific filled the horizon. A ship loaded with cargo containers approached the entrance to the bay. Otherwise, only the distant, craggy silhouettes of the Farallon Islands interrupted the endless expanse of ocean.

The sun behind her, Sunny gazed out to sea. It felt good to stretch her eyes. The sight of an endless series of swells rippling the water's surface all the way out to the horizon stirred her emotions. They arrived from a journey across hundreds or even thousands of miles of open water. So many endings. The ceaseless arrival of travelers, of journeys ending with a crash and an explosion of foam and spray.

They walked back to the truck and headed down into Rodeo Canyon. Bright orange poppies and purple lupin lined the road and climbed the hillsides. At the bottom, they passed stables, horses grazing lazily in a nearby meadow, and a snow-white egret stepping through tall grasses in the lagoon. A red-winged blackbird balanced on the tip of a reed, showing a flash of crimson with each adjustment.

The surf looked rough and disorganized, a chaos of waves and whitewater crashing into a steep depression it had carved into the shore. They walked out to a driftwood log washed up to the top of the beach and sat down. A cluster of surfers sat their boards a few yards beyond the breaking waves, facing out to sea. Periodically one of them would turn and paddle for a wave, usually pulling back at the last moment to let it slide away underneath him. Occasionally a guy would paddle hard and catch one, standing up for a few seconds before the wave closed out, enveloping him in foam. They watched a pair of surfers arrive and plunge into the icy water with their boards. They paddled into the line of breaking waves, struggling against the power of each wave in succession. They were forced underwater and shoved back toward the beach half a dozen times, coming up and resuming their struggle with determined strokes. One of them had paddled ahead six or seven feet. He crested the last swell easily, tipping over the top to join the pack in calm water. The other paddled hard behind him. The wave rose up and the surfer with it, his board more and more vertical as the face of the swell grew. Sunny and Rivka sucked in their breath in unison, anticipating an ugly backward tumble. The surfer paddled furiously and leaned forward, stretching to push the nose of the board up and over the top an instant before the wall of water gathered force and fell forward, crashing heavily downward with an angry blast of spray and foam.

They watched until their hands were red with cold, then walked back to the parking lot. A group of surfers, some in wetsuits, others in down jackets, all barefoot or wearing flip-flops, was gathered around the back end of an SUV.

"Hang on a sec," said Sunny. She detoured to approach the surfers. Rivka hung back, watching. Their talk fizzled as she walked up. There didn't seem to be any point to introductions or hey-how's-it-going formalities. "Do any of you know a girl from around here named Heidi Romero?"

Chins down, staring at their toes, they glanced at each other furtively. One of them, a teenager hunkered down in his jeans' pockets with the hood of his sweatshirt flipped up against the chill, looked up at her. "She the chick with the long black hair?"

"That's her."

"I think Hyder might know her."

"Where can I find Hyder?" asked Sunny.

The boy indicated the direction with his chin, keeping his hands shoved in his pockets. "Over there. Dude with the shaved head."

The issue resolved, they went back to talking waves and rides. The one they called Hyder, a bulky guy with a goatee, was sitting on the tailgate of a 4-Runner, pulling off his booties. When Sunny and Rivka walked up, he had just peeled his arms free of his wetsuit. His sturdy forearms and biceps were covered with tattoos, including a gothic cross, a dagger with a snake wound around it, and, from what Sunny could see, an ambitious dragon-like creature covering much of his back. He looked up at them with eyes the color of the water he'd just gotten out of. They met Sunny's with a jolt. She could hardly remember seeing more striking eyes in a more shocking shade of blue on anyone, let alone a girthsome, ink-covered surfer. They looked like blue-green marbles held up to the light. He was in his late thirties or early forties and his face was beginning to show the signs of middle age, with comfortable-looking crow's-feet around the eyes. He finished toweling off his shoulders and pulled on a T-shirt. Sunny and Rivka introduced themselves and he reciprocated with a surprisingly engaging smile.

"Joel Hyder," he said, shaking their hands and looking at them curiously. "What can I do for you girls?"

"We heard you might know Heidi Romero," said Sunny.

Joel Hyder gave her a stern frown. "Who told you that?"

"Those guys," said Sunny.

"What about her?"

"We're friends. We were just looking to hook up with other people who knew her, considering what's happened." Sunny studied his face, wondering whether or not he knew Heidi Romero was dead.

His expression softened and he went back to toweling off. "As long as you're not reporters."

"Reporters?"

"They were out here yesterday snooping around. I don't care for newspapers or TV news, and I don't like reporters. Vultures paid to prey on other people's tragedies."

"We're not reporters," said Sunny.

"Excuse me a minute." He wrapped the towel around his waist and gestured for them to spin around. Sunny had witnessed the surfer's towel dance before. The object was to pry yourself free of the tight, sticky wetsuit and pull on shorts or jeans, all without dropping the towel or exposing yourself. Especially for a man of Hyder's proportions, it would present a challenge.

"Much better. Now, tell me who you are again?" He stepped into flip-flops, tossed the hide of sandy black neoprene into the plastic bin with his booties, and tightened the drawstring on his shorts.

"Neat trick," said Rivka.

"Took me longer to learn that than it did to surf," he said, grinning. "So, how'd you know Heidi? Surfing?"

Sunny found it distasteful to lie, but, in the present circumstances, she found telling the truth even less agreeable. There was much to be lost and nothing to be gained by revealing how she had come in contact with Heidi Romero. Rivka took the lead. "We did yoga together."

"Did you? Where was that?"

"In Mill Valley."

"You mean the place across from the Cantina?"

"That's it."

"I go there myself now and then. I like to give the Marin moms a thrill. They love to see a guy who can barely touch his toes." He stared at them with his gemstone eyes. "And?"

Rivka faltered. "We only really knew her in that context."

"And now that she's dead, you wish you knew her better," he said.

"I guess so."

"Well, you've come to the right place. I surfed with her just about every day for the last year. You girls looking to learn? I make a good teacher. I taught Heidi and she was better than me within three months."

"Not me," said Rivka. "I'm afraid of sharks."

"You come with me, I'll protect you. I'll fight off any sharks that come around."

Rivka smiled awkwardly. "Thanks, but I think I'll pass."

He loaded his gear into the back of the 4-Runner and closed the hatch. They watched while he wiped down his board and hoisted it onto the roof, then went around the other side to tighten the straps down. He came back brushing off his hands. "Ladies, I suggest we continue this conversation over brunch. I know a place where the pancakes are out of this world."

They hesitated.

"Come on, I don't bite. At least not on the first date." He pinched at Rivka's waist and she jumped.

"I think we'll hang out here for a while," said Sunny.

"Don't be like that. I'll play nice, I promise."

"Thanks, but no thanks," said Rivka.

"Suit yourselves." He stroked his goatee and looked them up and down. "You girls ever been over to Heidi's place?"

"The houseboat?" said Sunny. "Not me."

"Me neither," said Rivka.

"It's over at the north end of Sausalito. I was meaning to go over there later, but we could go now if you want. That's my final offer. You come with me and you can snoop around all you want."

"We don't want to snoop around," said Sunny.

"Then what do you want to do? As far as I can tell, you're snooping around right now."

Sunny frowned. "Good to meet you. Riv, let's get out of here."

Joel Hyder grabbed Rivka's wrist. "How about just you come. You know you want to see where Heidi lived. It'll be fun. I can drive you home whenever you want."

Rivka glared at the hand on her wrist and he let her go. "Thanks, really, but no thanks."

"What are you two really up to?" said Joel. "Why are you here?"

"We told you. We're friends of Heidi's. We just wanted to see where she surfed," said Rivka.

"You saw it. Why bother me?"

"I'm sorry we bothered you. We're finished bothering you now." She rolled her eyes at Sunny.

"I don't get you two," said Joel. "You come all the way out here looking for some clue to who this acquaintance of yours was, then when you find it, you run away. I knew her better than just about anybody. Inside of an hour, I'll be sitting on her sundeck, playing my guitar, wishing her a good journey in the afterlife. If you don't want to come, that's fine with me, but you'll learn as much as there is to know about Heidi from looking around the houseboat. If you have unfinished business with her, maybe you should try to finish it while you have the chance. I'll tell you one thing, I'm not making this offer again."

Sunny looked at Rivka and back to Joel. "We can't go to Heidi's house."

"Why not?"

"You can't just break into somebody's house who's been murdered. We'll get arrested."

Joel scowled. "Forget I mentioned it." He got in the 4-Runner and started the engine.

Sunny made a face at Rivka. This was their only chance. She jogged up to the window and tapped on the glass.

He rolled it down. "What now?"

"Why are you going to her house?"

"Her father asked me to keep an eye on the place until he gets here. Besides, I don't need a reason. I used to hang out there whenever I wanted when she was alive. I don't see why I can't do it now that she's dead."

"Well, for one thing, there wasn't a murder investigation going on when she was alive. Her house could have evidence in it. Fingerprints, some indication of what happened to her."

"Her father owns the houseboat and he said it was okay to go out there. That's good enough for me. We can check with the harbormaster on the way in and make sure the cops are done with the place. I'm sure they've been all over it by now."

Sunny hesitated.

"I don't have time for this. Are you coming or not?"

Sunny studied the contents of the 4-Runner's cabin. It looked normal enough. "How did you know Heidi?"

"We used to date, a long time ago. Then we decided we were better off friends. Now, are you coming or not?"

They agreed to meet in an hour at the park-and-ride by the Sausalito off-ramp. "You can follow me from there," Joel said. "There are a couple of tricky turns."

Joel pulled out of the parking lot and turned up the road throwing gravel. Sunny and Rivka got in the truck.

"Do we go?" said Sunny.

"Curiosity killed the cat," said Rivka.

"I hope that's just an expression."

They burned the time at the upscale grocery Rivka called Whole Paycheck in Mill Valley. She put an organic tomato on the scale. "Look, it's a three-, no four-dollar tomato." They bought a papaya the size of a football, Asian pears, dates, a baguette, mixed olives, a wedge of Romano cheese, salmon jerky, and a bottle of cheap pink wine from Spain.

"I hope this is a good idea," said Sunny, back in the truck. "We have no idea who this guy is or what he's getting us into. And the way he was leering at you made my skin crawl. He could be dangerous."

"You're just freaked out by the tattoos. A little aggressive ink doesn't have to mean he's dangerous."

"It's not just that. Don't forget why we're here. The more I think about it, the more I think this is not a good idea."

"It may not be, but I think we should do it anyway. We came here looking for traces of Heidi and we stumbled onto the jackpot. Like he said, we'll get an up-close look at who she was, your curiosity will be satisfied, the dream ghost will leave you alone, and we can all get back to business as usual. I can't say I like the guy, but I don't think he's dangerous."

"At least there are two of us. We just have to be ready to run, scream, fight. Whatever it takes if things get sketchy."

"If you think about it, he's the one who should be suspicious, not us. He was just minding his own business. We're the ones who stalked him and lied about who we are."

"That's true. And we have our cell phones in case things get weird. Let's just keep our wits about us."

"Right. The cell phones will save us."

Sunny drove back to Sausalito and pulled into the lot, where Joel Hyder was waiting. He flashed them the thumbs up and led the way.

II

The harbormaster's office was little more than a storage shed with windows, set down under an acacia tree in between two parking lots. No one was in when they arrived. A note taped to the door said, "Back in five minutes." Joel tapped the note. "Starting when?"

"About five minutes ago," said a man striding up to them. "I left the dog in the house by accident this morning. She sleeps most of the day, but she can't stay in there forever. Had to pop home and let the old girl out for a pee." He was dressed East Coast nautical preppy, in khakis and a V-neck sweater over a button-down shirt and tie. He unlocked the door and they followed him into his outpost, where he hung his car keys on a hook by the door and took a pair of canvas topsiders from their place next to the coatrack. He sat at his desk and changed out of his worn leather topsiders and into the newer canvas ones.

"You live in town?" asked Joel.

"Just across Bridgeway, a couple blocks up the hill."

Joel jiggled the flimsy aluminum-frame window by the door. "What happened here?" he asked. The frame was bent and sitting crooked in the track, apparently from being jimmied open with a screwdriver or some other prying device.

"The local riffraff broke in again, looking for cash. We only keep a few bucks for incidentals. As far as I can tell, they got seven dollars. That's not much, but it's enough for a bottle of cheap booze, which is what they were after."

"You know who it is?" asked Joel.

"So far I can't prove it, but there's a crew of anchor outs who will do just about anything for a snootful. My money is on one of those characters. Now, what can I do for you?"

Joel introduced Sunny and Rivka. The harbormaster stood up and shook their hands with a stern grip. He scrutinized each of them carefully from behind thick bifocals, holding onto their hands longer than necessary. "Dean Blodger," he said. "You're friends of Heidi's, are you? How come I've never seen you around here before?"

He asked it in a folksy, friendly voice, as though making conversation, but Sunny was sure he was dead serious, based on the way he studied her face when she answered.

"We were in the same yoga class," she said. "We never socialized much otherwise. Just yoga and sometimes coffee afterward."

"Yoga class and coffee," said Dean Blodger. "I see." It was impossible to discern if his tone was sarcastic or fatherly.

"We're headed out to Heidi's place now," said Joel. "Are the police finished going over it?"

"The coroner's seal is still on the door, but they're done as far as I know. They certainly ought to be. There were at least a dozen officers here most of the day Friday and all day yesterday, turning the place inside out. Interviewed everybody, even me. Walked their tracking dogs up and down the docks and all over the parking lot. Those dogs make a mess. One of them got into the mud and tracked it all up and down the dock. The other relieved himself in the parking lot, right where anybody could step in it. You'd think police officers would know that we have laws about curbing your dog at the marina. It was still there when the last one of them left. You can guess who finally had to clean it up."

"That's rough," said Joel.

Dean Blodger scowled. "I just hope they find who they're looking for." He went back to his desk and sat down. "You're sure you want to go out there today? You can't break that seal without permission. They'll haul you off to jail."

"I've already spoken to the police. It's okay if you have permission from the family, which we do."

"Please yourself," said the harbormaster, turning to his paperwork.

"That guy makes me wish I had a dog," said Joel, walking fast. Sunny and Rivka hurried after him.

They passed an outbuilding for trash and recycling, then came to a weathered wooden portal announcing the entrance to Liberty Dock. The dock consisted of a wide plank gangway extending into the protected inlet between Sausalito and Tiburon. Floating houses sat close together on either side. Potted gardens of bright flowers, grasses, palms, succulents, and shrubs lined the way. The noise of cars dissipated quickly behind them, and soon the only sounds were the lap of water, a distant wind chime, and the thump of their footsteps on the planks. Each house was different from the next. There were sagging bohemian relics from the sixties, generic suburban tract homes, a pasha palace, and several twenty-first-century behemoths with all the posh trimmings.

Why was this place so inviting? And why was the light so marvelous? Sunny had rarely been anywhere so appealing. The tide was high and murky green water filled the narrow spaces between houses. That was it. The water made all the difference. Not the water itself, but the changes its presence produced. There were no garages, driveways, or front yards to these houses. There was no street. The lack of cars and pathways wide enough to accommodate them had reduced the setting to human scale. This was a human place, designed for the circumambulation of people, not cars.

As for the light, that was simple enough. It was the water again. Being on the water, there were no shadows from hill-sides, trees, or tall buildings. A ubiquitous golden sunlight enveloped everything, the way it did on a sailboat, making even ordinary objects crisp and radiant. A blue glazed pot holding a succulent with spade-shaped leaves seemed to glow, and even the dock's weathered gray planks had a silvery sheen. Shoved out on Richardson's Bay, the houseboats bathed in sunlight. Most of them enjoyed a straight-on, unimpeded view of Mount Tamalpais, a massive wedge of green from this point of view.

"What's an anchor out?" asked Rivka.

"The people who live beyond the docks," explained Joel. "There's a certain band of water where it's legal to drop anchor and stay there, indefinitely. Some of the houses aren't much more than rafts with shacks hammered onto them, but a couple of them aren't too bad, and some of the people are pretty inter-esting. There's also a bunch that don't bring much to the table, unfortunately."

They passed a house where a trim woman who looked to be in her early fifties was watering the potted plants around the gangway to her houseboat.

"Joel!" she cried happily when she saw them. "I worried we'd never see you again after all this terrible business."

"No such luck," said Joel. He made introductions. "Frank asked me to keep an eye on the place."

"How is he doing?" said the woman, a look of intense concern on her face. "He must be devastated."

"Like you'd imagine. The whole family is pretty shook up."

She nodded soberly. "Well, it's nice to see you in any case. I miss her already. She was a very positive addition to the scene around here. I liked hearing her voice, knowing she was there. Some mornings, if I happened to be outside, I could hear her singing in the shower. No secrets around here," she said, winking at Sunny and Rivka. "I don't know why these things have to happen. Tom down at the elbow—he has the place with the neon peace sign where the dock makes a hard left—he's having drinks Tuesday night in her honor. You should stop by if you're around."

While they were talking, another neighbor came out of a house on the other side of the dock. He was wearing a pink polo shirt tucked into his jeans and a cream-colored sweater tied around his shoulders, and had a silver iPod clipped to his jeans pocket. He was humming to himself as he put on a pair of gardening gloves and hefted a large, plastic garbage bin from his deck onto the dock, then dragged it behind him in their direction. When he reached them, he waved and took off his headphones. "Irene, any trash you want to get rid of?"

"Nothing today, Ronald, thank you." He resettled his headphones and left with a wave, dragging the trash can behind him down the dock.

"I've never known a man more diligent about taking out the trash," said Irene.

"I saw him messing around with the trash at about one in the morning one night," said Joel. "I was dropping off Heidi and there he was, doing something with the trash. Sorting out the recycling, it looked like."

"It's somewhat sad," said Irene. "He doesn't work as far as I can tell, and I've never seen him have a visitor. But he's always friendly, and I do appreciate his help. He takes out everyone's trash, if they'll let him. He's house-sitting for the Mendels until they get back from Prague." She took up her watering hose and turned to Sunny and Rivka. "Nice meeting you, and good to see you again, Joel. Enjoy the day, all of you. That's what Heidi would have wanted."

Heidi Romero's houseboat was by far the most unique and handsome of the lot. It had been a tugboat and still looked like one, at least from the outside. The hull and deck were painted shiny black. In the center of the deck, a tall cabin of wood slats rose up, topped by a cheerful window trimmed in cherry red. On the whole, the effect was decidedly maritime and vaguely Mediterranean, a souvenir conjured from a Grecian fishing village.

"Frank Romero, Heidi's father, converted this place," said Joel, lifting the edge of a potted aloe vera plant on the deck and removing a key from underneath. "He bought an old tug at salvage and remodeled it himself in the seventies. Heidi's lived here since she graduated from college."

"Where does her father live now?" asked Rivka.

"Up in Washington. He came down when he heard what happened, but he hasn't had the heart to come out to the houseboat yet. Says he can't stand to see it."

"Did she leave a key there when she was alive?" asked Sunny.

"Always. She was bad about losing things, especially keys."

Sunny frowned. "People must have seen her getting it."

"Maybe. Not much happens around here that everybody doesn't know about."

"And she never worried about someone using it to break in?" said Sunny.

"There's nothing inside worth stealing, and you take the key with you when you go in. Heidi was a very trusting person."

Joel examined the piece of paper stamped with the coroner's seal taped across the tugboat's red door. "Well, here goes." He lifted one corner of the tape and peeled it away far enough to open the door.

Inside was a Heyerdahlian paradise, complete with Polynesian straw hats, ukuleles, and tiki treasures mounted on the walls. The furniture was worn but comfortable, and there was evidence of various efforts at painting and drawing. Being a boat, the interior was entirely wood. The floor, ceiling, and walls were all covered in teak or redwood slats. It would have been morbidly dark if it weren't for two enormous half-circle side windows in the kitchen and dining area, and French doors off the living room that framed the view of Mount Tam and opened onto the rear sun deck. The corner next to the French doors held a cache of grubby, well-used surfboards and wetsuits, along with a mountain bike, beach cruiser, and an assortment of paddles, all shoved in a jumble against the wall. An open staircase led to a loft sleeping area and a bathroom with a window facing the dock. That would be where Heidi showered, and the open window explained why her neighbor could hear her singing. Joel touched a finger to the soot on the bedroom windowsill. "I didn't know they still used this stuff," he said, holding up a blackened finger.

Other than fingerprint dust, the house looked more or less in order. If the police had scrutinized the premises as thoroughly as the harbormaster said, they'd done an excellent job of putting everything back in place. Sunny made a mental note not to leave any fingerprints behind, if possible, just in case.

12

Joel Hyder opened the French doors. "The first order of business is a toast."

He went back to the kitchen for glasses. Sunny and Rivka stood on the deck taking in the view in the warmth of the mid-day sun, grateful to be away from the cold wind at the beach.

"My mom used to listen to Alan Watts on the radio," said Sunny. "A long time ago, when I was little. He was a Zen Buddhist. I think he lived here. Sometimes he would mention his houseboat in Sausalito and how they had swinging parties all the time. It was all very groovy."

Joel came back and opened the bottle of Champagne. He poured three glasses. "To Heidi. May she journey in peace, free from the menace." His face flushed red and clinched up with the effort to control his emotions. "From the menace that ended her adventures in this world." He set his jaw bitterly with the final words.

They drank and Joel went and sat down on the edge of the deck, facing away from them. He shook his head at some thought and wiped his eyes hard with the back of his hand. Finally he got up and refilled their glasses, then took a seat in a low canvas deck chair and sighed, smiling, his determination to enjoy himself renewed. Rivka sat down against the wall and Sunny took the other canvas chair.

They watched the water and the houseboats on the next dock over, and beyond them, Mount Tam. A woman in a canoe glided past, paddling the calm water with smooth, silent strokes. Overhead, a quintet of pelicans cruised west toward the open sea. There was the sound of water lapping against wood, the creaking of hulls against their concrete moorings, the occasional cry of a seagull, the distant ringing of a telephone. Sunny and Rivka took off their shoes and rolled up their jeans.

"This is heaven," said Rivka.

"The perfect Sunday afternoon," said Sunny.

"Glad you like it," said Joel.

They made another toast to Heidi's memory, drank, and finished the bottle. Joel got up and came back with a guitar, which he began to strum. It was all exceedingly pleasant. Sunny's mind drifted to slow, easy thoughts, few of which involved Heidi Romero. They slumped lower and let the sound of the guitar stand for all activity.

"I can't move," said Rivka. "I think maybe I should go look for some sunscreen, but I don't think I have the strength."

"Me too. It's the Champagne," said Sunny.

"And the heat."

"We should eat something before we lose the will to survive."

They went into the kitchen. Sunny examined the photographs stuck to the refrigerator. Snapshots of Heidi with friends and family offered the typical evidence of a brief, happy existence. Photographs taken with friends on road trips, at the beach, with her arms around family at her graduation.

"I hope she didn't drink this stuff," said Rivka, holding up a bottle with a snake coiled inside it, its white belly pressed against the glass. Other bottles contained a frog, a worm, and a cricket. "Where did she get them?"

"Vietnam?" said Sunny, pointing to a photograph of Heidi on the back of a moped being driven through a Southeast Asian village by a local boy in a white button-down shirt. Sunny took a dishtowel and opened the refrigerator. The inventory included soy milk, flaxseed, tempeh, lecithin, plain yogurt, soy sauce, oranges, and an assortment of wilted vegetables. She wondered what happened to the food in the refrigerator of a woman who is killed. Probably it would fall to Joel Hyder to clean it out eventually. She opened a cabinet. Green tea, honey, brown rice, oatmeal, a head of garlic. A wooden bowl on the counter held three apples and a lemon.

"Health food," said Sunny. "Hardcore." She opened the bottle of pink wine and carried it and the baguette out to the deck. Rivka followed with a cutting board heaped with the rest of the food they'd bought. They sliced the papaya in half. The light made its naked orange flesh unspeakably beautiful, and the hold of glossy black seeds shone like caviar. Sunny tore off a piece of baguette and loaded it with cheese.

"Salmon?" said Rivka, holding a dish of smoked fish out to Joel.

"No, thanks. I'm a vegetarian," he said.

"No meat at all?"

"Nope."

"How can you stand it?" said Rivka. "I would lose my mind if I had to face a lifetime without bacon, not to mention all the other succulent parts of the noble pig."

"To the pig," said Sunny. "Long may he reign."

"To our delicious friend," said Rivka.

"What did it?" asked Sunny, turning to Joel. "Did you just wake up one day and decide not to eat meat?"

"You could say that. I've been vegetarian since I lived in Japan. We went out to dinner one night at a very expensive sushi restaurant. The best in town. Their specialty was a certain kind of fish that they kept alive while they flayed it, right there at the table, so it would be really fresh. I had a mentor at the time who I considered very wise. I told him about how upsetting that dinner was for me, and he suggested I perform an experiment. He said I should go to the open-air market and buy two live sardines. Just two tiny little fish. One I should keep until I was really hungry, then I should kill it and fry it with some nice oil and lemon and eat it. The other I should again keep until I was very hungry, then I should take it to the harbor and set it free. The idea was to see which of the two gestures made me feel better. The first sardine was great, especially since I was so hungry, but the second one changed my mind. I'll never forget seeing it shoot away into the water. I've never eaten meat since."

Sunny stared at the bread and cheese in her hands. "I had a dream kind of like that."

"Like what?"

"I dreamed I was eating a fish that was still alive. It was looking up at me while I cut into it."

"Maybe your subconscious is trying to tell you something," said Joel.

"Maybe the fish is," said Rivka.

"When did you live in Japan?" said Sunny.

"Three years ago, after Heidi and I broke up. I sort of needed a change of scenery." He put down the guitar and refilled his glass of wine. "What do you suppose happened to her, anyway? Do you think we'll ever know?"

"She ran into somebody bad," said Sunny. "She crossed paths with the wrong person."

"It sounds like you believe in pure evil." He leaned toward her, his eyes growing intense. "I mean evil for evil's sake. Not accidental badness or ordinary malice or anything understandable. Do you?" He didn't wait for her to reply. "Because I think it does exist. I've seen it, and felt it." He sat back in the canvas chair and savored his thoughts. "I'll tell you something. I used to play football in high school. The coach was a big disciplinarian and ran a tight ship. He wouldn't let us drink or smoke or even swear. If he found out we did, we were off the team, no questions asked. It was all about strength and discipline. We thought of ourselves as a kind of elite corps, and we took pride in our clean living. I played defensive end. It was my job to break through the line and bring down the other team's quarterback. What you realize pretty quickly in that position is that you have to be aggressive, not just to win, but to keep from getting hurt. Collisions are not equal. One person delivers the blow, the other takes it. That was lesson number one: Always make the hit. If it looks like you are going to be involved in a violent situation, make sure you are the perpetrator of that violence, not the recipient. The other lesson was that the sensation of colliding with another body hard enough to rattle your bones and addle your head starts to feel good after a while. It sounds funny, but it's true. That shock of collision is painful at first, but over time it starts to feel good. Pretty soon you crave it, like a drug. Every once in a while I still get that hunger to crush an opponent, hammer him into the ground, and feel the crunch of bones and pads giving way underneath me. I think that's the nature of evil. When you start to crave that kind of power and release."

"That sounds more like testosterone than pure evil," said Rivka. "Or maybe some very old instinct being woken up. The inner Stone Age hunter. I think of evil as having to do more with coercion. The guy who tackles you to hear your bones crunch is a badass. The guy who tells you he's your best friend, then seduces your wife and teaches your kid not to trust you, that's evil."

"What I can't figure out is how they overpowered her," said Joel. "She was in great shape. It would have taken somebody strong."

"Maybe they didn't overpower her," said Sunny. "She was more likely tricked or drugged. Or maybe they had a gun. It's old-fashioned, but it still works. The gun is the great equalizer." Sunny studied Joel Hyder. She had a growing list of questions in her head for him, but she didn't want to put him on his guard. The trick was to get to them little by little. She decided to start with an easy one. "Why'd you two break up anyway?"

Joel yawned. He put down his wineglass and picked up the guitar. He played it softly. "We just seemed better as friends. I'm a decade older than her, plus some. At the time, we thought that mattered. I'm not so sure anymore."

"I think it matters," said Rivka. "I broke up with my last boyfriend for that reason. You have different priorities."

"What about recently," said Sunny. "Was she seeing anybody?"

Joel closed his eyes and rearranged his feet on the lip of the tugboat's deck. "She didn't have what you'd call a boyfriend, per se. For some reason, she didn't consider the guy she was seeing as boyfriend material. He seemed to be away most weekends, for one thing. She'd see him on Wednesday afternoons, Monday nights, like that. She never talked about him much."

"He was B list," said Rivka.

"Maybe even C, but there was nobody in the A and B slots as far as I know," said Joel, "and I think I would know."

"Maybe he was the one calling the shots and she was his B-list girl," said Sunny. "Did you ever meet him?"

Joel shook his head. "All I know is his name was Mark." He scowled. "Aren't you guys boiling? You should go upstairs and find some shorts. I saw a pair hanging on the towel rack in the bathroom and there's sure to be another pair somewhere."

"That's just a little too weird," said Sunny.

"It is really hot," said Rivka.

They climbed the stairs and found two pairs of board shorts without looking very hard. They changed out of their jeans and reemerged on the back deck, barefoot and wearing straw hats from the collection on the wall.

"That's better," said Joel. "You look good in her clothes. Jeans are a crime on a day like today." He went on softly playing the guitar, humming along occasionally. After a while, a neighbor started to play the piano. They could hear the notes as though the piano were directly in front of them. Joel put the guitar aside. A parrot screeched.

"That's Chopin," he said.

"I think it might be Mozart," said Sunny.

"I mean the parrot. The woman who plays the piano puts her parrot outside when she practices. His name is Chopin."

They sprawled on the back deck listening to the music. Rivka yawned and got up to investigate the rattling, metallic sound interfering with the piano's notes.

"It's shopping carts," she said. "People pushing shopping carts up and down the dock."

"They leave two of them at the entrance," said Joel. "For carrying groceries and garbage and anything heavy." The sun got hotter and the relaxed, foggy feeling from the wine gave way to a sticky lethargy.

"I could use a shot of espresso," said Sunny. "I'm so sleepy."

Joel heaved himself upright. "Me too. All there is is green tea. You guys must know Heidi didn't do coffee."

Rivka glanced at Sunny.

"I knew she took good care of herself," said Sunny, "but that kitchen is stocked with serious health food."

"She was hardcore. No meat, no dairy, no coffee, no refined sugar."

"Wow."

Joel pressed a finger to his forearm, checking for sunburn. He went inside and they heard his muffled voice from the front deck, apparently making a call. He came back with a bottle of sunscreen. "It's getting late. Should we go for a canoe ride before we take off?"

"Definitely," said Rivka.

The canoe was turned upside down on the dock directly below the sun deck. They flipped it into the water and climbed aboard. Joel and Sunny took up paddles while Rivka arranged herself in the stern, trailing a hand in the water. They paddled out to the end of the dock and into the channel, then explored the next dock over.

Joel suggested they make a loop, paddling between houses. They glided past downstairs windows almost at eye level, catching glimpses of a bedroom, a man at work at his desk, a woman putting away laundry. At the dock, they ducked down, lifting up wires as they slipped underneath with just enough room between the water and the wooden beams. At Liberty Dock, they chose a wide passage a couple of houses down from Heidi's. One house had all the curtains drawn. In the other, the man who liked to take out the trash was sitting stiffly on a couch watching cartoons with his sweater still around his shoulders and his headphones on. Sunny looked away, embarrassed to have invaded his privacy.

They paddled back out to the main channel and swung around the tip of Liberty Dock and back in the other side. They spotted the police officers standing at the tugboat's door about the same time the police officers spotted them. Sunny stopped paddling.

"Don't stop," said Joel softly, without turning around. "Just keep paddling, slowly, like nothing is wrong."

Rivka sat up, turning to face the group of officers now watching the canoe's approach.

13

They could hear the police knocking on the door while they hastily pulled the canoe out of the water and turned it upside down on the dock. Joel Hyder led the way inside. He opened the front door and stepped outside, closing it behind him. Sunny and Rivka went upstairs to change. A moment later, they heard Joel come back in. He shouted up to them from the living room. "They want to see you both. And they need IDs."

They gathered their shoes and socks from the sundeck and hastily put them on. When they joined Joel outside, he was trying to remember the name of the person he'd spoken to when he called the police to ask for permission to come out to Heidi's house. The officers were listening, but they looked skeptical.

"Let's just see if we can reach Heidi's father before we do anything else," said one of the cops. He turned to Sunny. "And you are?"

She introduced herself and handed over her driver's license. "Is this your current address, in St. Helena?"

"It is."

"And you were acquainted with the deceased?"

Sunny nodded.

"How did you come to be in her house today?"

"I came with Joel."

"You came with this gentleman. How do you know Mr. Hyder?"

Sunny blinked. "We met this morning. At the beach."

He ran the same questions by Rivka, who provided identical answers. The two officers conferred, then the talker told them to wait while he went to make some calls. His partner stayed behind to make sure nobody went anywhere. He and Joel struck up a conversation about surfing, something the police officer had always wanted to try. It was hot and there was nowhere to sit on the front gangway. Sunny was bathed in sweat by the time they heard the sound of the other officer's heavy boots clomping loudly up the dock. He handed them their IDs.

"I wasn't able to reach Mr. Romero to confirm your authorization." He made eye contact with each of them. "That means I'm going to have to ask you to get your things and leave. If you can confirm the family's authorization in writing, you can come back later. Otherwise, if I catch you out here again, I'm going to have to cite you. What I'm going to do now is give you a warning. You only get one, and this applies to all three of you, so no more visiting unless you are in the company of a family member or have written authorization from the current owner of the property. Do not remove anything from the property other than what you brought with you today, even if you believe it to be your own possession, as this house and everything in it is still part of an ongoing homicide investigation. On that note, if I wanted to, I could get real nasty about this, and if I get called out here again, rest assured I will do so. For now, let's just pack up, move out, and lock up."

"Who called you this time?" said Joel.

"They chose not to identify themselves."

"Ah, one of our bolder citizens."

The officer finished filling in the blanks on the forms on his clipboard and handed them each a citation. "We'll wait while you get your things."

They locked up, stowed the key under the planter, and walked down the dock followed by the two policemen. There were mercifully few witnesses. Only the preppy trash guy was outside, hosing off his front step. He gave them a friendly wave as they went by, oblivious to their police escort.

In the parking lot, Sunny and Rivka said a terse good-bye to Joel Hyder within earshot of the two officers and walked to the truck. Sunny was about to back out when she saw a white truck pull into the parking lot behind them. Dean Blodger, stone-faced and staring straight ahead, drove past, the Pelican Point Harbor logo on the side of his truck nestled in a circle of arched type. Sunny stared after it.

"Did you see that?" said Sunny.

"What?"

"Dean Blodger driving a white pickup truck with a circular black logo on the door."

"Who is Dean Blodger?"

"The harbormaster we met this morning. He's driving a truck exactly like the one I saw on Wednesday night."

"I thought you couldn't remember anything about the truck."

"I remember it was white and had a round logo on the door. That could be the truck."

"Nine out of ten work trucks are white, and logos are either circular or square. It's like looking for a medium-sized dog with brown fur."

"But this white truck belongs to a man who knew where Heidi lived. I could tell for sure if it had its lights on. What time is it?"

"Not late enough to wait around until dark. I vote for getting out of here before things get even more complicated. I'm too fried to deal with the police again, or Dean Blodger, or even Joel Hyder, who must be sitting in his car right now wondering who the hell we are and what we really want. He knew we were lying. Anyway, if that is the truck, we know where to find it."

Sunny drove out to the freeway and headed north. She floored the gas on the old truck to little effect going up the grade between Mill Valley and San Rafael. Rivka slumped in her seat with her knees propped up against the dashboard. They chugged up a second hill and over the other side. "I think the harbormaster must have called the cops," said Rivka in a sullen voice.

"Joel Hyder also made a phone call," said Sunny. "If the harbormaster were concerned enough to nark on us, he would have done it right after we got there. And if he did, it wouldn't have taken the fuzz four hours to respond. Whoever called did it right about the time we left for our canoe ride."

"Like around the time Joel made his call."

"Exactly."

"Why would he do that?"

"I don't know."

"What if the harbormaster didn't mind us being there initially," said Rivka, "but after a while he figured it was time for us to clear out?"

"Maybe, but it seems like a stretch. Another option is a stakeout. There could be somebody watching the place. If I were law enforcement, I'd watch to see who comes by snooping around. It's a cliché that criminals return to the scene of the crime, and clichés always have some truth to them. Steve explained it once. He said that crimes rarely go exactly as planned, assuming they are planned at all, so the perpetrator almost always has to rush or improvise at least part of it. That opens up the possibility of mistakes. Imagine if you committed a serious crime and wondered afterward, 'Did I leave the stove on? I know I turned off the iron, but did I leave clothes in the dryer?' They can't stand it. They have to go back and check."

"If they were watching, why did it take so long for them to bust us?"

"Maybe someone is just swinging by periodically to check things out," said Sunny. "Let's leave that for the moment. There's something else. I wonder if Steve knows about that key under the aloe vera. If everybody knew she kept a key outside, anybody could have made a copy. Or let themselves in and waited inside. For all intents and purposes, she did not lock her door. Also, that upstairs window looks like it's always open."

"You'd need a ladder to get in that window, and if you used a ladder, somebody would see you," said Rivka.

"Somebody tall and strong enough to pull themselves up might be able to do it." Sunny turned off the freeway and headed east toward Sears Point. "But they'd have to be small. Joel would never fit through that tiny window."

"Why would Joel want to climb through the window? You don't actually suspect him?"

"I don't know what to make of any of this right now, but all that talk about evil and crushing bones was a little off."

"His friend was just killed. I think it's a little harsh to accuse him of murder just because he said some strange stuff."

"You liked him!"

"I didn't *like* him, I just don't think he's a murderer. He seemed like an okay guy to me."

"I wonder how much of this Steve has turned up. I mean, does he know about Dean Blodger's truck? And Joel Hyder? And the guy Heidi was seeing on the down low?"

"You've got me. All I know is I'm done thinking about Heidi Romero for the day," said Rivka. "I'm beat. All that sun and relaxation took it out of me."

Sunny spent the rest of the drive turning over the facts in her head, and trying to think of a reasonable way to find the guy Heidi had been seeing. If she couldn't turn up anything more than his first name, she would never find him. Maybe it wasn't important. That was one person the police would track down, assuming he needed tracking down. Somebody close to Heidi had to know who she was dating, and the police would find them. Next she considered Joel Hyder. Despite her initial impressions, he seemed like a nice enough guy. And yet something about him bothered her. She couldn't put her finger on it. It wasn't the rough tattoos or the fact he'd lived in Japan. Plenty of people lived in Japan. That didn't make them ikebana experts any more than it made them adepts of Japanese bondage. It was something more subtle. A feeling. She searched her mind for what had triggered the sensation of distrust. Why didn't she trust Joel Hyder? He'd certainly bent over backward to help them. She went over their conversation. Other than his come-ons to Rivka at the beach, nothing in particular leaped out at her. He said he'd gone to Japan after he and Heidi split up. How bad was it? Did she break his heart? Could he be harboring a deep vein of resentment for Heidi Romero? Suddenly the thought clicked. That was it. That was what didn't fit. Heidi Romero would not have dated Joel Hyder. Sunny pictured the sweep of long black hair falling across Heidi's chest and the delicate feet with the perfectly pedicured toenails. She may have been a tomboy, but she had a feminine side. Sunny wished she'd taken a look in Heidi's closet when she'd had the chance. She was sure there would be sexy high heels and short dresses mixed in with the Tevas and fleece.

"I just can't imagine Joel and Heidi together," said Sunny. "He doesn't seem like her type."

"You never know. He has nice eyes," said Rivka. "And he seems thoughtful. Sensitive, at least. He's a good talker."

"I can't say why, I just don't see him fitting the bill."

"He didn't. It sounded like she jilted him."

"I wonder what her story was. She was twenty-six, had a college degree, was obviously very capable and disciplined, and yet she still worked retail. She couldn't have made much money at that job."

"She didn't need to. I bet she didn't pay her dad much rent."

"Of course! Her dad owns the houseboat. She was being subsidized. She didn't need a real job."

"If you ask me, he subsidized more than rent. That place reeked of Trustafarian. There was about a thousand bucks' worth of high-end face and hair product in the bathroom."

"Really. I didn't check."

"I always check. Bathroom products reveal all. Alex's bathroom, for example, contained generic supermarket shampoo, a bar of soap, and a razor. In Heidi's case, she may have been riding waves on Saturday morning, but she was cruising the Neiman Marcus makeup counter in the afternoon."

"That lends more support to my theory about Joel Hyder. This is a girl who dates guys with money."

"Maybe it's a girl who can afford not to."

Sunny smiled. "Indeed. Well said."

Well said or not, she didn't believe it. Something told her that sporty, rugged Heidi Romero liked to be wined and dined. Rivka sunk down even lower, curled up like a fetus, and closed her eyes. Sunny went back to mulling over the day. What was she to make of Dean Blodger? He was an uptight guy and a neatnik who probably took it upon himself to alert the police to strangers at Heidi's house, but was there more beneath the surface? Was there a way to tell how far a person was capable of going?

The first step was to get a look at the taillights on his truck. That was a problem that patience might solve. All she would need to do was drive down to Sausalito and wait around until he drove home after work, presuming it would be late enough to be dark. It wasn't the most appealing way to spend an evening, but it would be worth it to know one way or the other. She thought about Wednesday night and how the truck's headlights had illuminated her face as she stood by the side of the road. If that was the same truck, then Dean Blodger had now seen her twice. He'd even been introduced to her. In the unlikely event that he was the man who killed Heidi Romero, and if he recognized Sunny from that night, then her excursion to the houseboat had neatly bridged the gap for him. Instead of an unknowable, untraceable, anonymous witness, she was now a face with a name. It would be easy enough for him to find her. She silently cursed herself for being so careless, so foolish. How could it not have occurred to her before that showing her face and introducing herself all around Heidi's neighborhood might not be such a great idea? She drove the rest of the way staring sullenly at the road ahead.

Rivka let herself into her apartment and waved a weary hand. Sunny drove straight home. She tried to put the death of Heidi Romero out of her mind, thinking instead of the hot bath she would soak in, followed by the hot chocolate she would make herself, rapidly followed by the bed into which she would burrow, oblivious for a few hours to the existence of Heidi Romero's killer. Visions of domestic bliss evaporated as she pulled into Adelaide Avenue and spotted Sergeant Harvey sitting in his squad car outside her house.

14

Sergeant Harvey watched her in the rearview mirror as she pulled in behind him and parked. He got out of the car when she did. "Good evening, Sunny. Mind if we have a word?"

"My pleasure. Want to come inside?"

"Let's talk in my car."

Sunny went around to the passenger side and got in, sneaking a look at the squad car's array of black gadgetry.

"Why don't you start from the beginning," said Steve, "wherever that is, and explain everything up to the point where you and Chavez trespassed on Heidi Romero's property, dressed up in her clothes, and went for a spin in her canoe. Oh, and while you're at it, you might as well cover the part where you lie about how you know her."

Steve stared straight ahead, occasionally flexing his fingers against the underside of the steering wheel, while Sunny recounted the day's events. The dispatcher's scratchy communications interrupted her periodically, as did Steve, who showed interest when she mentioned that Joel said Heidi had been seeing a guy named Mark.

"Nobody we talked to knew about any boyfriends," said Steve.

"I thought that seemed odd. Pretty girl, single. There was bound to be somebody."

The story—especially the part where she and Rivka changed into Heidi's shorts—didn't sound too good, even to herself. When she was done, Steve said nothing for several seconds that felt more like minutes.

"Why?" he said, finally. "Why get mixed up in all this?"

Sunny made an involuntary sound like the pip of a squeaky toy. "It wasn't exactly intentional. I did set out to try to find somebody who knew her, just to see what kind of person she was, but after that, it all just sort of happened."

"You realize you just made the process of investigating this homicide and, should we get the chance, of prosecuting the guilty party, infinitely more complex. Now we have to go back to the houseboat and gather all the evidence from your tryst, bag it, document it, probably haul you and Chavez and this guy Hyder into the station for questioning, and possibly subpoena you for testimony if we ever get a chance to go to trial. All because you thought it would be a hoot to commune with the victim's lingering aura." He thumped the steering wheel with both palms. "Do you have any idea how many leads have come in that we need to track down? I've got people who say they saw her at Taylor's Refresher ordering a green tea milkshake and onion rings. People who swear she was walking a dog in Crane Park Wednesday morning. People who saw her in the post office with a man she seemed to be afraid of. We've got thirty officers from three counties working on this case, and half of them are riding my ass night and day wanting to know did we test the grass under the tree for semen and have we fingerprinted everybody who's ever set foot in St. Helena. We've interviewed close to a hundred people already. Do you think I really have time to be waiting for you to wander home so I can ask you, implore you, beg you to please stay out of this business?"

Steve contained his irritation with visible effort. He was breathing loudly through his nose, pulling each breath in and forcing it out like a mighty bellows. "You do realize that you could have gotten yourself arrested on top of it. Officer Mills would have been well within his rights to haul you in first and ask questions later."

"But we had permission."

"You spoke with Heidi Romero's next of kin?"

"Joel Hyder did."

"Joel Hyder said he did. What do you know about Joel Hyder?"

"Not that much."

"I happen to know that he didn't talk with anybody in Heidi Romero's family, and that her father has never heard of him."

Sunny said nothing. Steve controlled his breathing with visible effort. "So, now that you've made your inroads in the case, what's next?" he said, sounding casual.

"Next?"

"Yes, next. What will you do next about the death of Heidi Romero?"

Sunny looked at Steve for clues. "Nothing?"

"Not a thing?" said Steve, frowning.

"Nothing."

"Are you sure you aren't going to stake out the harbormaster's office to see if he killed her? Or invite Joel Hyder to dinner to see what else he might know? Or go snooping around the winery to see what you can turn up? Because you never know, those actions might all lead to valuable information."

"Am I catching a whiff of sarcasm? It smells like somebody is serving up a little sarcasm."

"Just answer the question."

"No, I am not going to do any of those things."

"Why not?"

"Because it's not my job, and because I believe in the talent and persistence of the good men and women of the St. Helena police force and their associates."

"That's correct. It is not your job. You are a material witness in a homicide investigation, which is enough to keep most folks tucked in bed at night. With you, it's an invitation to go making new friends with potential suspects."

"Is Joel Hyder a suspect?"

"I didn't say that. What I said, and perhaps not clearly enough, was if I catch you anywhere near Heidi Romero's home, family, friends, or acquaintances again, I will come down on you like ten tons of angry muscle. Am I making myself understood?"

"Yes, completely understood. I just have one more question. Have you discovered anything to connect Heidi with the winery?"

"We're following up on leads now."

"That could be tricky. If there is a connection, the people involved will try to hide it. They'll lie if they have to."

"You mean somebody might lie to cover up their connection to a murder?" said Steve. "I'm shocked."

"Ah, the sarcasm again. What about the harbormaster's truck? Do you think that's significant?"

"I think it's significant that nothing I've said has come anywhere near penetrating your skull. Now if you don't mind, I have work to do."

It was not an entirely pleasant end to the day. Sergeant Harvey had sped away from the curb in a contained but smoldering rage. Sunny felt, and was, thoroughly chastened. Nevertheless, she had achieved success. Her longing to know something about the girl left hanging in the tree had been sated. Heidi Romero was no longer a body, no longer a victim, but a person with a life and people who loved her. Sunny expected to enjoy a peaceful night's sleep free from the ghost of Heidi Romero. What's more, she had passed on all the details she had gleaned from her investigation to Steve, as well as her concerns. If any of the information she had picked up could lead to the guilty party, Sergeant Harvey would get there eventually. He had also set her mind at ease in regard to the harbormaster.

"I'll look into it," he had said. "He told us he was home watching TV the night Heidi disappeared. I didn't do the follow-up personally, but as far as I know his alibi checked out. Nothing in his interview raised any red flags. In fact, he's been very helpful. He knows just about everything that goes on in that community. But if it will make you feel better, I can put an officer outside your house for a couple of nights."

She had declined, and she could see that Steve was relieved. His department might be swamped with visitors from other departments, but they still didn't have the staff or the budget to keep officers up all night guarding local cottages from hypothetical threats.

She turned the lock on the front door and faced her living room. The lethargy that had weighed her down all day lifted. Her dealings with Heidi Romero were over, passed to those whose job it was to track down killers. She thought happily of getting up the next morning, going to Bismark's for coffee, and walking into work feeling refreshed and ready to whip the restaurant back into shape. Her greatest concern would be whether or not there was mouse scat on the counter, and if there was, she would create an ingeniously humane trap to capture the culprits and escort them to a better life in the great outdoors.

It was while basking in this spirit of renewal and optimism

that Sunny prepared herself a plate of shaved bresaola, arugula, and parmesan with a swirl of olive oil, a squeeze of lemon, and three cornichons on the side. She poured a glass of Etude Pinot Noir left over from dinner Friday night and carried both to the dining room table. The last thing she'd had to eat was a slice of papaya at the houseboat. She looked at the handsome plate in front of her, took it back into the kitchen, and covered it in cellophane. She poured the wine back in the bottle and put the glass in the sink. Twilight blue still lit the bedroom when she wiggled under the duvet in her clothes and fell deeply asleep.

She dreamed of waves and woke to solid darkness. The clock read quarter to five, a good time to get up. She showered in the dark, letting her eyes wake up slowly, and dressed while the tea brewed. Mondays meant a new menu, and she reviewed it while she sipped her tea. She read the words without hearing what they meant. The waves still occupied her mind. From a bluff she had watched them rising up on the horizon, blue walls coming toward her, each bigger than the last, and finally the one that would end the dream, the towering mass of water a thousand feet tall that would sweep away everything in its path. The sky was just beginning to lighten when she left the house.

The morning radio jocks ran down the weather and traffic as Sunny turned onto Adams, then Main. It was six o'clock, time for Bismark's to open. She pulled up to the café and parked in front. As she got out of the truck, she noticed a vehicle accelerated out of a side street two blocks up. Sunny stared at one orange taillight, one cherry red, receding into the distance. By the time she backed out and followed, pressing the old Ford for speed it never had, she'd lost them.

15

An era of tranquil productivity descended on the McCoskey quarters. Andre Morales spent Monday and Tuesday night at Sunny's house, arriving both times before nine o'clock and chasing her to bed before eleven. The subject of Heidi Romero did not come up. No one spoke of murder, sexual deviance, or mysterious white pickup trucks. They were not cautious. They left the windows pushed up to fill the house with night breezes and cold spring smells.

Sunny went back to her old work routine, preparing plates with a passionate clarity of mind she hadn't experienced in weeks. The tables filled with delighted guests, the staff went about their business with—there is no other word for it—blatant enthusiasm, both bussers showed up, and Rivka, through patience and careful observation, located the nest the mice had built and populated, tucked in a box of paperwork in a corner of the office, and evicted the entire family to the grassy border of the vineyard behind the restaurant, where their fate, while not guaranteed to be rosy, was nevertheless favorable to immediate extermination. Sunny convinced herself that the phantom tail-lights she had seen Monday morning had been a quirk of coincidence. There was sure to be more than one mismatched set of taillights in the world, and now that she was watching for them, she would undoubtedly see them everywhere. She even managed to ignore the white truck with the Pelican Point Harbor logo on the door that she was certain she had seen speed by on the main road one evening as she left work. She had promptly reported both incidents to Sergeant Harvey, not expecting anything to come of it, and nothing had, other than that Sergeant Harvey had suggested in future she contact Officer Jute with her tips and insights. She could think of only three interpretations of the two sightings. If they were not merely coincidence, and therefore meaningless, they could only be related to the murder in one of two ways. The killer either had remained in the area or had come back for some purpose. She briefly considered the obvious: What if that purpose was to monitor her schedule, to learn the patterns of her comings and goings, where she lived and worked, when she was alone? The thought prickled her skin.

She refused to believe it. This was a situation in which mental discipline was required. What else could be done? Even if her observations were correct and the white truck had been waiting outside her house on Monday morning and outside the restaurant Wednesday night, what could she do about it? Did she believe she was in enough danger to close the restaurant and go away in secret? Or hire a bodyguard? And what about the logo on the second truck? If it really was the Pelican Point logo she saw, then the person driving had to be Dean Blodger.

This is what they call paranoia, thought Sunny. She would refuse to indulge it. In all likelihood she had seen a set of taillights and a white truck, not *the* taillights and *the* white truck. Willfully and intentionally, she put all thoughts of murder and murderers out of her head and for the rest of the week went back to the ease and comfort of everyday life.

On Friday night, she sat down to dinner with Rivka, Wade, and Monty, a sure sign that life had returned to normal.

"What's with the hair?" Wade said to Rivka between bites.

"What d'you mean?"

"It's different."

"I wanted to try something new."

"What do you call that, pigtails?"

"Very sexy," said Monty, "in a hula hoops and popsicles sort of way."

"Don't perv out on me, Lenstrom."

"Rivka puts the hair in *mujer,*" said Wade, grinning and shoveling gnocchi in his mouth.

"Are you guys still doing that?" said Sunny. "I don't get it."

"Doesn't matter," said Wade. "We have more important issues to discuss, such as the agenda for tomorrow. Are you coming?"

"Where?" said Sunny.

"Infineon Raceway."

"You mean Sears Point? Only if somebody holds a gun to my head. You know I loathe that place."

"This is different. This isn't Nascar, it's vintage Ferraris and Maseratis. They're works of art. There won't be any hooligans."

"Just overage hooligans with money."

"Right. Chavez and I are going as Texas high rollers so we can schmooze our way into the VIP area. They always have a VIP area at these events. That's where they keep the free food and booze."

"That explains the upper lip. It seems to be some kind of epidemic around here."

"Tux Robinson never goes anywhere without his mustache and his woman."

"I'm wearing the bra with the built-in silicon boobs," said Rivka, "the trashiest pair of Lucite heels you've ever laid eyes on, and a cubic zirconia the size of a gumball."

"You're both insane," said Sunny. "What if you run into somebody you know?"

"I don't know anybody other than you guys, and Chavez is a shape-shifter. Nobody will recognize her once she's all tarted up, as long as she doesn't let the birds out," said Wade, referring to Rivka's tattoos.

"Covered. I'm wearing three-quarter sleeves," said Rivka. "Sun, you could come along as my best friend, Loretta, recently divorced and fabulously wealthy, but amusingly inclined to dress like a ten-dollar ho."

"Is there some object to this outing that I'm missing?" said Sunny.

"Threefold," said Rivka. "One, I get to wear the bra with the built-in boobs. Two, if we work it with expertise, we get a fancy lunch for free. Three, we mix and mingle with a crowd more exotic than Wade's mustache and more elusive than the Tibetan snow leopard. It's an anthropological adventure, like visiting Machu Picchu or joining a cult."

"Hang on, it's all coming back to me. These are the tickets Ted the fish guy gave us," said Sunny.

"Exactly. You should come. What else are you doing tomorrow?"

"Whatever it is, it's not going to involve a racetrack. That place is antithetical to my tree-hugger values. It's a noisy, ugly, crowded, sprawling swath of pollution-emitting pavement that does nothing but blight the land with cars and clog up the highway every time they have an event. I'd rather spend the day having the hair removed from my private parts."

"Ouch. I think you're being a little harsh," said Monty. "Unless that hair removal thing is more fun that it sounds."

"I can't argue with you," said Wade. "It's an eyesore. But, frankly, there comes a time in a man's life when he'll shake hands with the devil himself if it means he can wear a mustache and fake a Texas accent for the afternoon."

"How did Ted the fish guy get tickets anyway?" said Sunny. "It doesn't seem like his scene."

"His daughter is dating one of the guys from the Ferrari dealership in Marin," said Rivka. "That's our secondary mission, to check this guy out. Ted thinks his intentions are less than honorable."

"He cares enough to kiss up to the father," said Wade. "That's a good sign."

"Lenstrom, are you in on this nonsense?" said Sunny.

"You know I can't grow a mustache," said Monty, "and I'd look stupid in one of those bras. Besides, I have to work at the wine shop. Bill is trapped in some god-forsaken cabin in the Idaho wilderness for a week. He calls it a vacation."

"You'll see," said Wade. "The whine of those engines clears the cobwebs out of your head like nothing else. You get a contact high just seeing the cars go that fast."

"Maybe, but I'm not dressing up. I'll be your sane local friend entertaining you for the weekend."

They sat around the living room after dinner sampling the collection of port and Armagnac that Sunny put out on the coffee table. Wade stretched out on the couch. "Lenstrom, it's now or never. Five more minutes and I won't make it up from this couch until morning."

"Let's roll."

Rivka followed soon after. "You should come with us," she said, lingering by the door. "It'll be fun, and you know you could use a change of scene to liven things up. It's been dull around here this week. We'll meet new people. New *kinds* of people. People who think food is something you eat, not something you do for a living."

"It just doesn't sound like my scene."

"That's the point. Haven't you had enough of your scene? We're leaving at eleven. Call me if you change your mind."

Sunny finished cleaning up and putting the dishes away. It was still early by Friday-night standards and for once she felt like getting dressed up and going out. She would call Andre at eleven and see when he would be done working. Maybe they could drive into San Francisco and hit a late-night dance club. She paced the house, looking for something to do. Everything was picked up and none of the more involved projects waiting for her attention appealed to her. She turned on her laptop and searched for the racetrack's Web site. Maybe she should go, she thought. Rivka was right. She could use a change of scene, and she had nothing else planned for the day other than to drop her knives off for sharpening, not exactly the highlight of a weekend. The front banner on the racetrack's site proclaimed the imminent arrival of the Ferrari Challenge. She scrolled down the schedule of events. Races, lunch, the unveiling of the latest Ferrari and Maserati models. She studied the event description, attempting to divine what her Saturday would be like based on the adjectives they'd used. When they said "exciting," did they mean, "hot, loud, and boring"? Was "exotic" and "well-organized" euphemistic for "of interest only to the deeply committed aficionado of sports cars"? The list of sponsors was a hodgepodge of Fortune 500 companies and local businesses that catered to the wealthy. Among the makers of cell phones and PCs were some of the valley's most expensive hotels, restaurants, florists, and wineries. The Vedana Vineyards logo was near the bottom of the page where she almost didn't notice it.

She called Rivka. "I'm coming, but I'm not dressing up like Loretta."

"Suit yourself. But wear something a little upscale so we don't have to ditch you when we go VIP."

16

Ferrari red was everywhere. Rows of vintage roadsters in a dozen shades of lipstick red were parked across the lawn between the concessions and the racetrack, where men in Ferrari red shirts could mill between them, peering in at the dashboards. Red moving vans lined the raceway with pit crews dressed in red uniforms lingering nearby. Rivka picked her way down the gravel road from the ledge where non-Ferraris and Maseratis were made to park.

"When we find the people in charge, you do the talking," said Rivka. "It's going to take all my concentration not to fall down in these shoes."

"Don't you worry, darlin'," said Wade. "I've got you covered." He turned to Sunny. "Do you think the bolo tie is too much?"

"Yes, but I also think the mustache, Western suit, rodeo belt buckle, and accent are too much."

"It looks good, doesn't it," he said, grinning. "Is that a new dress?"

"So old it's new. I found it in a trunk at Catelina's house a few months ago. She wore it to her sister's wedding in 1955."

"Very Audrey Hepburn. How old is Catelina these days?"

"Eighty-something. And she can still chop onions faster than me."

They strolled through the vintage cars, then headed for the main attraction, the tent where the new models were on display. Wade showed a healthy interest in the Maserati Quattroporte and let the salesman talk him into sitting in the Ferrari 612 Scaglietti.

"My palms are moist," he said, when he came back. "That car makes me feel like a cheerleader on her first date."

"I thought you were acting," said Sunny. "I was going to be impressed."

"You want to see acting, watch me work this crowd. See that guy over there? He's the man in charge."

"How do you know?" said Rivka.

"See how he's looking around, watching for new arrivals, seeing if everybody has what they need? He looks like the bride's mom at a garden wedding. I'm going over and warm him up, then you come by and give him the silicon treatment. We'll see if we can earn our pasture."

Sunny and Rivka watched Wade walk up to the man and introduce himself. A few minutes later they were laughing and the boss was slapping Wade on the back like an old friend. He patted down his jacket pockets and handed Wade his business card. Wade waved them over.

"Salvio, I want you to meet my beautiful wife, Rachael," said Tux, "and our charming hostess here in Napa, Ms. Sonya McCoskey."

They made quick work of the small talk and Rivka closed the deal, inquiring demurely whether there was anywhere out of the sun that they could have a nice glass of wine.

"Please, you must be my guests for lunch," said Salvio. "Enjoy yourselves. You see this white tent in the middle? It's there. I have to walk around. For me, it's all business today, meeting the people. But you go and eat, drink some wine, relax. Show them my card if you have any difficulty." New arrivals distracted him momentarily, and he turned back to them with an expedient air. "Tonight we will make a dinner at the winery Niebaum-Coppola. You know it? You go there, seven o'clock. Tell them you are with Salvio. We make a good time." He pumped Wade's hand and gave Sunny and Rivka each a breezy kiss, then hailed the new arrivals and glided away.

"I think your kiss was more sincere than mine," said Sunny.

Rivka adjusted the display of bronze cleavage that was the centerpiece of an outfit engineered to stop traffic. "I don't claim to understand the power, I just deploy it as needed." She turned to Wade. "What did you say to him? That guy was ready to take you home to mama."

"I dropped a few choice details about the collection of Testa Rossas from the sixties I keep out in the horse stables back in Houston."

"Doesn't it bother you to lie?" said Sunny.

"Not while I'm in costume. Everything I've said is genuine Tux."

They dropped Salvio's name at the entrance to the hospitality tent and entered a place where, ironically, everything was free because they were assumed to be rich. The tables were draped in white. An epic floral display stood on the center table, with smaller versions dotted around the room. Along the left edge of the tent ran a continuous table loaded with salads, antipasto, pastas, and main courses. In back was dessert, cheeses, fruit, and coffee. On the right, several local and Italian wineries were offering tastings.

Sunny filled her plate and left it at the table while she went to meet the people pouring Vedana wines. They introduced themselves as Ové and Daniela Obermeier. Ové was the winemaker at Vedana. Unless Daniela was Ové's sister, Monty Lenstrom had been wrong about him being a single playboy type, or at least about him being single. He was tall and blond with a nose that started in the middle of his forehead and descended straight down to two generous nostrils. It was an ancient nose, the same that had been worn by Norse seamen, warriors, and woodcutters for centuries. He had a crooked slice of a smile and an endearing gap between his front teeth, one of which showed a slender gray fissure. Sunny decided he was handsome without being attractive. He poured her a glass of Cabernet Sauvignon and explained its virtues. As he did so, he let his blue eyes roam over her with promiscuous liberty. She swirled the wine and tasted. Daniela stood by with a second bottle at the ready. Daniela Obermeier was younger and, pouring the second wine, said she handled publicity and tastings for Vedana. If Ové was fifty, Daniela was in her mid- or early thirties. She wore her brown hair down, her eyes made up, and a diamond pendant around her neck, sitting in the V of her red silk blouse.

Sunny chose her favorite and requested two more glasses for the table. "Are the owners here?"

"They're not," said Ové, hesitating.

"But they'll be at the Niebaum-Coppola dinner tonight," said Sunny.

He smiled. "Exactly. I can introduce you then."

"I look forward to it."

She went back to the table, where Wade was listening to a little gray-haired man swimming in an enormous red Ferrari shirt detail the attributes of the vintage race car he took around to these sorts of events. The man's wife was looking to Rivka for support in her trials. "We compromise," she said in a conspiratorial tone. "We go to three races each summer, and in September he takes me to Europe. That's been our arrangement for fifteen years."

Rivka took the glass Sunny handed her. "Well?"

"Mission accomplished."

The grandstand overlooking the racetrack faced a postcard view of the wine country's green hills and distant mountains. A feathery breeze brushed their cheeks. On the track, vintage Ferraris with white and black numbers on their doors rolled into place, arranging themselves for the start. Some were cherry red, curvy, and voluptuous. Others were leaner, with longer lines and paint jobs the color of cinnamon Tic Tacs.

"Listen to those engines!" said Wade. "So deep and pretty. Close your eyes. It's like the thunder of horses running."

Rivka leaned back and crossed her legs in her high, clear sandals. She looked over her sunglasses at Sunny. "Glad you came?"

"Definitely. I stand corrected, it's kind of nice out here."

The announcer delivered the final pronouncements and the engines roared into action. A dozen roadsters accelerated toward the opening curve. They watched until the pack disappeared into the turns at the western end of the racetrack.

"Did anybody spot the guy dating Ted the fish guy's daughter?" said Sunny.

"I looked, but not very hard," said Rivka. "All I know is he's a salesman and his name is Luciano."

"It shouldn't be that hard," said Wade. "They don't have that many salesmen. I want to have another look at that Maserati before we leave anyway. We can figure out which guy is Luciano and give him the once-over."

"You looking to buy?" said Rivka.

"You never know," said Wade, stroking his mustache. "I could use a new car. I'd only have to sell one acre of Skord Mountain and that baby could be mine."

"Wait, I'm having a vision," said Sunny. "It's raining. I am wrapping a chain around the bumper of your hundred-thousand-dollar sedan so I can pull it out of the cascading, rutted mud slick known as Skord Mountain in winter."

"Good point. I might as well sell the whole homestead and move to town. Then I can afford the coupe as well, and a garage to keep them in."

"I never thought of it that way," said Rivka. "You would be pretty nicely set up if you sold Skord Mountain."

"So, the old man is looking a little better now, is he?" said Wade. "You girls think you're dealing with a country bumpkin, but I'm a diamond in the rough, baby. I've got potential. This particular rustic behind happens to be sitting on a grape-flavored, dust-covered, poison oak and rattlesnake–infested gold mine."

They fell silent while they watched the race cars round the eastern turn and head toward the straightaway in front of the grandstand. The thrilling, high-pitched whir of the engines going full throttle slingshotted past.

"Oh, how I love that sound," said Wade. "Makes my heart go pitter-pat." He watched the cars accelerate out of sight. "If you think about it, a car has a certain significance in our lives. It's your vehicle for experiencing the world. Like your body."

"The rationalization process has begun," said Rivka. "He's going to talk himself into a second mortgage for a fancy sports car."

"As long as it has high clearance and four-wheel drive," said Sunny.

"The automobile is a statement to the world about who we are," said Wade.

"That's true of every possession," said Sunny. "If Rivka chooses to wear clear plastic sandals that are impossible to walk in but sexy to look at, it says that being sexy is more important to her at that moment than being comfortable."

"Cars say more than shoes," said Wade. "You change shoes all the time, but most people only drive one car."

"But some people don't care what car they drive."

"And that would be evident by the car they drive."

"Okay, what profound statement about my character does my car make?" said Sunny.

"That you are sentimental, resistant to change, and attached to familiar textures and sensations," said Wade. "You like that truck because its windows roll down manually and the upholstery is scratchy. Of course, that wouldn't be evident to everyone. I know you better than most. But anyone could tell by your car that history is more important to you than money."

Sunny watched the cars come around the backside of the track and head into the hairpin. "I am not resistant to change," she said. "I just like things the way they are."

They watched the rest of the race and the next two after, then Wade slapped his hands on his thighs. "Let's go find our boy Luciano."

In the new car tent, Wade worked the sales group while Rivka and Sunny stood in line for espressos. Sunny dropped a lump of sugar in the tiny paper cup and stirred, watching the crowd. She recognized Dean Blodger before he turned around, and sucked in her breath. "Guess who's here," she murmured to Rivka. "Our friend the harbormaster."

"The guy from the houseboats?" Rivka scanned the crowd. "Yep, that's him. That's weird. Why is he here?"

"Let's find out. Wait here."

Sunny surprised him while he was inspecting the hood ornament on the new Maserati. "Dean Blodger! What brings you out to the racetrack?"

Dean met her eyes coolly. "Same as you, I presume. Ninety years of fine Italian engineering."

Sunny smiled. "I didn't realize you were an admirer."

"How would you? A five-minute meeting does not reveal a man's soul."

"Indeed."

She thought of the taillights receding down Highway 29 early on Monday morning and the glimpse of the white truck with the Pelican Point Harbor logo on the door on Wednesday night. It had been accelerating away up the highway as she pulled up to the stop sign outside Wildside's parking lot. She had convinced herself it was nothing, that she had been mistaken about the logo, and that it was only one of hundreds of white work trucks that must drive up and down the valley on a given day. "We seem to cross paths quite a bit these days," she said. "For a guy from Sausalito, you spend a lot of time in Napa."

Dean Blodger stuck his thumbs in the pockets of his khaki pants and gave her a smug look. "You inspired me," he said, "with your commute from St. Helena to Mill Valley to do yoga with

Heidi Romero. That's more than an hour each way. If it's worth it for yoga, it's worth it for a day at the races."

Sunny felt a rush of anger bring the heat to her cheeks. She did not like to lie, and it was even worse to be caught at it. "What do you want?"

"Me? I'm just here to pay my respects to the trident's marque. We've waited a long time for a new Maserati." He pointed out the logo. "You see? Every Maserati bears the weapon of the sea king. With his magical trident, Neptune could control any body of water. The perfect car for a man in my line of work."

Sunny stared at the harbormaster, searching his face for an explanation. Why was he here? Was he stalking her?

"It's a masterpiece," he said, standing back. "But you don't seem much interested in cars, Ms. McCoskey. Why are you here, I wonder?"

Wade walked up while Sunny was staring at Dean Blodger, considering her response. Wade held his hand out and introduced himself. Dean reciprocated. They fell silent.

Wade looked from Sunny to Dean and back again. "*Vámanos?*"

"*Lista.* Dean, I'll be seeing you around."

"Will you?"

"Bet on it."

They met Rivka and headed for the car. "What was that guy's story?" said Wade.

"I don't know," said Sunny, "but I think it's time I found out."

They had just enough time to drive home, shower, and change before dinner. Wade dropped off Rivka first.

"Don't forget you still have to be Rachael Robinson tonight," said Sunny.

"I know," scowled Rivka. "My feet are killing me."

Wade drove to Sunny's house, where he kicked off his shoes and took possession of the couch. Sunny showered, then sat in front of her laptop in her bathrobe and searched the web for anything about Dean Blodger. Nothing.

17

Pea gravel crunched underfoot as they made their way through the French garden toward the music and party sounds at Niebaum-Coppola. The winery doors were flung open and women in cocktail dresses spilled into the courtyard like bright flowers. Sunny and Rivka stepped gingerly in their heels. Wade stopped a server with a tray of sparkling wine and commandeered three glasses. "Ladies," he said, handing them around. Another server came by with spiced tuna tartare with sesame on rice crisps. Wade popped one in his mouth and picked up another. "Nice setup," he said between bites, surveying the scene. "Remind me to crash parties here more often."

Sunny selected a crisp and the server moved on. "Ten bucks says the next tray is goat cheese with tapanade."

"Worse. It's mini quiches," said Rivka.

"I hope you two are not going to pick everything apart. It ruins it for those of us who truly appreciate free food."

"I'm not picking, I am merely registering concern. Fusion confusion leads to spoiled appetites, not to mention flatulence," said Sunny.

"You're right. I think it's happening already," said Wade.

"Please."

"You brought it up." Wade tapped his glass against hers, then Rivka's. "Remember, you're not food snobs tonight, you're here to make me look like the guy with the well-endowed wallet."

They mingled, introducing themselves to the other guests and mining them for useless details about where they lived, what they did for a living, and how they came to be sipping bubbly with the Ferrari people. Those they met worked for the big corporate sponsors, for various Ferrari and Maserati dealerships, or for corporate headquarters in Maranello. A group from a big telecommunications company were drinking martinis fast and getting rowdy, including a chorus line of young female executives in formal gowns who were linked arm in arm and beginning to break into song. "Volare" was quickly becoming the theme song of the night. Sunny watched for Ové and Daniela. She followed Wade and Rivka as they circulated through the winery's gift shop, then made their way upstairs, sampling squash blossoms with queso ranchero, endive with blue cheese and candied walnuts, and skewers of chicken breast with Thai dipping sauce from the silver trays along the way.

"Thailand, France, Mexico. I'm so confused. We're going to make it all the way around the globe before we sit down to dinner," said Sunny, watching a tray of oysters on the half shell go by.

"What's your problem?" said Wade, reaching for one. He knocked it back and deposited the shell on the next waiter's tray.

"I just don't understand what's wrong with a sense of unity. Why do we have to be all over the map? What we are experiencing is a culinary cacophony. It's like having a jazz drummer, a cellist, and the lead singer from Black Flag jamming together in your garage while you try to find a wine that goes well with all of them."

"Spoken like a woman who hasn't eaten toast and sardines for the last nine out of ten meals. This is a feast," said Wade.

"Sure, you can feast," said Rivka. "You're not squeezed into a spaghetti-strap straightjacket. Guys are so lucky."

Wade finished chewing the oyster. "You'll never make it on the party girl circuit. You and McCoskey have the goods but you lack commitment. You're going to be back in your jeans by the end of the weekend, I can tell."

"Are you kidding?" said Rivka. "I'll be back in jeans by the end of the night. This getup is a costume, Skord, not a lifestyle change. I have no intention of going around trussed up and hobbled on a regular basis."

"I don't see why not," said Wade. "How old are you these days, twenty-four?"

"Twenty-five. You may recall the birthday celebration you hosted recently."

"Right. I don't want to be the bearer of grim tidings, but that twenty-five-year-old action doesn't stay fresh forever."

"Sun, when do I get to throw my drink in his face?"

"Soon. Or now, if you like. Wait, I'll get a refill and help."

"All I'm saying is, you girls don't exactly work it on a day-to-day basis. Look at McCoskey. Who would have guessed she'd clean up so nice? She keeps that body tucked away like it's a matter of national security. You think it will last forever, but let me tell you, when it's gone, it's gone. If I were blessed with what you two have, I know what I'd do with it."

"I can just picture you as a woman," said Rivka with a wide smile on the brink of tipping over into laughter. "Tux Robinson, hot babe. You would be such a slut."

"And proud of it. I just hate to see all that potential wasted on jeans and work boots," said Wade. "A man has a right to his opinion."

"This from the man who hasn't bought a new T-shirt since 1985," said Sunny. "You sound like Sean Connery. What's in those hors d'oeuvres, catnip?"

"All the pomp and finery is going to my head. It's been a long time since I was off the mountain."

They were examining the display of movie memorabilia when double doors swung open, revealing a dining room like the loft of a barn, with plank floors and exposed rafters. Tables draped in white linen were set with silver, china, and a sea of glasses. A server in white gloves circulated among the guests, urging them to choose a table and take a seat.

"Salmon salad with ginger and green onion to start. Sourdough bread. Sweet butter. Followed by filet mignon with baked potato and some kind of innocuous vegetable. All edible. Something-something chocolate with a streak of raspberry whatever for dessert. Inedible. Five large says I'm at least eighty percent accurate. Any takers?" said Sunny.

"By five large you mean five dollars, right?" said Wade.

"Right."

"I'll take salmon fillets with dill cream sauce and new potatoes," said Rivka. "More asparagus. Mixed baby greens to start. With pickled beets. I'll see your inedible chocolate-raspberry whatever for dessert."

"You're on. Those beets are wishful thinking," said Sunny. "Wait, we can't sit down until we find the Vedana people. I'll watch for Ové. When I spot him, Wade, you pounce and work your charisma."

"Check," said Wade. "Who is Ové again?"

"The winemaker at Vedana. I met him at lunch."

They lingered in the entrance to the dining room, watching the guests trickle in. Sunny spotted Ové coming up the stairs with Daniela close behind. "There he is. The tall guy with the blond hair."

Ové and Daniela hesitated at the entrance, scanning the roomful of empty tables and the people milling around between them. Wade and Rivka took the opportunity to stroll over and introduce themselves. Sunny followed, feigning surprise to find her dear old friends from Texas talking with her new acquaintances from lunch. Another couple joined them and introduced themselves as Bruce and Kimberly Knolls. Ové added that Bruce and Kimberly were the owners of Vedana Vineyards, and that Sunny was the chef and proprietor of Wildside in St. Helena.

Kimberly Knolls put a slender, bejeweled hand to her throat and opened her eyes wide at Sunny. "What a coincidence! We had my birthday luncheon there. Remember, honey?" she said to Bruce. "I told you the girls took me out." She laid two perfectly manicured fingers on Sunny's wrist. "Our meal was impeccable. Flawless."

"Thank you. I'm delighted to hear it." Sunny tipped her head at Ové curiously. "Funny, I didn't think I mentioned the restaurant."

"You didn't. Everyone knows Sunny McCoskey in St. Helena." He gave her a hearty wink to go with the smile he was wearing.

"Really. I didn't know."

"Ové never forgets a face," said Daniela.

Ové continued to stare at her. She looked away uncomfortably. When she looked back, he gave her another wink, smiling placidly, while the conversation turned to the day's events at the racetrack. She smiled back stiffly, wondering if it had been a second wink or only a twitch. A twitch seemed most likely. She turned to Bruce Knolls, who was telling the story of how he'd met the director of the Ferrari dealership and struck up a friendship. Bruce looked about fifty, with short brown hair and basic Northern European good looks. He carried himself with confidence, like a man who has achieved his life goals with time and energy to spare. Sunny took inventory while he talked. He was wearing a submariner Rolex and, judging by the cut and fabric, a Brioni jacket. Even on sale, a jacket like that could set a guy back a couple thousand dollars. The Rolex might be white gold or platinum, but she was ready to guess steel. Bruce Knolls had wealth, but not outrageous wealth, and discriminating taste without the need to flaunt his worldly advantages to excess. Definitely a steel Rolex man. It was equally clear that he was a second lifer, one of those men who migrate to the valley of dreams to try a second marriage and second career, only this time on his terms. There would be no children, no late nights at the office, and no worrying about making ends meet every month. This time around, his work and marriage would be about passion and personal fulfillment. This time, he would focus on what really mattered before it was too late to enjoy it.

His second wife was nothing short of dazzling. Kimberly Knolls had attracted and held the room's attention from the moment she entered it. The effect was partly due to her choice of attire. She was wearing a strapless gown, full-length, and made of shimmering white satin. It had a slit on the side that ran up to her hip, exposing a petite but shapely leg. Her golden skin contrasted beautifully wherever it met the white satin, as, for example, at the clean white line of the bodice. Around her neck was a diamond choker that lived up to its name, sitting high on her neck and fastened snugly. The leftover chain fell down her back to a teardrop emerald that rested between her shoulder blades. She wore her black hair pulled back tightly, drawing attention to delicate features and eyes heavily made up with black liner and frosted shadow. She looked to be of Asian or possibly Polynesian descent, and somewhere in her thirties or early forties. She might have looked younger if it weren't for a certain fatigue discernable around the eyes and mouth. As beautiful as she was, up close she gave the impression of being very tired.

The group moved toward a nearby table. The white-gloved server went through again, urging them to take their seats. Rivka picked a spot and Ové took the place next to her, with Daniela on his other side. Sunny chose a seat opposite them, next to Wade, who sat next to Kimberly Knolls. Bruce Knolls sat next to his wife. Wine was poured. Sunny asked Kimberly how she and Bruce had met. Kimberly laughed and told the story of how they'd fallen in love from a distance at a resort in Cancún, while each of them was there with someone else. Bruce tracked her down when he got back and the rest was history. Servers came around with wine, and the discussion turned to Bruce's goals for the winery.

Sunny glanced across the table and Ové met her eyes, his mouth expressionless, and winked at her again. She started. Obviously Ové Obermeier suffered an embarrassing nervous tic. Sunny made a mental note to politely show no reaction if it happened again, and turned toward Kimberly, leaning in so she could see past Wade.

"Wasn't that terrible about that poor girl who was killed?" she said. "When I read about it in the paper, I could hardly believe it could happen in St. Helena."

Kimberly stared. Bruce replied for her. "It is utterly tragic. We've started raising money for a scholarship in her name, but that won't bring her back of course. I'm sure her family is devastated."

"You took it upon yourself to create a scholarship in her name?" said Sunny. "That's incredibly generous."

"Do we have to talk about such a morbid topic at dinner?" said Kimberly. She put her hands on the table and straightened the silverware with fluttering fingers. "I'd like to forget about that business for just one night."

Bruce put a hand on his wife's. "It's been hard for us. The girl who died was left at our winery. Maybe you didn't know. That's where she was found."

Sunny made what she hoped was a shocked and mortified face. "How awful. I'm so sorry. I had no idea. I read the article but I didn't even notice where she was found. You didn't know her, did you?"

"Of course not," snapped Kimberly. "Don't be ridiculous. Some maniac just decided to ruin our lives at random."

"Let's change the subject," said Daniela loudly from the other side of the table. "I personally would love to hear more about the race cars Tux and Rachael collect back in Texas."

"You won't hear it from me," said Rivka, playing the wife. "I stay out of that car business. I don't think Tux even likes me to go inside the stable where he keeps them. He treats them like his newborn babies. We have to keep our hands in our pockets and lower our voices when we're anywhere near them."

The table chuckled politely, grateful for the effort to lighten the mood, while Bruce stroked Kimberly's hand and whispered to her supportively. The first course arrived and Rivka made a face at Sunny when they saw the plump filets and mixed vegetables. While they ate, Wade entertained the table with descriptions of each of his race cars and the international adventures it took to acquire them.

"I once flew all the way to Milan just to see a car. It was exactly the car I wanted, and there were only three of them in the world, as far as I could tell, and two of them weren't for sale. I though I was the luckiest cowboy west of the Mississippi. The only problem was, turns out the guy selling it didn't own it. I didn't find that out until after I'd paid him. Took three weeks chasing him all over the countryside from Roma to Palermo to get my money back."

Sunny ate her dinner without tasting it and listened to the conversation without participating, keeping to herself so she could think. It was understandable that Kimberly would be upset, but it struck her as the wrong kind of upset. Instead of being saddened or shaken by what had happened, she seemed angry. It was the kind of anger that suggested resentment, or perhaps barely contained fear. Given the situation, it was reasonable for her to be frightened. Or was it? Was there really any direct threat to her? If it really was a random act, as she said it was, then she had little to fear. But if she suspected the girl had been left there for a reason—and Sunny had never believed the girl was left there at random, there being nothing random about the careful presentation she had encountered—it would be very unnerving indeed.

The police knew nothing to link the Knolls to Heidi Romero, that much seemed certain. Sergeant Harvey would have said so, or at least hinted at as much. If Kimberly Knolls was frightened, and if the police knew nothing, then Kimberly Knolls had a secret. She looked like the kind of woman who had a lot of secrets. What if she knew exactly why Heidi Romero was left at her winery, but she didn't dare tell the police. Then she would be alone, waiting for her fears to come get her. Did Bruce know?

Whatever it was that connected them to Heidi Romero, were they trying to hide it together?

Sunny looked around the table, realizing she hadn't heard anything anyone had said in quite some time. Ové looked at her and winked. She was certain now he had an unfortunate tic, and she replied with an encouraging smile.

Her wineglass had been refilled without her noticing. The more she thought about it, the more certain she was that Kimberly Knolls was hiding something. The question was how to find out what it was without causing a scene. Unable to come up with a way, Sunny tuned back into the dinner conversation. Bruce Knolls was explaining where he sourced his grapes, and what he paid for them. Daniela looked at Sunny and smiled, giving her a solid wink. Sunny stared. Daniela smiled coyly. If Ové had a tic, perhaps, from years of living together, Daniela had picked it up. Or maybe it wasn't a tic. Maybe he started doing it on purpose, liking to establish a jovial camaraderie with new acquaintances, and she had picked up the habit. Between dinner and dessert there was more winking by both Ové and Daniela, and a commotion from Rivka's side of the table. Wade looked at them. "What's going on over there?"

"Nothing," said Rivka. "I thought something disgusting was crawling on my leg, but it turned out to be nothing."

When dessert arrived—a thoroughly edible apple tart with vanilla bean gelato—Sunny realized her time was running out. She leaned past Wade. "Kimberly, how did you come to name the winery Vedana? I'm not familiar with the word."

"It was called Acorn Flat when we bought it," said Kimberly. "We wanted something more exotic and evocative. I liked the way *vedana* sounds. In Buddhism, you could say it's almost a negative term. It means sensation, which is what causes attachment to experience. That attachment leads to pain, which keeps the whole wheel of samsara turning. But we thought it was a beautiful word that could be reinterpreted, albeit in a slightly naïve Western sense, in a positive light. Sensation, like attachment, has its good side, from our perspective." She leaned over and gave Bruce a kiss on the cheek.

"Where did you study Buddhism?" asked Sunny.

"At the Zen Center in Marin. Years ago."

"Zen is Japanese, isn't it?" said Sunny. "Did you ever go to Japan?"

"No. It wasn't like I was a student of religion. I practiced meditation at the center and read some books. I was in a difficult place in my life at the time, and I found sitting meditation helpful."

Sunny thought for a moment. If she was going to get any of her questions about Kimberly Knolls answered, she was going to have to be more direct, and quickly. People were already getting up and mingling with other tables. At that moment, her lucky break came from the other side of the table.

"I love Japan," said Daniela. "Tokyo is such a sexy city. There's nothing like it in Europe or the Americas." Her eyes were half closed and her head dipped as she looked across the table at Sunny. She swallowed what was left of her wine and laughed out loud, leaning into her husband. "Ové loves Japan, don't you, darling?"

Ové took the glass gently from his wife's hand. "It is a fascinating place. If you consider the contributions Japan has made to world culture, especially considering the size of the country, it's really quite remarkable. Geisha, samurai, Godzilla, sushi, Zen, the kimono, the tea ceremony, ikebana, tatami. So many things I love are Japanese."

"And the latest contributions, manga comic books and anime films," said Sunny.

Ové's eyes lit up. "You are absolutely right. You still have to go to Japan to get the best manga and anime, but it's finally starting to catch on here. Some of those films are works of art. Future classics."

"You're forgetting the truly great contribution," said Rivka. "Pokémon."

"Every culture has its weak points. Pokémon and pachinko I could live without."

"Aren't some anime films pornographic?" said Sunny.

"Some are, but most aren't. Either way, they can be quite beautiful." This statement was followed, no surprise, by a wink.

Sunny took a gulp of Merlot. "But aren't they terribly violent? I've never seen one, but my boyfriend said they're extremely degrading to women and usually involve torture and bondage scenes."

"As opposed to Western pornography, which isn't degrading to women?" he said. "At least nobody gets hurt making bondage cartoons. You can't say the same thing about pornography shot with real people."

"Quite true," said Sunny.

The conversation rolled to a stop and stayed there. Daniela had her eyes closed and her head against Ové's shoulder. Kimberly excused herself. When she came back, she and Bruce said good night. Ové coaxed a thoroughly tipsy Daniela out of her chair and persuaded her to walk with him and collect their coats. She stopped to plant a kiss on Wade Skord's forehead. "I like him," she told her husband loudly on their way out.

Wade scrubbed at his wiry gray hair, looking embarrassed. "Let's get out of here. I'm beat."

"You can't drive," said Rivka, "and I can't even walk. We're going to have to sleep here."

"When did everyone get all loosey-goosey?" said Sunny.

"How could you not? They poured about a dozen different wines."

Sunny noticed for the first time the collection of wineglasses, all of them full, crowded at the top of her plate. "Come on, I'll drive."

18

A ghost landscape waited outside. The moon, a lopsided yellow spectacle that filled the valley floor with shadows, loomed over Atlas Peak like an alien visitation. Sunny kept her eyes straight ahead on the parking lot, avoiding the hillside covered with oak trees rising to the right, wary of catching a glimpse of any unusual shapes the shadows might hold. She was relieved to reach the car. Wade handed her the keys to his old Volvo station wagon and they got in.

Rivka closed her door with a loud sigh. "That might be the strangest dinner party I have ever attended."

"I thought it was fairly civilized," said Wade from the backseat. "Except the part where McCoskey went fishing for murder suspects and nearly gave Kim Knolls a nervous breakdown."

Sunny backed out and headed down the winery's long driveway. "Awkward, but necessary, not that it yielded much. What did you think of Kimberly Knolls?"

Wade whistled. "A very tidy package. That was a naughty man's naughty dream girl if I've ever seen one."

"What makes you say that?"

"Just a feeling. In my experience, contrary to the familiar saying, you can tell quite a bit about a book by its cover, and that cover said, 'I'm a nasty, naughty girl who likes a good, hard spanking.'"

"Saucy critter!" said Sunny. "Do you think so?"

"I know so. Wade Skord didn't fall off the pumpkin wagon just yesterday. I've circulated among plenty of bad girls in my time, and I'm ready to bet the vineyard that Kimberly Knolls has a naughty streak six lanes wide. If Bruce Knolls, that lucky devil, isn't turning her over his knee on a regular basis, I'll hand in my bachelor's card and become a nun."

"The world is a much more mysterious place than a person would ever imagine," said Sunny. "Why would anyone want an *elective* spanking? That's like getting a parking ticket for fun."

"If Wade is right, I know the perfect man for her," said Rivka. "Our friend Ové Obermeier should be just her kind of guy."

"I wondered what was going on over there," said Wade. "It looked like you were tangling with a marmot under the table."

"More like a weasel. It's amazing how much trouble a guy can cause with one hand. Finally I had to stomp on his foot with my heel."

"Ouch, the sting of the stiletto. I think I saw that," said Wade. "I distinctly remember seeing him grimace."

"That explains another very perplexing aspect of dinner," said Sunny, and told them about the winking epidemic. "I actually felt sorry for him. I thought he had a tic."

Rivka rolled back in her seat with the giggles. "I love it! He's getting all pervy on you, and you think, 'That poor man! I must reach out to him in his time of need!' I love how you thought they *both* had tics!"

"I think I feel a little insulted," said Wade. "Nobody groped my knee or winked at me. You could have at least given me a suggestive nudge, McCoskey. I feel like such a wallflower."

"You should have sat next to Daniela," said Rivka. "I'm sure she would have made it worth your while. I thought she was going to crawl in your lap on the way out."

"You noticed that, did you? I figured it was my imagination."

"The part where she threw her cleavage in your face and nuzzled the top of your head should have been a clue," said Sunny.

"It just proves that you put enough wine in a girl, she'll fall for just about anybody," said Rivka.

"Meow!" said Wade. "Hey, so, you think they were swingers?"

"Swingers!" said Rivka. "I've never heard anyone actually use that word."

"What else do you call it? I think they were cruising for a side dish to the marital main course."

"Don't make me lose my dinner," said Rivka. "Hey, nice job, by the way, faking the Ferrari connection. For a while you almost had me believing in your Testa Rossa collection out in Houston."

"It was Ventura County, not Houston, but everything else was true. I owned every one of those cars. Put them together one piece at a time with my own hands. The only part I left out was that they were only about ten inches long."

"Explain," said Rivka.

"Back in the days before cable and TiVo, young lads like myself liked to kill the hours by assembling highly accurate models of our dream cars. My favorites were the beautiful new Testa Rossas they were bringing out in the late fifties and early sixties, what they call *vintage* models these days, but back then they were brand new and what everybody dreamed of owning, or even just seeing. I had a whole collection of them. I even had the 1956 Maserati Tipo 300S, a masterpiece from the moment it was born."

"It's all coming together now. Little Wade Skord taking out his adolescent frustrations sniffing model glue out in the barn," said Rivka.

"And dreaming the sweet song of the Italian twelve-cylinder redhead," said Wade. "I knew I would see those cars race someday, hear the basso profundo of the engines at the starting line and the howl of them flying by, and afterward have an elegant dinner in the company of two sexy young things. I just didn't realize it would be such a long wait, or that one of them would be such a smartass."

Sunny glanced at the moon, hanging like a yellow stone in a dull black sky. "That's a lot of chemistry for one winery. Riv, what's your take on Kimberly?"

"For once, I agree with Skord. Kimberly looked like the kind of woman who eats men for breakfast. I don't know what she's doing with Bruce. He seemed like a nice, ordinary guy. She's all action. Did you see the nails? And the choker? That was a fuck me outfit if I ever saw one."

"So we have Ové the groping winker and his winking accomplice Daniela," said Sunny. "We have Bruce Knolls, the enigma, who may be a nice, ordinary guy, or who may simply have a better poker face than everyone else, and we have Kimberly, the wanton beauty with a case of nerves. In my opinion, somebody at that table has something to do with Heidi Romero." She thought for a moment. "And then there's Dean Blodger. Is it possible to believe he was at the racetrack today by coincidence? No, it's not. But why would he go there?"

"The same reason you did," said Rivka.

"Yep. To get a look at Bruce and Kimberly Knolls," said Sunny. "But how would he know they'd be there?"

"The same way you did. It's probably posted on their Web site."

The Volvo's occupants fell into a meditative silence as the road narrowed and the trees planted on either side reached together overhead, their branches thrumming a flickering pattern of moon shadow on the hood of the car as they drove toward home.

19

Certain chores at Wildside could not wait until Monday morning. Least urgent was the tower of unopened mail on her desk, but that was what Sunny tackled first, since it was more inviting than doing inventory on the walk-in, figuring out why the grease drain on the grill was sluggish, and baking a fresh supply of biscotti. Even the payroll sounded fun compared to cleaning out the grease drain. Andre was right, she thought, tearing open another bill. If she expanded the restaurant like he suggested, and started serving dinner and staying open on weekends, she could do more business, bring in more revenue, and afford to hire more staff, which might ultimately liberate her from cleaning out the grease drain, not to mention working the line all day Monday through Friday. On the other hand, there was plenty of evidence to suggest that expanding the restaurant's hours would only expand her own and make it that much more difficult to maintain her standards. "More money, more problems," was what her father said plenty of times, usually on a Sunday afternoon while trying to repair some new piece of equipment that was supposed to make life simpler.

She had finished opening the mail, taken inventory, made a list of what to order for the week, completed the payroll, and, against all inclination, crawled under the grill, unbolted a section of pipe, and stuck her arm into the drain up to the elbow, the better to scrape away the clogged-up grease, when she heard knocking. She waited, presuming she was mistaken. To her surprise, it sounded again, this time louder and more insistent. She wiggled out from under the grill and found a rag, wiping the black grime off her hands as best she could. The knocking continued impatiently from the front door.

"Coming!" she called. "It's Sunday and we're not open, but I am coming to the door anyway. Just one second, please." Sunny did not have to open the door to know who it was. It would be a tourist convinced that her continued happiness and well-being, as well as that of her friends and loved ones, hinged irrevocably on a reservation for four at noon on Tuesday, and that her possession of a major credit card entitled her to as much. Instead, she was surprised to see Kimberly Knolls standing on the threshold, looking the picture of affluent professionalism. She did not stay there for long. Sunny moved aside as Kimberly walked in without waiting for an invitation.

"We need to talk. Are you alone here?" said Kimberly.

Sunny took two chairs down from a table in the dining room. "We're alone. Have a seat. Would you like something to drink? I'm going to get a lemonade for myself."

Kimberly declined. Sunny went into the kitchen and came back with two glasses. She put a glass of water in front of Kimberly and sat down with her lemonade. Mrs. Knolls, dressed in a sleek gray pants suit and heels, was as well groomed as Sunny was slouchy, sweaty, and grubby.

"What can I do for you?"

Kimberly moved her sunglasses to the top of her head and stared into Sunny's eyes with a fierceness that some people would have found intimidating. A few years ago, Sunny would have been one of them, but running a restaurant and all it entailed—demanding near perfection from her crew, dealing with arrogant customers, handling the county and city authorities—had toughened her to such displays. Kimberly gave it her best shot, nevertheless. She leaned toward Sunny. "First of all, I know who you are. I found it all out this morning. I don't know what you think you're doing, but it is not amusing. I'd like a complete explanation of last night, and if I'm not satisfied you've told me everything, I'm going straight to the police."

"I'm not sure what you mean," said Sunny.

Kimberly's lips narrowed angrily. "You think the fact that a young woman died is some kind of invitation to play games?"

"No, I don't think it is. Do you?"

"I'm not the one going around telling lies," said Kimberly. "You pretended you didn't know anything about the murder when you know more than anyone else."

Sunny bit her lip. "That's true. I'm sorry I deceived you. I wanted to hear what you thought about the murder, see if you knew anything about Heidi Romero, if you had any theories. That's why I went to the Ferrari dinner last night, to try to talk to you. But the police asked me not to tell anyone I was the one who found her, so I had to pretend I only knew what was in the paper."

"And are you satisfied now? We don't know her. We don't know anything about her. It was a random act of violence that happened to land in our laps. It was just our miserable bad luck, and hers."

"Do you honestly believe that? Because it seems very odd to me. It just doesn't fit. If you saw what I saw that night, you would find it very hard to believe there was anything random about that particular act of violence. It was . . . orchestrated. Choreographed. What's the word? Curated."

"Murder rarely seems normal, does it? And the fact remains, we know nothing about any of it. Our winery caught the attention of a killer. In the scheme of his demented logic, it somehow made sense to leave her there. We may never know what that logic was."

Sunny studied her. There was no hurry. She took her time, gathering her thoughts and her courage. Kimberly Knolls wasn't going anywhere.

"We have a very unpleasant situation on our hands. A young woman, a fine person by all accounts, is dead. Her killer is free. And you know something that has you in a panic. I don't want to make any of this more difficult for you, but under the circumstances—"

"I am hardly in a panic. It is an unpleasant situation. But it's also over. Whoever killed Heidi Romero is long gone. They chose our winery to make their demented statement. Beyond that, none of this has anything to do with Vedana."

Kimberly looked even more tired, and more beautiful, than last night. Sunny drank her lemonade. Finally she said, "That sounds to me like what your husband tells you at night when you're scared. Only he doesn't know everything, does he? As I was saying, under the circumstances, with a killer out there running around, I'm prepared to do whatever is necessary to get to the truth. I have never believed Heidi Romero was left there at random, and I'm even less inclined to believe it now. On the contrary, I think you know plenty about that girl and why she was left at your winery, but you'd rather sit and wait and hope nothing more will come of it than tell what you know, or what you suspect."

"You're wrong," said Kimberly, taking her sunglasses from her head and placing them on the table nervously. "I don't know anything about her."

Sunny read the word PRADA upside down on the stem of the sunglasses and idly wondered what such objects cost. "Then why are you so scared?"

Kimberly gave her an amused look. "What makes you think I'm scared?"

"The fact that you're here, for one thing. I think Heidi Romero's murder makes you nervous in more than the usual ways. The police haven't said much about what happened to her or exactly how she was left, but the kind of questions they've been asking probably has you good and worried, and you want to know more. You're here to find out everything you can from me. You need help, and I might be the only safe place for you to look for it. The worst part, I would imagine, is being alone. You can't confide in anybody. You can't even share your fears with your husband, let alone the police. All you can do is wait."

Kimberly looked at Sunny with an expression of naked despair. She put her hands to her face, covering her mouth. "I don't have to tell you anything," she said in a voice that was barely a whisper. She reached for the water and drank thirstily.

"No, you don't. In fact, I have work to do. And since nobody left a dead body at my restaurant, I don't have to worry about any of this. Heidi Romero is not my problem, she's your problem. You can tell me what's really going on, and maybe I can help you, or you can go on staying up all night wondering when the next body will be found, and when it will be your turn. It makes no difference to me."

Kimberly put the glass down hard. "I didn't even know her. I've never even heard of Heidi Romero until last week."

"Then tell me what you do know," said Sunny. "Wait, let me enhance your motivation. Here is what we're going to do. If you don't share enough of your story to satisfy my curiosity right now, my first phone call after you leave will be to Sergeant Harvey. As I understand it, he's been inches away from getting a search warrant for your home and office for the past week. This conversation could be just what he needs to finally get it."

"What are you talking about? I haven't said anything that would remotely interest the police."

"The fact that you came here to threaten me is enough."

"I didn't threaten you!"

"Didn't you? I thought that was how this conversation began."

"I just wanted to . . . I was angry about last night."

"And I'll just tell Steve you came by after meeting me at dinner, desperate to know more details about the murder, asking a million questions. The police don't believe any more than I do that that girl was left at your winery at random. They know someone at Vedana knows something about her. Imagine what they could find with a search warrant. It's remarkable what can be recovered from a hard drive these days, for example. Deleted files, deleted emails, Web sites you visited three months ago. As I understand it, it's all still on there if you know where to look. And then there are the cell phone records."

A disturbing look came over Kimberly's face and she rose up from her chair, aiming a solid slap at Sunny's cheek that definitely would have hurt and certainly would have made it more difficult not to lose her temper. Luckily, a childhood of roughhousing and slap fighting had served her well. She read the intention accurately, saw the hand en route, and reached up in plenty of time to catch Kimberly's delicate forearm before the blow could reach her. Sunny spent her days getting a kitchen workout that pumped up the veins in her forearms, brought definition to her biceps, and hardened her grip until she could flip eggs in a cast-iron skillet with a flick of the wrist. Even an enraged Kimberly was no match for her strength. Sunny let go and almost smiled, seeing that Kimberly was about to try it again. "How dare you accuse me!" she fumed instead. "How dare you imply I've done anything wrong."

Sunny matched her glare unapologetically. "I'm not implying anything. I'm quite confident you've done something wrong. I think you know why that girl was left at your winery tied up like an erotic sideshow at the Folsom Street Fair. As far as I can tell, you have two options. You can take action on your own, or you can sit around and wait for somebody else to make the next move. Whether it's the police or the killer that makes it, either way it's not likely to improve your quality of life."

Kimberly turned away with a look of disgust and seemed to crumple inward. "What do you mean by erotic sideshow? How was she tied?"

"She was hanging from the oak tree in front of the winery with her hands tied behind her back. She was naked except for hemp rope worked around her body, almost like a corset. From what I've been told, it was a kind of Japanese-style bondage called shibari. Does that mean anything to you?"

Kimberly released her hair from its ponytail, letting it fall down around her face. She removed each of her rings and stacked them on the table, then sat staring at her hands, twisting and rubbing them as if trying to remove some invisible binding. Finally she said, "That's right, that's what it's called. If I'd never heard of that word, none of this would have happened."

20

Contrition evaporated swiftly from her pretty face and she went back to looking defiant. "Boredom can be dangerous," said Kimberly Knolls. "I was bored." She looked away. "It doesn't matter why I did it. I'm not sure I even know. Boredom. I let go of the reins of my life, and some dark, hidden part of me took over. I did it, that's all that matters."

Sunny waited. Kimberly would tell her now, if she was patient. Asking questions or trying to encourage her would only risk making her change her mind.

"I was reading the personals online, exactly six months ago. I remember because we had just had our third wedding anniversary. Anyway, I was playing around and I found a listing that appealed to me. A guy looking for something edgy and anonymous. Edgy was exactly what I was looking for. Something forbidden. I contacted him and we exchanged emails for a while. He was articulate, witty, intelligent, and he could tell what I wanted. He sent me pictures of what he was going to do to me." She picked up the elastic and tied her hair back again. She took a drink of water and lifted her eyes to Sunny's. "I liked them. I liked the pictures he sent. I hated them, but they did something to me I could not resist."

"What were the pictures of?"

"Girls tied up, all different ways. Some of them looked beautiful. He said he was an artist. He said I would love it. I thought he was probably right. In the beginning, I never even considered meeting him. I just wanted to flirt with the idea. Then I thought I could do it once and get away with it and no one would ever know. If we did it just right, neither of us would know the real identities of the other, and we could vanish back to where we came from. It would be our secret forever. I knew if I got it out of my system I would feel better, then I could forget about it and everything would go back to normal. I needed a release."

Kimberly reached for her purse. Sunny watched her, wondering what she would do if Kimberly did something unpredictable now. What if she had a gun? She took out a pack of cigarettes and a lighter. They both took one. Sunny went behind the bar and came back with a ramekin, two glasses, and an open bottle of Chardonnay. She filled the glasses. Kimberly held the lighter for her and Sunny inhaled, the orange glow of the burning tobacco registering her commitment to the conversation. The cigarette tasted bad, but they were in a bad place. She pulled again on the cigarette, exhaling a thick plume of smoke. "Go on."

Kimberly drank the wine and looked relieved. She almost looked like she was enjoying herself. Part of her still liked the story. "I was very careful. We never revealed our real names. Just anonymous email addresses. All I knew was that he lived north of San Francisco. He knew I lived in the wine country. I suggested we meet at a big hotel where I was unlikely to be noticed by anyone I knew."

"Which hotel?"

"We went to that one in Sonoma with all the Russians. The Flamingo. He offered to put it on his credit card so I wouldn't have to give my name at all. He told me to go to the room on a certain day at a certain time. He would be waiting. I didn't think I would really go, and I told him that. He said he would be there anyway, hoping I changed my mind. The day came, and I got in the car, and I drove there, almost without thinking. It was like someone else had control of my body. I sat in the parking lot for an hour, trying to decide what to do. Finally I went to the room where he said he would be waiting.

"Have you ever felt two things at once? Two conflicting emotions? I hated him and I loved him at the same time. It was the worse day of my life and the best."

Sunny felt nauseous, whether from the cigarette or what Kimberly was saying, she couldn't tell. One question couldn't wait any longer. "What did he look like?"

"I don't know. It was dark in the room, and when I came in he grabbed me at the door and blindfolded me. When it was over, he told me to count to five hundred before I left the room, and I did. I never saw him."

"But it wasn't over when it was over," said Sunny.

"He continued to email me. I told him it was a one-time thing, that I was happily married and I never intended to see him again. I canceled that email account and assumed that was the end of it. Then he started calling the house." She crushed out the cigarette and took a drink of the wine. "I was lucky. I answered the phone once, and managed to delete messages three other times without Bruce hearing them. They were terrible messages. At first he said he was in love with me, that he couldn't live without me, and that I had to come back to him or he would go crazy. Then he started saying that nobody could take me away from him, that I was his forever, and he would do anything to get me back."

"You talked to him?"

"No. As soon as I heard his voice, I hung up."

"And the number?"

"I wrote them all down. A couple of times he was in the room at the Flamingo. One of the numbers was blocked. The fourth was the phone booth at that gas station on the south end of town."

"In St. Helena?"

Kimberly nodded.

"You didn't contact the police," said Sunny.

"How could I? Like you said, I'm in this alone. I couldn't tell anybody, not even Bruce."

"How did he get your number?"

"I was very stupid. I brought my purse with me to the room. I thought I was being smart by taking my wallet out and leaving it in the glove compartment, but I forgot about my business cards. I assume he looked in my bag at some point while I was there and found them."

Sunny crushed out her cigarette and moved the ramekin to another table. "This was when?"

"I met him in late October. The phone calls came about once a week through November. Then I never heard from him again. I assumed it was over. Even after the police called us and said they had found the body of a young woman at the winery, I never imagined it was connected. It was only after the police kept asking questions about our marriage and our personal lives that I started to worry. They asked me a dozen different ways if I ever suspected Bruce of having an affair, if I had had an affair, if we ever went to sex clubs, if either of us was into bondage. I could tell there was something funny going on."

"Why Heidi Romero? What did she have to do with it?"

"I don't know. If she was tied the way you say, I'm sure it has some connection to the man I met. He talked the whole time about the beauty of shibari as an art form, how a woman tied that way was like a work of art. But I don't know what the connection could be. I'd never met or even heard of anyone named Heidi Romero until she turned up dead. The only thing I could think of was he wanted to scare me into seeing him again."

"Has he called you?"

"No, nothing."

"And you told the police none of this?"

Kimberly Knolls looked at her hands and shook her head. "Of course not. It would mean losing everything. It wouldn't bring that girl back, and it would end my life as well. Can you imagine the scandal?"

"Scandal? Bad press is the least of your problems. Do you think the person who did this won't do it again? Can you actually live with the fact that you have information that could put a murderer behind bars, and you're not going to share it because you're afraid of upsetting your husband? What about when the next body turns up? Are you going to be able to live with yourself then?"

"I don't know anything that could put him behind bars. He's probably halfway around the world by now. Telling the police what I know would only destroy my marriage and nothing else."

"He used a credit card at the Flamingo. Even if it wasn't his, it belonged to someone, and it could lead to some kind of trail. Which day in October did you meet there?"

"Listen, I can't go to the police and I won't go to the police, and neither will you. If you do, I'll simply deny everything. I have witnesses that you approached me last night, that you crashed a dinner party for that purpose, and that you pretended to know nothing about the murder. I'll just say you are obsessed and you've been harassing me."

"And I suppose you'll sleep like a baby tonight, knowing once and for all that that message was meant for you."

"I'll never sleep like a baby again as long as I live. Life goes on."

Sunny shook her head. "This isn't over, and you know it's not over. Heidi Romero was his way of getting your attention, probably so you'll be more cooperative next time he contacts you. It's the beginning, not the end. For your own safety as much as anyone else's, you need to come forward with everything you've got."

Kimberly Knolls stood up and buttoned her jacket, tugging it down in front and smoothing the creases from her trousers. She put each of her rings back on and picked up her handbag and sunglasses. "What I did and what happened to Heidi Romero are both in the past. The past is gone. Only three people know what I just told you, and two of us will never admit it. That just leaves you." She put on her sunglasses. "Thanks for the wine."

21

Everything is relative. Cleaning out the grease drain sounded like a terrible way to spend a Sunday afternoon until the alternative was to call Sergeant Harvey and set a series of events in motion that neither Sunny nor Kimberly Knolls would enjoy. She considered various strategies. One was the truth. Call him up and tell him exactly what had happened. Kim would lie about it. Steve would grill both of them. Then he would start looking into it and find, presumably, that Sunny had been telling the truth. Another was to leave an anonymous tip. Leave a message saying Kimberly Knolls had had an affair with a guy who was into bondage in October at the Flamingo Inn. That would give them enough to get them going.

A third, more daring strategy was to call Dean Blodger down at Pelican Point Harbor with Kim Knolls listening in on the line, or have Kim call him directly. If the harbormaster was her man, she would recognize his voice. Sunny thought of Dean gripping her hand that morning in the harbormaster's office. He was stronger than he looked. If he was the guy Kim had met, the guy who'd killed Heidi and dragged her up to Napa, the last thing she wanted to do was have any more contact with him, even by phone.

And then there was the other option. She could simply forget what Kimberly had told her. As long as no one else got hurt, it wouldn't matter one way or the other. It was refreshing to imagine doing nothing, to think that Kimberly was right, the past was gone forever, over. If only that were the case. The ramifications of the past live on in the present, that girl hanging limp and dead proved it, and Sunny knew in her heart that a man who could do that to Heidi Romero was possessed by an illness too powerful to just go away. That kind of force did not dissipate. It would grow, searching for a new outlet, or it would wait for the next irresistible opportunity. Whatever he might have started out as, he had become a monster, and he would go on committing the acts of a monster. It was his nature now.

She made quick work of the grease drain and went out to the garden to pull weeds, working with manic energy. The light had softened and a pink glow edged the Mayacamas Mountains. She tugged up handfuls of oxalis and field grasses ferociously. Their presence seemed a blatant affront to order and productivity that would no longer be tolerated. What do you call this state of mind, she wondered, in which it was crucial to think clearly and decisively and yet impossible to do so? She saw stars straight ahead and black zones at the corners of her vision. How long had it been since she'd eaten? There would be food at home. For now, the soil in her hands meant everything. She kept going back to what Kimberly had told her, hearing it again and again. *If I'd never heard of that word, none of this would have happened.*

Was it her duty to turn this information over to the police? Sergeant Harvey would listen, then he would check the story out with Kimberly. If she denied it, the worst that could happen was Steve would shake his head at Sunny and chastise her for getting involved again by going to the Ferrari event. He would ask her, again, to stay out of police business. Best-case scenario, there might be something in it that would lead the police to Heidi Romero's killer.

The light turned somber and the air cold. She went inside and washed her hands. The only item left on her list of chores was the biscotti. She looked around at the silent kitchen and the dark windows. In the mood she was in, Wildside would feel lonely once it got dark, and she never liked the look of those windows at night, especially since one of her pet fears had been realized last year, when she'd looked up during a late-night baking session and seen a face looking in the window. All week long she had avoided thinking about the white truck that kept showing up in St. Helena. She didn't think about the driver, and how he might be wondering if she could identify him. And she had not been thinking about Dean Blodger, and how he'd turned up at the racetrack. However, staying late alone at the restaurant was a good way to start thinking about those things all over again. It would be much more pleasant to bake at home. She gathered a box of supplies, locked up, and went out to the truck. Her cell phone was wedged in the ash tray. She could call Sergeant Harvey on the way or when she got home, if that's what she decided to do. It could even wait until morning. Sunny pulled onto the highway, not thinking about anything, not even Kimberly Knolls.

"What are you doing?" she said, cradling the phone against her shoulder while she sifted flour.

"I just came in," said Andre Morales. "I'm beat. We did 388 on a Sunday night. Crazy."

"Want to come over?" said Sunny.

"I could do that, if I do it soon, before I get too tired to deal. I'm pretty foul at the moment. I need to rinse the kitchen grunge off. What's all that clanging around?"

"I'm baking biscotti. I just put the aniseed in the oven, and now I'm going to finish the dough for pistachio orange with white chocolate frosting."

"Isn't it sort of late for that kind of project?"

"I didn't feel like going to bed. You know what they say, 'Idle hands are the devil's workshop.'"

"I don't think they meant when you're asleep. Is everything okay?"

"Everything is fine. I've just been thinking too much."

"What about?"

"Just fretting. Assorted worries, concerns, fears. You know, the stuff nightmares and wrinkles are made of. I'd like to forget about it all for a while. It would be nice to see you."

"In that case, I'm yours. I'll be there in half an hour."

"I'm supposed to have dinner with another VC in San Francisco tomorrow night," said Andre.

"Where are you finding these guys?" said Sunny.

"Through Emily, mostly. She's completely behind the expansion concept. Vinifera has been great, but she agrees it's time to take the next step and do something that will really get people's attention. Being alive means growing. You can't just sustain the status quo. That's stagnation."

Emily was Andre's agent, a tiny powerhouse of a woman who could fit through a doggie door and still kick butt at the negotiating table as well as on the tennis court. Until she met Andre, Sunny didn't know a cook needed an agent.

"Why is everything comfortable termed stagnation? What happened to stability and consistency? And isn't there anything to be said about what rate of growth is healthy? That's how herbicides kill, by overstimulating growth so the plant depletes its resources and literally grows itself to death."

"I know, small is beautiful. Less is more. Slow food. Do you want to join us or not?"

"What time?"

"I'm not sure. It depends on when we meet. It might be early."

"Where are you going?"

"I'll have to check on what's open on Monday night. Maybe somewhere old school, like Bix."

"Give me a call when you know what time. If I can get there, I will. I'd like to see what a venture capitalist looks like." She nestled into his arms and rested her head on his chest. "Are you going to the knife shop?"

"Yeah. I'll go by there early and see if they can get them done the same day. You want me to take yours too?"

"Would you? They need it bad."

"No problem. You can make it through a Monday without them?"

"I have my old knives at the restaurant. They'll do the job for a day."

Andre was still asleep, resting on his side with the sheet tucked under one arm, when she slid out of bed. She showered and put water on for tea instead of making a racket grinding coffee beans, and watched the dancing blue flames surge against the kettle until wisps of steam rose out of the spout. She took her tea out to the patio and sat in a spot of pale early sun, feeling the brisk air on her skin like cold water. When she had finished her tea, she crept back into the bedroom to get dressed. Andre grumbled and turned over without waking up. Sunny pulled her favorite blue sweater over her T-shirt, grabbed her shoes, and went out to the living room to put them on. She left a good morning note on the table with four biscotti, gathered up the rest, and let herself out as quietly as possible.

While she warmed up the truck, she returned to her thoughts of the night before. She couldn't put it together. The only solution she could come up with didn't fit well enough. It could be forced into place, but it didn't click down smoothly and solidly the way the truth always did, fitting each piece of the puzzle perfectly. Assuming the man Kimberly Knolls met at the Flamingo Inn was the killer, it was still a stretch to see him leaving Heidi Romero's body at the winery. The threat did not seem specific enough. What did such a grand gesture accomplish? Was he saying he would do that to Kimberly if she did not comply with his wishes? If so, why hadn't he contacted her to make his demands known? Did he simply enjoy frightening her? And why the winery? Wouldn't it have been more compelling, if the message was intended for Kimberly, to leave the body at the Knolls' home?

There was always the possibility that Kim was lying. Sunny put that possibility aside. She was telling the truth, she was sure of that. But did she tell all of it? If she was willing to meet a stranger at a hotel for an anonymous bout of daring sex play, it was reasonable to assume that other excursions against boredom were not out of the question. An obvious choice was right under Kimberly's nose. From what Sunny could tell about Ové Obermeier, he would be a willing participant in just about any tryst. What if Kimberly had shared her new hobby with him? Or vice versa? Kimberly might easily have left out how she got interested in shibari in the first place. She didn't say specifically that the man at the hotel had introduced her to the concept.

None of these questions was likely to be answered this morning, thought Sunny, breezing past Bismark's without stopping. And there were more questions. Why did Dean Blodger show up at the Ferrari event? Was he the one driving the white truck she'd seen around town? Who was this guy named Mark that Heidi was supposedly dating? Why did Joel Hyder lie about having permission to go to the houseboat? And why was he so amenable to their company? He was obviously attracted to Rivka, but was that the only reason?

Wildside was still dark when she pulled into the parking lot. She turned on the lights, cranked the oven up to 450 for warmth, and tuned the stereo to classical music for a lofty, efficient mood. Then she went into her office and sat at her desk. She picked up the telephone and stared at it, imagining how the conversation would go. She put the phone down. No matter how she worked it through, squealing to Sergeant Harvey didn't feel right. On one hand, what Kimberly had told her might easily lead to the capture of a genuinely dangerous individual. On the other, it might not. It was entirely possible the two events were not at all related. Either way, Steve would inevitably question Bruce Knolls about it and, unless Bruce was a man of unusually expansive, philosophical, and adventurous understanding, that would be the end of his marriage to Kimberly.

Sunny thought about it some more. The root of the problem was that an intimate confession of the sort Kimberly had made needed to come from Kimberly. If Sunny went to Steve now, the conversation would be about how she wasn't supposed to be involved and she should stay out of it and what was she doing tracking down the Knolls and how could she prove any of this anyway? If Kimberly went to him, he would have something real, direct, and substantial to tackle.

She gazed around the office. Cookbooks were stacked in

towers on every flat surface, including the floor. A ray of dawn light angled in the window and lit a carved wooden bowl filled with leafy mandarin oranges. Brown, orange, green, all boldly stated. From the top of the bookshelf, the rusty metal rooster that presided over the room stared down at her pensively. If only she could persuade Kimberly to go to the police. At that moment, she harvested the fruit of a good night's rest, abbreviated as it was. Sleep had done its work. In the light of morning, she realized the obvious. Kimberly would go to the police on her own. She knew she was in danger, and she knew others were as well. She had already taken the first step, she had told Sunny. Now the truth had had a taste of the open air and it would wiggle and squirm until it got out again. Sunny felt better immediately. Yes, Kimberly Knolls would call the police on her own, she was sure of it. If not today, tomorrow. Unless Sunny had seriously misjudged her character, Kimberly would go to the police, and she would do it soon. The impulse to relieve herself of the burden of secrecy would grow over the next day, maybe two. After that, if she didn't give in, the impulse would wane. If she didn't crack today or tomorrow, she wouldn't do it at all. Sunny would wait until Wednesday morning. If Kimberly hadn't called the police by then, she would do it for her.

She leaned the chair back and put her feet on the desk. "You hear that, Randy?" she said to the rooster. "That little bird is going to sing. I'll bet my last bottle of sixteen-year-old Sicilian balsamic on it."

Satisfaction was short-lived, replaced swiftly with new concerns. Some questions couldn't wait any longer for Steve or Kimberly to take action. She dug in her purse for the slip of paper where she'd written the telephone number, spent a moment organizing her thoughts, and picked up the receiver. Joel Hyder answered on the second ring.

22

He was breathing hard. "Sorry, I was just coming in from outside. Who is this?" Sunny explained again.

"Oh, right. Of course, Heidi's yoga buddy. What can I do for you?"

"I just wondered if the police had contacted you about the man Heidi had been seeing."

"Why would they?"

"I gave the investigating officer in St. Helena your name and number. That night after we were at the houseboat, the Sausalito police called him and reported what had happened, and he came by my house about it. From what you said, I had the impression maybe nobody else knew Heidi was seeing someone, and I thought he would be interested. He acted like he was, so I'm surprised he never followed up."

"Well, nobody has contacted me. And I haven't even had time to go by the houseboat since we were there. I feel kind of bad about it, since I said I'd watch the place."

Sunny considered that for a moment. "Can you think of anything else about this guy she was seeing? Anything she said about him that might be useful?"

"You trying to track him down?"

"I'd like to talk with him."

"What for?"

A few seconds went by while she tried to think of a good answer to that question, one that would encourage Joel to share whatever he knew about the topic without revealing what Kimberly had told her. She couldn't think of one. "This is going to sound strange, but I can't tell you. All I can say is that I recently came across a piece of information that might be related to Heidi's murder, and based on that information, I have a hunch meeting the man she was dating could lead somewhere."

"Let me guess, you can't tell the police about this either."

"Not yet."

Joel sighed loudly, finally catching his breath from the jog to the phone. "Well, hell, I guess I don't care one way or the other if you talk to the guy, assuming you can find him. I don't have much to go on. She said his name was Mark. I know he was gone a lot."

She took a pencil from the jar on her desk and grabbed a notepad. "What about his job? Did she ever say where he works or what he does for a living?"

"If she mentioned it, I don't remember. I do remember he took her with him to New York once. I think she said he was going out there for some kind of board meeting. He seemed to have money, at least enough for dinners out and a few trips. They went down to Hawaii for a few days, and up to Tahoe to ski a couple of times."

She wrote down NY, board meeting, Hawaii, Tahoe. "Anything else? Do you know where they met?"

"I think they met at Caffe Trieste."

"So he probably lives in Sausalito."

"Maybe. I couldn't say for sure. I just don't know much about him. We exchanged maybe ten sentences about the guy. We never talked much about the people we were dating. I didn't exactly want to hear about her love life in detail."

"Because you still loved her?"

"Something like that."

"Any idea what the guy looked like?"

"None."

"I guess that's that. Mind if I ask you one more question?"

Joel laughed coldly. "I'll answer one more, if you'll answer mine first."

"Fair enough." Sunny put the pencil in her mouth and allowed herself the pleasure of sinking her teeth into it, the wood giving way under her incisors. She examined the marks, moved the pencil over the width of a molar, and bit down again.

"You said you used to take yoga with Heidi in Mill Valley," said Joel, "and sometimes you'd have coffee afterward. I happen to know those two statements are outright lies. Who are you, really? And what were you really after that day out at the houseboat?"

Sunny took a moment to decide what to say.

"Hello?" said Joel.

"I'm here. That's a reasonable question. How did you know we were lying?"

"Because Heidi was a trained yoga instructor. She didn't like the style of yoga they teach at that place you're talking about, and she never would have practiced there. She also didn't drink coffee."

"So you knew we were lying even out at the beach."

"Yep."

"But you took us to the houseboat anyway."

"I wanted to know what you were up to. Keep your friends close, and your enemies closer, as they say. Then the cops came and I never got to find out what you were really up to."

"Hang on, back up. If Heidi didn't drink coffee, what was she doing in Caffe Trieste?"

"Who knows? They don't make you drink the stuff. Maybe she ordered tea. I've been in there with her for a glass of wine at happy hour. Don't change the subject. Why do you care what happened to Heidi?"

"Very simple," said Sunny. "I found her body. She was left near my house and I found her Wednesday night while I was out walking. I never knew her when she was alive."

Joel Hyder whistled. "That's too weird to be anything but the truth."

"It's the truth. It was a terrible thing to see. Afterward, I couldn't get the image of her out of my head. I thought maybe I could dilute it with impressions of who she was when she was alive. The only thing we had to go on was she lived in Sausalito and liked to surf. Rodeo Beach seemed like a good place to start."

"Makes sense, I guess."

"Now my turn. Why did you lie about having Heidi's family's permission to go out to her house? You're not supposed to be watching it. The police told me her father doesn't even know who you are."

"You mind hanging on a second while I get a cup of coffee?" She heard a cabinet door close and then the sound of a spoon against a ceramic cup. He took a loud sip. "Ah, that's better. Unlike Heidi, I don't function without the stuff. I was just brewing when you called." He took another audible sip. "Well, it sounds like we're going to air all the dirty laundry this morning, or try to." There was a pause. "Sunny, where are you right now?"

"Me? In St. Helena."

"You live up there?"

"Yes. Why?"

"I thought if you were nearby we could meet. This kind of conversation is better in person."

"I can't get away right now. Besides, I'm okay on the phone. I'm listening." Joel was in the mood to talk and she wasn't about to let him off the hook. If they arranged to meet later, he might not be so willing.

"You have to understand who Heidi was," he said. "She was beautiful and powerful and gentle all at once. There was nobody else like her."

Sunny waited, listening to the sound of him breathing. It was the controlled in- and-out breathing, slightly louder than normal, of someone trying to steady himself through a surge of emotion.

"The fact is, Heidi Romero never much liked me. I tried to date her plenty of times. I loved her. I was in love with her for a long time. Like I said before, that's why I took that job in Japan teaching English, to try to forget about her. But it didn't work. I came back a year later and it was just like before. I'd do anything to be near her." He stopped and she heard the controlled breathing. There was a soft thump and she knew he'd put the phone down. A moment later he cleared his throat and went on. "I'd see her now and then at the beach, and we would talk for a few minutes. Small talk, like acquaintances. It's true that I taught her to surf. We hung out a few times at her place, but she was just being nice to a lonely guy who couldn't get over her. Once, when she went traveling, I took care of her place for her. After she died, I just wanted to be near her for a little while longer. Sort of like you. When you and your friend came along, it gave me the perfect excuse. I figured nobody would pay attention if we were all there together."

Rivka didn't show up for work until almost ten o'clock. By then, Sunny had done all the prep work for the day, including butchering and preparing all the beef, pork, fish, and poultry. Luckily, through necessity and time, her squeamishness about meat was beginning to fade. She was blanching tomatoes when she heard the back door slam. Rivka appeared looking disheveled.

"What happened to you?"

"Sorry. Crazy night. I overslept."

Sunny observed the raspberry lips and rosy chin. Someone had been kissed thoroughly enough to sustain minor damage to the surface areas in direct contact. "Do I know him?"

Rivka perked up. "You know that guy who was selling wild greens and blackberries at the farmers' market in the park last summer?"

"The one with the hair like a cross between Don King and Buckwheat?"

"That's him. I ran into him last night at the D. Vine. One thing led to another and we ended up staying up all night talking. He's a genius."

"Talking-talking or talking-getting-it-on-like-two-wild things?"

"Little of both, but mostly talking-talking. You should see his body. Brown, silky muscle all over. He can toss me around like a rag doll."

"Is that desirable?"

"Not if it's too rough. But just rough enough is definitely desirable. You know, sometimes a girl likes to have her hair pulled."

"I knew I was missing something."

"I keep telling you, you should grow it out."

"Even if my hair was long, I don't think I'd like somebody pulling it. Are you seeing him again?"

"We have a date on Thursday night."

"Oh, good. I'll plan to be in early on Friday."

"You should be happy for me! I've been like a turtle in its lonely shell for the last four months. How much can a woman take?"

"Don't be a goose, of course I'm happy for you. No one deserves the company of a loving man with big hair more than you. Speaking as your boss, I prefer the lonely and well-rested Rivka who gets to work two hours before me and channels her sexual frustration into maniacal diligence. But as your friend, I'm delighted you stayed up all night snogging with the local weed and berry man."

"*Weed* is a subjective term. Plenty of people think watercress is a weed. One man's weed is another man's salad."

"Words to live by."

"Guess who called me again on Saturday," said Rivka, stirring the four-hour tomato gravy.

"Who?" said Sunny.

"Joel Hyder."

"Fascinating. What did he want?"

"Apparently just to hang out."

"How many times is that?"

"Four altogether."

"He's persistent."

"A little too."

"Did you ever get to talk?"

"No, all messages. I called him on Friday, but I got his machine."

"I'm not sure about him. All that stuff with Heidi freaked me out. He's obsessed. And a confirmed liar."

"We're liars too. One-sided crushes always seem creepy, but everyone has one eventually. We all get our turn to look like big, dopey losers. I think he's okay. I'm not sure I want to hang out, but I don't mind talking on the phone. I thought he seemed kind of interesting."

"I called him this morning," said Sunny.

"What? Why?"

"I decided to take the direct approach. I wanted to know why he said he knew Heidi's father when he didn't."

"And?"

"Like I said, he was obsessed with her."

"Obsessed or in love?"

"That's a judgment call."

No residence, no occupation, no last name, no physical description. Finding Heidi's boyfriend, if you could call him that, was not going to be easy. In fact, it was going to be impossible unless she found something more to go on. Sunny decided to focus on questions more likely to yield answers, such as whether or not the taillights on Dean Blodger's white pickup truck matched those she had seen the night Heidi Romero was killed. Rivka staggered through the day's work and went home with a feeble wave. Sunny finished up, got in the truck, and headed south. A few miles down the road, Andre Morales called the mobile to say he and the venture capitalist were getting dinner around seven.

"He's ready," said Andre. "We're talking about opening the new place in Sonoma. He also likes Scottsdale. He says it's booming out there. And New York. He says New York is still worth doing."

"That's huge."

"It's still just talk. You never know. If you start driving in, I can let you know where we'll be for dinner once you get here. We haven't picked a place yet. You should meet this guy. He's ready to get serious about opening a new place, maybe two. He has deep pockets and he's ready to move. He could be the ticket to expanding Wildside like we talked about."

"I don't think I could make it there in time. I have a couple of things to take care of in Marin, and I'd have to go back home and change, then drive all the way back down again."

"What's in Marin?"

Her mind went blank. "Green Gulch. I want to talk with them about growing some proprietary stuff for Wildside."

"Interesting. Listen, I'll give you a call when we know where we'll be. Maybe you can come in anyway. Whatever you're wearing is fine."

"I'll keep the phone on."

"Hey, I left you something at your house. That item you asked me to get."

"The knives?"

"I left those too, but I meant the other item."

"Great, thanks. Which other item?"

"The DVD. You said you wanted to see an example of anime, so I procured one, but then after I left it I sort of regretted it. I don't think you should watch it. It might upset you, just when you're starting to forget about that whole ordeal."

"I'm sure it will be fine. It's just a movie, and I'm curious."

"I don't see what good it can do. If I'd been thinking, I wouldn't have left it. You think you'll come tonight?"

"I'm not sure. Probably there won't be time."

"That's a no. What about tomorrow?"

"Definitely. I'll be home at the usual time."

"Good, because my week gets crazy after that. There are more reservations on the books this Thursday and Friday than we've ever had before."

"That's great! Vinifera is really taking off."

"Yeah, things are on fire. About tomorrow, I was thinking we could drive over the hill to that little French bistro off the square in Sonoma. The one that's even smaller than Wildside."

"La Poste?"

"That's it. La Postage Stamp."

"Sounds good to me. I like their deep-fried artichokes, and that weird artichoke and mâche salad they make with poached eggs and bacon."

"Then we shall eat artichokes. It's been a while since we were out, just the two of us."

"Weeks."

"I'm looking forward to it."

"Me too."

She put the phone away and turned her attention to the green hills and slow traffic. The drive gave her time to think. Lift up the film of tourism, and Sausalito was still a sleepy seaside town. The tourists tended to stay on the two or three blocks of the main drag. The locals kept to different schedules and mostly different venues, and they knew each other. Somebody among the employees and regulars at Caffe Trieste would know Heidi, and they might also remember who she liked to have a glass of wine with after work.

Joel said Heidi and Mark had been to New York, Hawaii, and on ski trips to Tahoe together. Even for the most ardent jetsetter, that implied at least two months of association, and probably more like three or four. She and Andre had been seeing each other for just over two months and they had photographs of each other, taken the day they went out to the lighthouse in Pt. Reyes. Anybody who took a romantic trip to New York would take pictures. There was the one in Central Park, the one on top of the Empire State Building, the one on Fifth Avenue. The setting was too cinematic to resist. In Tahoe, there would be the shot at the top of the summit, and the one sitting in the snow after a wipeout. Sunny tried to remember the pictures on Heidi Romero's refrigerator. Were any of them skiing or New York? There were several beach shots, but she couldn't remember if they looked like Hawaii or not, or if there was a man who could be Mark in any of them. Whether it was on the refrigerator or not, there was sure to be a picture of the man named Mark somewhere in Heidi's house, unless of course the police removed them. If only she had thought to look for one when she was there. Then she thought of the aloe vera plant on Heidi's front deck, and the key Joel Hyder had removed from underneath it.

23

Where there had been water, now there was mud. It had been high tide the first time she visited the houseboat, and pretty bluish-green water had washed up all the way to the parking lot. Now there was nothing but ugly greenish-brown slime between the pavement and the first house. Canoes and rowboats that had tugged at their lines jauntily last time now sat askew, grounded. Sunny started down the dock carrying a bouquet of stargazer lilies. If anyone asked her, she was here to leave them at Heidi's door as a memorial.

To reach the tugboat from the dock, it was necessary to descend a sloped gangway to the level of the boat's concrete mooring, then proceed along a plank walkway and finally up another sloped gangway to the level of the boat's main deck. On the lowest part of the walkway, near the water level, something shiny attracted her attention. She paused for a better look. It was a small, rectangular piece of metal about the size of a belt buckle. The ancient lust for buried treasure awakened. She set the flowers down and kneeled on the walkway, reaching out over the turbid water as far as she could. It was just out of reach. She could reach it easily if she put one foot in the water, but that would be one foot too many. To sink into that glutinous ooze up to the ankle only to grasp a bit of tinfoil, an old Zippo lighter, a bleached beer can sticking out of the filth was too much. It might be something that belonged to Heidi, but it was certain to be of little value. Even when the tide was in, the water was shallow. If she'd dropped something important, she would have retrieved it. Buried treasure was rarely that.

Sunny put the flowers she'd brought next to the door and looked around, pretending to take in the view. She pulled her sleeves down over her hands and lifted the aloe vera pot. The key was still there. The red door swung open silently and she slipped inside. Gold light hit the potted palms crammed into the corners and warmed the wood surfaces all around. A sublime, timeless silence filled the space. She had the urge to stretch out on the couch and study the view of Mount Tam through the French doors until she could see it with her eyes closed.

Instead, she studied the photographs taped to the refrigerator. There were no standouts in the boyfriend category. Of the males in the pictures, one was the clearly indigenous driver of the Southeast Asian moped and one looked good to be her father. One young, attractive guy appeared in several pictures. The family resemblance and total lack of chemistry suggested a brother. The only other shots that included men was a triptych showing her being hoisted onto the shoulders of two surfers who drop her in the third frame. Neither of them looked like the kind of guy who attends board meetings in New York. They looked more like the kind of guys who attend classes at the JC. That was it for the refrigerator, which was just the easiest place to look. She hadn't really expected to find what she was looking for there. If Joel was right and Heidi was keeping her romance under wraps, posting his picture on the refrigerator was the last thing she would do.

The dining room doubled as the study with a wall of shelves and a built-in desk. At one end of a full-size table, tucked under the stairs that led up to the loft, were a printer, a scanner, and a detritus of cables where her laptop had been. Probably the police had removed it, a comforting thought. Their first move would be to read her recent emails and check out the Web pages she'd visited. If she was chatting with anybody about meeting up for a bondage workout, they would find it. Extremely unlikely, based on what she knew of Heidi so far. She had seen nothing to suggest much of an edge, or even a hidden erotic aesthetic. The bad girls Sunny knew kept tokens of their romps around the house. There would be the tell-tale snapshot of the infamous Halloween costume if nothing else. They were the ones in the French maid costume, and there was always a picture. It wasn't Heidi's style.

A single shelf of well-worn books held novels by Paul Coelho, Jim Harrison, Milan Kundera, García Márquez, and Barbara Kingsolver, plus a book of poetry translations by Robert Bly, *Seven Years in Tibet,* and a six-pack of spirituality and self-help paperbacks of the Buddhist persuasion. The desk was piled with mail, drawings, and magazines. Sunny lifted a few of the stacks, checking them at intervals for interesting content. The sketches were mostly still lifes of flowers and plants, boats, her guitar, and her surfboard. She grabbed a kitchen towel and opened each of the drawers under the desk, finding nothing of particular interest. One contained the usual desk supplies and odds and ends, the next paints and brushes, another computer parts and cables. The bottom drawer was crammed with cards and letters she had received. Sunny hesitated, tempted to snoop. She closed the drawer. There was no need to invade Heidi's privacy any more than necessary, and while letters were bound to contain interesting personal information, would any of it be pertinent to her murder? Whoever killed Heidi would not have sent her a postcard beforehand announcing as much. However, the boyfriend who was away frequently might be a letter writer. He was more likely to be a text message and cell phone guy, but it was worth checking. She opened the drawer again and checked each of the envelopes and letters. Nothing from anyone named Mark.

Having found nothing downstairs, she climbed the ladder-steep stairs to the loft. Above Heidi's dresser was a mirror with several photographs tucked into the frame along the bottom edge. Two were the small school portraits relatives mailed out. Probably nieces. A third was a snapshot of a guy, probably in his mid-forties, standing on the deck of a sailboat. Sunny picked it up. A breeze blew back his sandy brown hair, and he was giving the camera a nice, relaxed smile full of white teeth. At first she thought it had to be Mark, except the man was wearing a wedding band. Sunny examined the photo more closely. There were no visible landmarks to indicate where the picture might have been taken, but the light was crisp and bright like a nice day in Marin. His eyes shielded behind sunglasses revealed nothing.

She looked around the rest of the room. The bed had not been made. It still wore the impressions of Heidi's last night's sleep. From her perch in the top of the tugboat, she could lie in bed and watch the light change on the mountain out the window. Sunny squatted down so the neighbors wouldn't see her if they happened to look in, and pulled the pillow off the bed. It smelled of sun and dust and only very faintly of sleep. She tossed it back in place.

Across from the bed was a closet. Sunny examined her desire to hunt through it. At what point did the quasi-legitimate search for hints about who Heidi was seeing give way to a morbid romp through a murder victim's effects? Rivka would certainly look.

Sunny opened the closet door. Jeans, tiny T-shirts, tank tops, shorts, fleece, Gore-Tex. She dressed cute, not sexy. The sexiest item was a denim miniskirt. As for shoes, there were slaps, running shoes, sneakers, clogs, and, still nestled in their box, a lone pair of black high heels with a peek-a-boo toe. These were of recent vintage and expensive. The matching black cocktail dress was not far away, hanging next to a black cashmere overcoat with a Barney's house label sewn into the collar. All three had no doubt been purchased in New York, either by the mysterious Mark or by Papa Romero's Platinum Amex. Other than those three items, there was nothing new. There was also nothing excessively short, nothing constructed of string and glitter, no fur, no feathers, no outrageous heels, and nothing transparent, tight, or shiny. It was, in other words, a naughty girl's nightmare wardrobe.

Sunny closed the closet door and checked the bathroom. Rivka was right, there was a horde of pricey hygiene products arrayed on the counter and in the cabinet. Sunny picked up a bottle of La Mer face lotion. If working in a sporting goods store still paid like the rest of mid-range retail, it would take about three days to net enough cash for a bottle of this stuff. Clearly supplementary funding was coming from somewhere.

Sunny looked at the picture of the guy on the boat again. It had to be Mark. He was good-looking, confident, older, and athletic. He fit the bill. This was the man who would like his new lover to wear the elegant black coat and black heels. This was the man who would appeal to a sophisticated young woman who chose to buy into the affluent lifestyle on a selective basis. He was also married. That would explain why Heidi didn't advertise her relationship with him, and why there were no pictures of them together. Married men did not document their affairs, or at least the smart ones didn't.

She put the photograph in her pocket and went back downstairs, using the kitchen towel to remove her footprints as she went. The kitchen towel posed a dilemma. Hang it back up? It was obvious it had been used to wipe up the floor. Take it with her? Too risky. She decided to rinse it out in the sink and hang it back up where she'd found it. When that was done, she put the key back under the planter and walked down the dock as casually as possible. There was no way to know if anyone had seen her or was watching from the windows, but she didn't run into anyone. In the parking lot, the door to Dean Blodger's hut was open and a plump woman in a billowy purple dress stood guard in front of it.

"Excuse me," said the woman. "Excuse me! Is that your car?"

Sunny looked around. "Which one?"

"That one." The woman indicated a silver Saturn blocking the gangway.

"Not guilty."

"You know whose it is?"

"No idea." The woman stood with her hands on her broad hips, staring at the Saturn with indignation. She had dark, glossy skin and a direct gaze like an accusation. Sunny walked over. "Is Dean Blodger around?"

"Dean went home. Be back tomorrow morning at six sharp. I'm going to tow that car if nobody moves it. That's a loading zone. You can't park there."

"Are you the harbormaster when he's out?" asked Sunny.

"I am the assistant harbormaster all the time. Vurleen Rose," said the woman. "And you are?"

Sunny introduced herself.

Vurleen narrowed her eyes and looked her up and down. "I see everyone who goes in and out here. I haven't seen you before. You visiting somebody?"

"I was just leaving some flowers at Heidi Romero's place."

Vurleen shook her head slowly. "I feel mighty sorry for that poor girl. She never did nothing to deserve to be killed. But I truly hope people aren't going to start leaving flowers at her house. All those flowers and cards pile up and wilt and blow around. It makes a terrible mess."

Sunny laughed. "I'll go back and get them if you like."

"Don't bother, darlin'. One bouquet of flowers won't make no difference. What'd you leave?"

"Stargazer lilies."

"Oh, that's nice. That's a nice flower. It's when they start to pile up that's a problem. I managed a building once where a man jumped out the window one day. Nice guy. Everybody liked him. We had people leaving jars of flowers from their gardens, candles, cards, fruit, you name it. I thought they would burn the place down with those candles." Vurleen pattered her fingers over the shiny walls of hair slicked down to either side of her head, savoring the memory. "Went on for weeks. Every morning, same thing. Flowers, candles, cards, little packages all piled up along the wall where he died."

"That's terrible."

"Well, turns out he'd been robbing the company blind for a decade. It was talk to the judge or talk to his maker, and he chose his maker. Heidi Romero was a different story."

Sunny was beginning to like Vurleen, who sees everyone who goes in and out of Liberty Dock. "What do you think happened to her?"

"Only the good lord knows. The dead tell no tales. If I had to guess, though, I'd say it was getting messed up with that man she was seeing. He come in here with that fancy car of his. He didn't even bother to take off his wedding band. I saw it with my own eyes. He was always trying to sweet-talk me, but I ain't gonna sweet-talk with any man stepping out on his woman. I do not approve of such activities, I don't care who the girl is. I told Heidi she was doing wrong, but she wouldn't listen to one word of it. That's the way, though. That's what money will do to you. Pretty soon you don't know who you are and you're stepping out on the woman you swore to love till death do you part."

Sunny nearly pulled the photograph out of her pocket in her excitement. She remembered just in time where it had come from. "You mean Mark? You think he killed her?"

Vurleen looked at her with the mixture of profound contempt and pity reserved for the irritatingly stupid. "Him? Why would he kill her? He was the happiest man alive. Pocket full of money, wife at home cooking dinner, and that pretty young thing on the side whenever he liked. He wouldn't kill nobody. I don't think he took an extra breath in case it might upset things. Now his wife, that's a different story though."

"You think his wife killed her?"

"Or made arrangements," said Vurleen with a sage look. "A man runs off with a pretty young thing like that, makes a woman mighty resentful. No jury I was part of would blame her for taking steps to resolve the situation."

"Was he the only guy Heidi was seeing?"

"The only one. That's what I could never understand. Why go with someone else's man when she could have had her pick? Pretty girl like that could have had anybody. Even that cold fish Dean Blodger was practically obsessed with her. He would never admit it, but I saw clear as day. He couldn't wait for ten o'clock every morning when that girl would sashay down the dock to her car. Dean Blodger would be glued to the window watching her while he pretended to listen to his phone messages. That poor little girl. But you can't say she didn't deserve it, messin' around with another woman's husband. None of my business, I got to tell it like it is, though."

"You think Dean had a crush on her?"

"Dean Blodger may be all tied up like a ball of dime store twine, but he's still a man. He was right there with the rest of them whenever she walked by. When she said jump, he said, 'Yes, ma'am.'" Something beyond Sunny attracted Vurleen's attention. "Good night, Ronald!" she called out sweetly, waving.

"Good night, Miss Rose," said the man across the parking lot with equal honey. It was the guy Sunny had seen on the dock last time, when she was with Joel Hyder talking to one of the neighbors. He was the one who liked to take out the trash. He picked a leaf off the windshield of an old beige sports car, got in, and fired up the throaty engine. A moment later it chugged out of the lot. Behind them, they heard it accelerate loudly toward the freeway.

"We're losing all the good ones," said Vurleen. "That Ronald Fetcher has been a rare pleasure to have at Liberty Dock. Clean, quiet, courteous, friendly. A real gentleman. If everyone was that helpful, my job would be easy."

"Is he moving?"

"Got to. The Mendels own the place he's been watching. They'll be back before the end of the week. What was your name again, darlin'?"

"Sunny. Sunny McCoskey. Good luck getting that Saturn to shove off."

"I don't need luck, missy. I've got the law on my side."

24

Caffe Trieste was in between crowds. A sprinkling of customers dotted the sidewalk tables, and a few others were hunkered down inside. Jason, Rivka's pupil in the school of fine espresso making, wasn't there. Instead, two men, one tall with gray hair, the other short with black hair, both stocky, stood behind the counter. Sunny showed them the photograph she'd taken from Heidi's bedroom.

The short man shook his head. "Never seen him."

The tall man gave him a disgusted look and made a gesture like he would knock him in the back of the head. "Idiot. This guy's been in here at least a hundred times. He keeps a boat down at the marina. Hey, Antonio! Tonio! What's that guy's name with the Baltic 37 with the black sails?"

"You mean the smartass with the turtleneck?" said Antonio, a rumpled oldster wearing a plaid trilby hat and loafers with white socks. A backgammon game was set up between him and an old man in a well-worn suit sitting across from him, who was busy plucking at his long strands of eyebrow as he considered his next move.

"Yeah, that's the one," said the tall man. "What's his name?"

"Weisass," Antonio called out. "I mean Weisman." His friend jiggled with laughter. "Mark Weisman."

"Mark Weisman," said Sunny. "He keeps his boat here at the marina?"

"That's right. He comes by for breakfast on his way down."

"Any idea how I could reach him or where I could find the boat?"

"You mean which slip? No idea. It's easy to spot with the sails up, since it's the only one out there with black sails. With them down, you'll just have to hunt around until you find a Baltic 37. You know what that looks like?"

"Not a clue."

"It'll be thirty-seven feet long, for one thing. And a sloop, so there's only one mast. And the Genny will be black. You'll only see it rolled up, but it will still be different from everybody else's. Why are you trying to find him?"

"I need his help. Did you ever see him with a girl named Heidi Romero?"

"The one who was just killed?" A look of profound skepticism came over his heavy face. "That I never saw. I read in the paper she lived down in one of the houseboats, but I didn't recognize her. I don't think she came around much." He raised his voice again. "Hey, Antonio, did this Weisman ever come in with a girl named Heidi? Young girl, long black hair."

"If he did, he kept it secret from the missus," said Antonio, triggering another round of chortles from his gaming partner.

Sunny thanked them and walked around the side of the café, down to the water. The gate to the marina was locked, so she waited. After a few minutes, a trim, friendly-looking man and his dog came along and opened it.

"Thanks," said Sunny. "You don't happen to know where I can find Mark Weisman's Baltic 37, do you? The one with the black sails?"

"It's down on C Dock. But he's not around. He's been away for weeks."

"Do you know where?"

"Yes," said the man, his eyes sparkling. "I do. Do you?"

Sunny laughed. "Am I being nosy?"

"Technically, this marina is private property. You need a pass to get in here, and you need to rent a slip to get a pass. How do you know Mark?"

"I don't," said Sunny. "He knows a friend of mine. Any idea when he's coming back?"

"I couldn't say. Last I heard he was in Europe. And you are?"

"Sonya McCoskey." She took a business card out of her purse. "I'm just trying to find a way to reach Mark. The sailboat is all I have to go on so far."

"You could try leaving a note. He'll come back here eventually." He called his dog and headed up the gangway.

Sunny walked up to C Dock. All the boats looked alike, and most of them seemed about thirty-seven feet long. They had names like *Bodacious* and *Vanity Fair* and *Seventh Heaven*. She might not have figured out which one belonged to Mark Weisman if she hadn't stopped to watch a seagull crack open a mussel, eat it, and discard the shell onto the dock. It dipped back into the water to forage for another, and Sunny walked over to see where it was getting them from. That was when she noticed the name. Painted in black, swooping script along the bow of one of the boats was the word *Vedana*.

The *Vedana* was sleek and well-maintained. The canvas covers on the mainsail, wenches, and tiller were all brand new, and the deck and hull were pristine gray teak. The ropes tying it to the dock were still white. Sunny climbed aboard and called out if anyone was below decks. All was quiet. Both of the hatches were locked. She peered in through the tinted glass at the kitchen and seating below. Everything seemed perfectly normal. There was no way to tell if Mark had been there lately, or if the boat had been neatly battened down for weeks. She took out the photograph and compared it to the boat. Everything in the picture matched perfectly.

The sun slipped behind Mount Tam and the air cooled off quickly while she waited by the gate for someone to let her out. A sailboat motored toward the dock and slid into its place. There was a flurry of activity, with crewmembers adjusting bumpers, shouting, and jumping off to tie off ropes. When they cut the motor, the evening quiet returned and she listened to the rigging of a hundred swaying boats chime gently against an equal number of aluminum masts. In the end she had to wait until the new arrivals had hosed off the deck and stowed all their gear to let her out. At the café, the tables were filling up with the young, well-heeled paycheck crowd, just off work and eager to unbutton over a noisy glass of wine.

She walked past and got in the truck. There was no hurry to do anything about Mark Weisman and the *Vedana*. She could sit right here as long as she wanted and sort out what it meant. A couple, laughing, their arms around each other, walked by on the sidewalk. She closed her eyes. The world was not all darkness. That night she'd found Heidi Romero's body had run like ink into every part of her life, coloring it with a muddy darkness. She had allowed it to permeate her thoughts and obscure every other concern. Had she given any real attention to Andre Morales lately? Or her restaurant? Or her family? Or anything that ought to matter? Had she thought of anything other than Heidi Romero? Heidi's death had pulled her life into its wake, dragging her along after it, an unrelated, superfluous, accidental hanger-on, trailing after the disaster that had struck her. Nobody planned for Sunny to leave a party in the middle of the night and walk out into the darkness. Her whim had caught fate by surprise. She was never supposed to be part of what happened to Heidi Romero, but she had walked out of her place in the warmth of Andre's home into the cold night, where she had crossed into a world of darkness and been caught up in it, snared by an ankle and dragged.

She stared at the photograph of Mark Weisman and wished he wasn't wearing sunglasses. The smile looked authentic enough. The hand that gripped the sailboat's cable was held neither too firmly nor too loosely nor at an awkward angle. Still, without the eyes, his character remained opaque.

Try to keep it simple, she told herself. Sort through the facts. Mark Weisman owned a boat named *Vedana* and dated a girl named Heidi, who turned up dead at a distant winery named Vedana, possibly while he was out of town. Other than that connection—boat to Mark to Heidi to winery—no other connection between boat and winery had turned up. Could the two names overlap coincidentally? Not plausible. *Vedana* was too unusual a word. Or was it? After she named her restaurant Wildside, she'd been surprised to discover all the other businesses of the same name. Maybe the world was peppered with enterprises and vessels named Vedana. More facts. Kimberly Knolls met and had sex with an anonymous man. No name, no description. This man is connected to Heidi's body both by his sexual proclivities and by his association with Vedana Vineyards, e.g., Kimberly. What if Mark Weisman was the man Kimberly met at the hotel in Sonoma? If that were true, it would make the connection between the name of his boat and the name of the winery coincidental, since, presumably, he already owned a boat named *Vedana* when he met Kimberly without knowing the name of the winery she owned. Not plausible. To arrange to meet an anonymous lover and find that she owned a winery of the same unusual name as your boat would be a very strange coincidence. What if Kimberly's adventure had nothing to do with Mark Weisman? That would make the shibari connection between her adventure and Heidi's body coincidental. Possible. Bondage was certainly not an unusual fetish, and, even if she lived in the bush and spent all day in a kitchen, Sunny knew enough about sex to know that there were trends in erotic activities as much as in bathroom towels, breeds of dogs, cocktails, and any other aspect of human activity. Shibari might simply be the latest acquired taste from the scandal crowd to go mainstream. In that case, nothing made any sense at all, at least as far as Mark Weisman was concerned. If there was no other connection to the winery than the name, and if he did kill Heidi, he would not have left her there. It exposed him to suspicion without being direct enough to be a good taunt to the police.

Which left her back where she started, clueless about the events that led to Heidi's death, and in lawless possession of a souvenir from her house.

A white plastic chair stuck out of the glossy mud next to the dock, along with the domed top of a barbecue, an evening slipper, assorted cans and bottles, and a two-by-four painted yellow and bristling with rusty nails. The tide had gone out still farther in the last hour, stranding the houseboat community in a quagmire of debris. Sunny made her way as quickly and quietly as possible down the dock. A woman was watering her plants in the twilight. Otherwise, she saw no one.

She entered Heidi's place the same way as before and stood in the kitchen letting her eyes adjust to the gloom inside. She considered the light switch. Was it more suspicious to turn on a light in a dead girl's house, or to be seen going into a dead girl's house but not turning on the light? She imagined the sight of a yellow glow, visible up and down the dock, coming from a house known to be deserted. It would attract attention like a beacon. She waited until she could make out the heavy wooden table, the desk with its stacks of papers, the two stairs up to the living room. Out the French doors, the mountain stood in silhouette against a Moroccan blue sky.

She climbed up to the loft and froze, listening. The creak of wood settling its weight against its mooring sounded remarkably like careful footsteps on a wooden floor. She was seized by the temptation to go downstairs and be sure no one had come in behind her. She listened again. Now there were definitely footsteps. They sounded close enough to be on the boat. She thought of the sound of the shopping carts people used to ferry heavy loads up and down the dock. Whoever was walking was on the dock, not in the house. It was a trick of acoustics. She stepped forward and returned the photograph to its place on the mirror, her heart thumping, then slipped into the bathroom to peer out the window. A silhouette was walking away down the dock. She turned to go back downstairs and realized she had forgotten the kitchen towel. She went down to the kitchen, grabbed it, climbed back up, then backed her way down, removing her footsteps as she went.

In the kitchen, she rinsed the towel out as she had done before and hung it back up to dry. Someone, Vurleen or a neighbor, had put the stargazer lilies she'd left outside in an old mayonnaise jar filled with water. Sunny stashed the key back under the aloe vera and stepped lightly down the gangway. Since she'd arrived at the houseboat, the lights along the dock had come on. One of them, positioned on the dock directly above, flooded the catwalk with a soft yellow light and reflected off something shiny in the mud. It was the same piece of metal she'd seen earlier in the day, lying just out of reach. She could see now it wasn't a can. It was rectangular and made of brushed aluminum. A credit card case, or a folding makeup mirror for your purse. She kneeled on the catwalk and reached, stretching her hand out as far as she could. The silver rectangle sat several inches beyond her fingertips.

Under the dock, an old newspaper lay moldering in its plastic bag. She pried it from its resting place and laid it in the mud between the catwalk and the shiny square of metal, resting her weight on it with one hand and stretching out with the other. Her fingers came together around the piece of metal and she shoved her weight back to the catwalk. She considered the newspaper. Throw it away or put it back where she found it? Safer to put it back where she found it. She tossed the newspaper back into its place under the dock and was sitting on the catwalk examining her treasure when a voice called down from the dock.

"The tide reveals all kinds of interesting things. What did you find down there?"

She looked up slowly into the face of Vurleen's friend, the guy taking care of one of the houseboats while the owners were away. "Looks like an iPod," she said, trying to come up with a reason to be sitting where she was sitting, just in case. "Know anybody who's lost one?"

He pulled the corner of an iPod out of the side pocket of his khakis. "I've got mine. Haven't heard of anybody else losing one. I wouldn't imagine it matters much either way. I'd say that one is gone for good. Might make a nice paperweight." He lingered, looking down at her. "Are you the one who left the flowers?"

She nodded. "I came by to see if they were still here. Somebody put them in water."

"Probably Vurleen. That woman thinks of everything. She takes very good care of us."

Sunny stood up and climbed the ramp up to the dock. "We've met once before, sort of, when I visited last time with some friends. I'm Sunny McCoskey." She wiped her hand on her pants and held it out.

"Ronald Fetcher," said the man, with a warm, natural smile. "Pleasure meeting you." He was dressed Ralph Lauren preppy as before, with a cable sweater around his neck and a polo shirt underneath. "You must have been close with her," he said, indicating Heidi's house.

"We were friends."

"Since we're here, do you mind if I ask you a rather forward question?"

"You mean about Heidi?"

"Yes. As a friend and a peer of hers, you might have some insight on a topic that's been tickling my curiosity."

"Now I'm curious." If Ronald Fetcher wanted to exchange gossip about Heidi Romero, she wasn't going to do anything to discourage him.

"Not that it's any of my business, mind you. Just something nagging at me."

"Fire away." She gave him a smile of encouragement.

Ronald glanced up and down the dock, as though expecting someone to be eavesdropping on them. "It's just this. Frankly, I couldn't understand it. Why would a girl like that, a young woman with everything going for her, why would she waste her time with a married man? What was it about that guy that was so special?"

Sunny watched his face. Did Ronald Fetcher have a thing for Heidi too? Or did his concern find its roots in the protective paternal impulse? Or was he simply a voyeur and a scandal-monger, mining for details of her personal life? "The usual reason?" said Sunny. "I don't think most people have affairs on purpose, do they? It's too messy. They fall into it by accident. The attraction overwhelms them and they can't help themselves. Before they know it, it's too late."

"You're being generous. If you ask me, it was the money. Or a daddy complex. He was twice her age."

"Was he rich?"

"He wasn't poor. You never know how much a guy like that is really worth, but it was more than nothing." He inched closer to her and put his hand on her sleeve, speaking with an air of intimacy that made her want to pull away from him. "I'll tell you something else. Those two had a knock-down, drag-out catfight a few days before she disappeared. Everybody heard it. He was furious because she'd called him at work and his PA told his wife. He said she did it on purpose to drive a rift between him and his wife. She was livid. She said that that was the final straw, she was tired of sneaking around and didn't want to see him anymore. Then he really came unglued and accused her of using him for sex." He gave her an awed look and waited for her to react.

"Interesting," said Sunny.

He seemed disappointed at this response but soldiered on. "Is this the twenty-first century or what? The older man accusing the mistress of using him for sex. That was the last we saw of him."

Sunny manufactured an appreciative smile while she studied his face. He obviously enjoyed other people's lives. He gave the impression of being idle. Did he work? Or just hang around other people's houses? "Vurleen said you're moving."

"That's right. I found a place up in Guerneville for the summer. On the river."

"Nice spot to be in for the summer," said Sunny. "Very relaxed. Especially if you don't have to commute to work."

"Not as nice as this spot," said Ronald, gesturing to the surroundings. "Still, nothing lasts forever."

A seagull squawked overhead. Sunny looked out toward the water and the distant high-rises of San Francisco, stone gray in the dusk. She turned back to Ronald. "I should hit the road. It was good to meet you, again."

"Likewise." He shook her hand for the second time. "Take care of yourself."

Sunny walked out to the parking lot clutching the iPod in one hand. The harbormaster's office was dark, the door closed and locked. She felt an illogical pang of guilt. Illogical because even if Vurleen had still been there, she would not have left the iPod with her or even mentioned it. It belonged with Sergeant Harvey if it belonged anywhere. She had already decided she would try to discover what was on it herself before she turned it over to him. The risk of its being ignored in a storage box somewhere at the police station was too much. She would try everything she could think of to extract whatever information it held before she handed it over. There would be music, certainly, but people kept plenty of other things on iPods. There could be photographs, contacts, to do lists, documents. Anything that could be on a computer could be on there. When her curiosity was satisfied, or if the device refused to come back to life, she would turn it over to Steve and hope he had technical contacts who could work their magic and extract the data from its memory.

Past the harbormaster's hut and the acacia tree standing guard over it, a wider outer parking lot led to the street. At the entrance, Sunny glanced automatically both ways before crossing to the truck, then stopped and looked right again. There it was. Waiting at the stoplight was a white pickup truck with mismatched taillights. All she could see of the driver was an outline. The light turned green, and the truck pulled up and made a right. On the door was the Pelican Point Harbor logo.

25

By the time she started the old Ford, turned it around, and drove up to the stoplight, the white truck was long gone. It didn't matter. Dean Blodger's truck was the truck, that was all she needed to know.

Her heart pounded. She dug in her purse for her cell phone. She needed to talk to Sergeant Harvey. Make that Officer Jute. She put the phone down. Before she talked to anybody, she needed to organize her thoughts. In fact, was it really so urgent that she report what she'd discovered? Couldn't it wait until she'd had a chance to unwind a little? She wanted to sound calm and together when she talked to the police. Dean Blodger wasn't going anywhere, and Mark Weisman was already out of reach. It had been a tiring day.

She foraged in the glove compartment for music and found a Beach Boys CD. She rolled down the window to the cold air and turned up the volume. *Wouldn't it be nice . . .*

It took the entire greatest hits to get home. She was back at the beginning, replaying her favorites, when she turned onto Adams. *Round round get around, I get around . . .* The cottage on Adelaide was dark when she pulled up, as of course it would be, since she lived alone. She never got entirely used to that. How long until the day she would come home to a light on, somebody else home, somebody expecting her? Too long. Forever, she thought gloomily, if past experience was any indicator of the future. She picked up the mail on the way in. Andre had left her knife kit and the movie he'd mentioned on the dining room table. She headed straight for the refrigerator, grabbing the phone on the way. She dialed Wade Skord's number. This was no time to be alone. "Have you had dinner?"

"Nothing I couldn't forget about. You cooking?"

"If you're eating, I'm cooking. Nothing fancy. Looks like I can scrape together a refrigerator clean-out pasta. I've got, let's see, two Meyer lemons, a red bell pepper, a red onion, some of those big capers we love, a little leftover salmon, and, in the herb department, a bunch of fresh parsley. Wish it was dill. Anyway, we're good for a carbfest, and soon. I'm starved."

"I'll be there in half an hour."

Monty Lenstrom had eaten already. "But I could use a glass of the soft stuff," he said. "Work kicked my ass all day long. I need to sit on the couch and stare at a blank wall for about twenty minutes, then I'll head over."

Rivka picked up her mobile. "I'm at the market. You want anything?"

"A baguette, if they're worth having. And a pineapple. I have a strange craving for pineapple. Unless there are apricots or cherries. The first cherries should arrive any day."

"One baguette, one pineapple, early seasonal dream fruit optional. You sure you don't want some chocolate sauce with that? Maybe a side of mac and cheese?"

"Tonight I'll eat anything."

She put the phone down and turned her attention to the tiny, mud-caked device she'd left on the counter on her way in.

This one had an extra nugget, a white rectangle of plastic, plugged into the top of it with a perforated metal area, probably a microphone. Ronald Fetcher was probably right, it was sure to be ruined for good. Still, it was worth a try. Rivka once dropped her cell phone into a tub of lime vinaigrette. The tech gurus in customer service in Bombay suggested she rinse it in warm water and leave it somewhere warm to dry out. Sometimes all the water evaporated from the inner mess after a few days and whatever it was worked fine again. Sometimes, they regretted to inform her, one had no choice but to go back to the store and select a replacement model. This was the way with cell phones dropped into tubs of lime vinaigrette. Sunny rinsed the player under the tap, wondering if this was also the way with iPods found at low tide in local harbors. The stream of water ran over the casing and into the tiny holes with disastrous efficiency. Certainly there was little hope it would ever sing again. She patted it dry and left it on the windowsill, then went to find a pair of headphones. She found one plugged into the portable CD player she never used and brought them back. They fit into the port and she put them on, to no point since the device was dead as a stone. She hit all the buttons. Still nothing. No life on the screen, not even a crackle over the headphones. She put it back on the windowsill and turned to the refrigerator.

An hour later, the three of them—Rivka, Wade, and Sunny—sat down to pasta, mixed greens, and bread and butter. Sunny passed a bottle of chilled pink wine. Rivka rhapsodized about her recent telephone conversations with her new crush while they loaded their plates.

"Who are we talking about?" asked Wade skeptically.

"Remember the sexy guy selling those incredible blackberries at the farmers' market last summer? Super puffy hair, great lips."

"I remember the crazy hair and the blackberries. The sexy lips part may have escaped me. He had some kind of an accent. What is he, Caribbean?"

"Jamaican. Love the accent." She stuffed a heap of mixed baby greens in her mouth. "Totally irresistible," she said with her mouth full.

"Irresistible." Wade assumed a worldly expression. "Sounds like you're telling me this guy puts the afro in aphrodisiac."

"Very funny," said Rivka.

"I can't believe you used that before Monty got here," said Sunny.

"I tried to hold off, but I couldn't contain myself."

Monty Lenstrom turned up near the end of dinner bearing a bottle of Schramsberg. He went into the kitchen and came back with four champagne flutes, which he filled and passed to each of them. Sunny turned the bottle. "Brown label. The good stuff. And of a certain age. This must be important."

"Only the best for my dearest friends." Monty stood and raised his glass, his eyes moist behind wire-rim glasses. For a moment no one spoke. Their glasses frosted over and bubbles rose in steady, luminous streams. "My people, I have news."

"Oh my god," said Rivka. "You did it."

"That's right. Friends, it is my great pleasure to announce that you are looking at the future Mr. Annabelle Reins."

Sunny gasped. "I don't believe it!"

"Believe it," said Monty. "I've always known she was the one. I knew the moment I laid eyes on her."

"That would have been, let me see, about seven years ago," said Sunny.

"I've been busy. What's your point?"

"No point at all. I salute your conviction, and caution, and Annabelle's patience. You make a lovely couple. To Monty and Annabelle."

They chimed and sipped. Wade stood up. "As the senior male of the tribe, allow me to propose a toast to the end of a record-breaking run of bachelorhood, if you can call it bachelorhood when you've been living with a woman since the week after you met her. To Monty and Annabelle, may she one day grace us with her presence."

They drank to the happy couple and hashed through the usual congratulations and inquiries. Would they do it this summer? Not likely. Too soon. Probably not until the fall. This wasn't a shotgun wedding, was it? Was Annabelle expecting? Certainly not. As far as he could tell, all she was expecting was a solid carat of bling, maybe more, since, considering they already owned a house, lived in it together, and didn't need a new toaster or bath towels, not much else would change after the big party. Any venue selected? Hardly. He just sprang it on her over the weekend. When this flurry of talk had run its course, a satisfied pause came over the table. Good food, good news, glass of bubbly in hand, the end of another solid Monday, and still plenty of time to brush, floss, and knock off eight hours before the whole business started again tomorrow. Sunny pounced on the moment of tranquility. "I went down to Sausalito this afternoon," she said. "I found out some interesting stuff."

She described how she'd discovered that the mysterious man Heidi had been seeing was named Mark Weisman, and that he also owned a sailboat named *Vedana*. She repeated her conversation with Vurleen, the harbormaster's assistant, and how she'd corroborated that Mark was married and suggested his wife would go homicidal if she discovered his betrayal, and that she'd thrown in the comment that Dean Blodger, the harbormaster, was smitten, or possibly even obsessed, with Heidi. Then she told them about seeing the mismatched taillights on Dean Blodger's white truck.

"There's plenty to go on, but where it goes is still beyond me. You tell me how it all fits together. I can't figure it out."

Wade frowned. "I don't like this, Sun. It seems obvious enough to me who killed Heidi, and equally obvious that you're playing with fire by hanging around down there. This Dean Blodger character is your man. You saw his truck at Vedana Vineyards. You saw the same truck at the place the girl lived. His assistant says he was glued to the window whenever she went by. Then he turns up here in town, not to mention at the racetrack. We don't know if he followed you there or if he went to check them out like we did, but either way, he's showing way too much interest in topics related to you and that girl. I don't need anything more to convince me. I think it's high time you got the police in on this, like tonight, like right now, and ask them to loan you a bodyguard while you're at it."

"I agree," said Monty. "It's not safe to be here alone."

"Dean Blodger worries me too," said Sunny. "The trouble is, the Dean theory leaves two big holes and no good way to explain them. Why would he transport the body an hour away and leave it tied up in a tree? It makes no sense to risk being seen like that. And what about the boat?"

"Maybe he was trying to throw suspicion on the boyfriend," said Monty. "Or maybe there's a piece missing. Just because we don't know why he did it doesn't mean he didn't do it."

"Hang on a second," said Rivka. "Back up. I still don't see how Dean Blodger could have done it. First of all, everybody up and down that dock knows him. They're going to notice if they see him carry off Heidi Romero. And there's no way he could have done it silently. Sun, you remember how sound carried in that place. If she so much as squealed, everyone for half a mile would hear it."

"That's simple enough to explain," said Monty. "All your well-informed date rapists know you can buy chloroform off the Internet for less than it costs to take a girl to a movie. Or you can make your own with nail polish and pool chlorine. It's just like on TV. You sneak up behind her, hit her with a rag full of chloroform, and she's yours. This guy is stationed right there in the parking lot. All he has to do is watch for her, call her over, dose her, and let the creepy fun begin."

"I don't want to know how you know that stuff," said Rivka.

"College," said Monty.

"Exactly how they did it isn't all that important," said Sunny. "It matters ultimately, but not in relation to who did it. The fact is, anybody who wanted to abduct her could have. I can think of a dozen different ways. You could break into her house with a credit card. The front door had no deadbolt and a nice, wide gap between the door and the door frame. Or you could make a copy of the key while she was out. You could grab her off the back deck while she was sunbathing, or in the parking lot. Or in the parking lot at work, or better yet while she's out on some trail riding her bike. She could have been lured somewhere where she was vulnerable. These things aren't difficult. She might even have been seduced. Killers have been known to be charming."

"Not by Dean Blodger," said Rivka. "That guy couldn't seduce the last woman on earth if she'd been living alone in a cave for six months."

"My money is on the winker," said Monty. "I would have made a citizen's arrest on that guy right there at the table."

"You mean Ové? Innocent," said Wade. "If anyone at Vedana is guilty it's Kimberly Knolls, or possibly Bruce Knolls. She's way too slick and he's too quiet for my taste. Never trust a guy who doesn't drink too much and make an ass of himself at a formal dinner party among strangers."

"I still say how they did it is not as important as why they did it," said Sunny. "When we know why, we'll know who. Leaving all the inexplicable pieces out of it for the moment, I'm with Wade. All Vedanas aside, Dean Blodger scares me most because he has a motive, and he is directly connected to the murder."

"What's his motive?" asked Rivka.

"If he was in love with Heidi, he might have done anything to get his hands on her. Once he'd forced himself on her, he would have to kill her to keep her quiet."

"That sounds sort of thin to me," said Rivka. "Joel Hyder was obsessed with her too, but I don't think he did it. What's Dean's direct connection?"

"The truck."

"Also sort of thin. You saw his truck, not him. Somebody else could have taken it. He left the keys hanging right there on the wall in his office."

"You're right," said Sunny. "I forgot about that. He put them on the hook by the door. And somebody broke into his office right around the time Heidi disappeared." She thought a moment. "Except the office is open in the daytime, so there's no need to break in, and at night he'd have the keys with him, since he would need them to drive home."

"Not necessarily," said Rivka. "Remember he said he lived nearby? Maybe sometimes he walks home."

"So, assuming for a moment that he walks home with some regularity," said Sunny, "and assuming he has a pattern the killer can rely on, which is fairly safe to assume since Dean Blodger is a creature of habit if he is nothing else, someone could have broken in and taken the keys to the truck, used it to deposit Heidi at Vedana, and returned them. Why?" She thought again. "To make it look like Dean did it. Or, if it was Dean, to give himself an out."

"I think you guys are barking up the wrong suspect," said Monty. "Sun, you need to follow your own advice. Look at why, not how. Sure, any passing sociopath could have nabbed her. That's true of all of us, all the time. All you really have to go on is where and how she was left. Find somebody connected to the winery or the rope business, and you've got your man. For now, that suggests Mark Weisman, even if we can't think of a reason for him to have done it. He's the only one connected to both the girl and the winery."

For now, that suggests Mark Weisman and the man Kimberly Knolls met in a hotel in Sonoma, thought Sunny. If they were one and the same, or if Kimberly's Internet hookup was Dean Blodger, she was getting close. Wade was right, it was time to alert Sergeant Harvey, even if it meant admitting she'd been back to the houseboat at Liberty Dock.

"There's more," said Sunny, thinking what an understatement that was. The faces around the table waited eagerly. She couldn't disclose what Kimberly had told her, and she would resist the urge to share her find in the mud. If she was going to withhold evidence from a murder investigation, it only seemed prudent to do so with discretion. "I was talking with one of Heidi's neighbors tonight, and he said Heidi and her boyfriend had a loud fight a couple of days before she disappeared." She related the argument as Ronald Fetcher had given it to her.

"There," said Monty, looking over the top of his glasses meaningfully. "I rest my case."

26

Wade searched Sunny's cottage, including the closets, the pantry, and under the bed, then went outside and toured the perimeter. He even walked up and down the block checking for suspicious cars. When he came back, he extracted a solemn promise from Sunny that she would telephone Sergeant Harvey within the hour. Only then would he agree to leave her alone in the house for the night.

"Don't you think the harbormaster or Mark Weisman or whoever the bogeyman du jour is would have come to get me by now if he was going to come at all?" said Sunny, watching Wade check behind the shower curtain. "You're making me paranoid."

"Since you mention it, that is exactly what I think," said Wade, satisfied there were no murderers hiding in the bathtub. "Otherwise I would never leave you here alone. But I still want you to call Steve tonight."

"I will."

"You promised me."

"And I will do it."

Everyone cleared out by eleven. When they'd left, Sunny locked all the doors and windows, checked the whole house one more time herself, and went for the phone. Steve Harvey was in the middle of watching a movie with Sarah Winfield, resident yogini.

"Sorry to interrupt."

"It's okay, it's a rental," he said. "We can pause it."

"Anything I've seen?" said Sunny.

"*Dirty Harry.*"

"A classic."

"Sarah says it glorifies violence and revenge."

"Indeed. That's the whole point. What's Clint supposed to do, suggest the bad guys try some breathing exercises and a few downward dogs to relax those destructive impulses?"

"I don't think that will help."

"Tell her it's about mindfulness. That scene at the beginning with the bank robbery is a celebration of his superior powers of awareness. He's a crime-fighting Zen master."

"Who packs a .44 Magnum."

"Let me guess, you picked the movie. Word of advice. Next time, let her pick."

Steve sighed. "To what do I owe the honor?"

"You're not going to like this."

"I never do. People don't call my mobile at eleven o'clock on a Monday night to invite me out to pizza. I'm listening."

"First of all, does the name Mark Weisman mean anything to you?"

"What does it mean to you?"

"I asked first."

"I'm wearing a badge."

"Fine. Mark Weisman, owner of the *Vedana*, a sailboat docked in the Sausalito marina, as well as lover of Heidi Romero, recent victim of apparent homicide. Alleged to have had a loud argument with the deceased shortly before her disappearance."

"Very good. A little too good, as a matter of fact. I guess you didn't take my advice from last time to heart."

"I did, but then circumstances intervened."

"What circumstances?"

"That's not the important part. The important part is Mark Weisman."

"Weisman was in Germany starting four days before Heidi went missing," said Steve. "Verified by his office in Frankfurt. Verified by his office in San Rafael. Verified by the very helpful and courteous staff at Lufthansa Airlines. Verified by his wife. Verified by phone by Mr. Weisman himself. I'm sold on the story. Next topic."

"So you don't make anything of the connection between the two Vedanas?"

"I didn't say that. But I believe Mark Weisman was out of the country during his girlfriend's murder, and I believe he is still there. If he comes back, we'll want to have a talk with him."

"What do you mean, *if* he comes back?"

"Well, if he is involved in Heidi's death, Germany is a great place for him to be, and I'm sure he knows that. We have a hell of a time extraditing suspects from abroad. There's no budget for sending somebody over there to track him down, for one thing. The paperwork's a nightmare. I gotta get somebody who speaks German. Even with way more to go on than I've got, I'd be spinning my wheels. The best evidence against him is if he doesn't come back. That tells us something. In that event, we keep gathering evidence, we watch, we wait for a chance to nail him."

"What about Dean Blodger?"

"Why don't you tell me about him."

Sunny sighed. "Harbormaster at Liberty Dock. Said to have had a crush on Heidi. Drives the white truck with mismatched taillights I saw leaving Vedana Vineyards the night of the murder. Leaves his keys clearly visible in his office, which is often left open. Is that enough, or shall I go on?"

"If you've got more, be my guest."

"Spotted recently by me around St. Helena, twice. Turned up at the Ferrari event where Vedana Vineyards was a sponsor. He was tailing somebody, whether it was me, the Knolls, or the Obermeiers, I don't know which. And speaking of the Obermeiers, what do you make of Ové?"

"The winemaker? Once again, I'd like to hear your thoughts first."

"He's lecherous enough to be overtly inappropriate in a formal social setting. He spent an entire dinner winking at me across the table. He may not be dangerous, but he is certainly motivated and daring when it comes to women. He's a pathological winker. How deep his impulses run is another question. There, I've spilled my guts. Please tell me you're looking into the white truck at least."

"*At least*. Have a little faith, McCoskey. I don't make it my top priority to keep you informed on my investigations. But since you ask, yes, we're working on linking up the white truck. Yes, we've talked with Dean Blodger, several times. Yes, I am aware that Mark Weisman owns a boat named *Vedana* and was in a pickle with his wife and his mistress, with whom he had recently had a nasty quarrel overheard by at least three people. And yes, I picked up on the concept that Ové appreciates the company of the ladies, maybe even a little more than is healthy. What else have you got?"

"Isn't that enough?"

"Can you tell me who I should arrest and why?"

"No, I can't. But I do have something else."

"Spill it."

"Has Kimberly Knolls contacted you recently?"

"Ms. Knolls? No, she hasn't contacted me. We interviewed her a couple of times after the body was discovered, but that was over a week ago."

"If she talked with someone else, another police officer, would you hear about it?"

"You mean about this case?"

"Yeah."

"Then I'd hear about it. I get cc'd on anything related or potentially related to my cases, especially Heidi Romero. Why would Kimberly Knolls need to contact me?"

"I was just curious."

"Do you have any other curiosities you would like to float, or can I go back to Mr. Callahan and his Zen handgun of justice?"

"Just one more. You never talked to Joel Hyder."

"True, we have not spoken as yet."

"Why not?"

"I'm keeping an eye on him, don't you worry. Sometimes you don't gain anything by talking. Sometimes it's better to wait and watch, see if somebody will make a move on his own. Believe me, Joel Hyder isn't going anywhere that I won't know about."

"How is that?"

"Little run-in he had outside a bar in Oakland last year. He's still on probation." Steve paused. Sunny waited. She had the impression the TV she could hear in the background had caught his attention. After a moment, he went on. "I'll tell you what, Sunny. You're worrying too much about all this. We've got it under control. Not that I don't appreciate your insights and contributions, but it sounds like you're letting this thing get under your skin. I can understand that, and I'm sympathetic.

But you've gotta understand that murder investigations can go on for a very long time. You'll wear yourself out thinking about it, and if you get yourself involved you could easily mess up the investigation. Unless you join the police force or remember something you forgot to tell me about that night, it's better to just forget about Heidi Romero and get on with your life. We'll handle it. When I've found the responsible party and the evidence I need to prove it, you'll read about it on the front page of the *Napa Register*. Okay?"

"Okay."

"Get some rest. You sound tired."

"Right. Will do."

She hung up the phone and sat staring at the empty fireplace. Steve was right, she should go to bed. There was nothing she could do. He already knew everything she'd discovered, except for what Kimberly had told her. She would wait one more day. If Kimberly hadn't talked to the police by then, she would call Steve, make her very last disclosure, and be done with it. She stretched out on the couch and put her feet up. Everything had its price. The price of a day of anonymous sex was about to come due for Kimberly Knolls. That was the last thought she remembered before the sun shining in the living room window woke her six hours later.

"Jason, you know, the blackberry dude, called me last night, late. We had this amazing conversation about how when you have sex with someone, it's not two people in bed together, it's really four," said Rivka, right before she shoved a bowl of crepe batter under the mixer and hit the switch.

Sunny waited until the machine stopped and she could hear again. "Explain."

"He was saying how our brains are made up of different sections that handle different tasks. You've got the base brain that all animals have. The brain stem. They call it the lizard brain because it goes back to the reptilian age, when we were all lizards and there weren't any big thinkers around. The lizard brain is the part that handles subconscious impulses, like breathing, eating, and procreating. The basics. Then you have the higher brain where conscious thought happens. That's the lumpy gray part. What he was saying is, when you're in bed together, there are really four minds jockeying for position. Two lizard brains trying to get their freak on and make a new generation of lizards, and two higher minds trying to form a deep and lasting spiritual bond, move in together, maybe buy a house. The lizard brain and the cerebral cortex are essentially in conflict. They have conflicting objectives. Lizard is single-minded, knockdown kink. Lumpy gray is all love and harpsichords. That's why sex is so confusing and full of contradictions."

"Is it full of contradictions?" said Sunny, wishing they could wrap up the subject swiftly and move on. These conversations with Rivka inevitably made her feel like she'd been doing it wrong all these years, or possibly had missed the point entirely and never really done it at all.

"It is in my experience. Part of me wants the guy to bring flowers and kiss my hand and read me Pablo Neruda. The other part wants him to throw me on the bed and get busy. I always wondered what was up with that. Now it turns out the reason it feels like there are two people in my head who want two different things is that there really are two minds in there with two different sets of goals. Three actually, since there's also the middle brain controlling emotions. That's the part that really messes things up."

Rivka disappeared into the walk-in and came back with an armful of stainless-steel bins covered in plastic wrap. She left again and returned with a bag of onions and a bottle of red wine vinaigrette. "I mean, I always wondered about that stuff, but I never really thought about it. Then last night when we were on the phone he started talking about how the rift between our sexual minds and our conscious minds gets bigger and more confusing and full of contradictions all the time. Because our conscious minds are getting more and more refined and sophisticated, but our lizard brains are still as primitive, carnal, and violent as ever. Our basic nature is fight, eat, fuck, repeat, not necessarily in that order, meanwhile the guy driving thinks he's above it all. He just wants his strawberries and cream."

"That's a refreshing perspective," said Sunny. "I thought we all agreed that we were basically devolving and becoming more violent as a species, as demonstrated by cable television and spring break in Baja. I kind of like the idea that we're getting more refined."

"Maybe we're not improving overall, but we're definitely becoming more intellectual, more centered in our heads. We identify with our higher brains, not our reptilian brains. Which is as it should be, otherwise we'd still be living like lizards, but it's getting more exaggerated all the time. The more we focus on the higher brain with its cerebral pursuits and primness and detachment from the physical, the more alienated we become from this other very basic part of ourselves. We're never going to escape the fact that we are animals, and that sex is this very physical, basic, grungy, unequal, aggressive scene that is an undeniable part of us, no matter how superior and moral we might think we can become. I can be as eloquent and influential a feminist as I want to be, but somewhere inside me I'm still going to hunger for a big, strong man. It's hardwired into the brain stem. To deny it leads to repression, which leads to frustration, shame, anger, and ultimately violence." Rivka cut into another onion, trying to turn her head away from the fumes. "The whole topic came up because we started out talking about how Americans lose their minds if somebody shows a breast on television, but it's okay to show bodies being pulled out of rubble, people being shot and tortured, maniacs hitting each other in a ring. You know, how various aspects of American culture—our Puritan heritage, for example, but also the more recent hero-savior complex—have repressed the erotic impulse. Shoved down under the surface, it festers and turns into shame, frustration, and anger, then reemerges as an addiction to violence."

"Here, let me take a turn," said Sunny. Rivka went to throw cold water on her face and Sunny took over dicing onions. "You talked about all that last night?"

"Yeah," she called from the sink. "We were on the phone for at least an hour. It was incredible."

"You think he's trying to tell you something? I mean, other than that he's an insightful conversationalist?"

"You mean like he's some kind of wild lizard-man in the sack?"

"Exactly."

She looked up from the paper towel she was using to scrub her face dry. "I've got my fingers crossed."

Sunny finished the onions and went back to her station. She took out the three knives she liked to use for butchering. One was eight inches long, slender, and gently tapered like a blade of grass. The other was six inches and narrow, shaped with a curve at the end for hooking under joints and skin. The third was a classic chef's knife for chopping. All three were marvelously sharp. The Italian shop in San Francisco where Andre had taken them sharpened knives to perfection. With knives this sharp, a piece of meat surrendered all resistance.

She started with the chicken. The smell of raw meat was still a problem, as was the cold touch of it. Only time would strip away the associations of that night. Someday, she reassured herself, the sight of a pristine pink salmon fillet or a pale, tender pork loin would make her smile with anticipation again. She took up the meat shears, deftly snipping at the tendons and cartilage of the chicken on the block in front of her, rendering it neatly flat for roasting. "Joel Hyder call you anymore?" she said.

"Not since Saturday."

"Good."

A strange sourness deadened her senses gradually. By the end of the day, her arms and legs felt leaden. In her mind, darkness reigned. Rivka's talk from the morning haunted her with violent visions, with scenes dominated by primitive cruelty. Humanity seemed a barely contained tide of murderous, purposeless aggression, brimming up under a meager surface of civility and kindness. She longed for the past. For Catelina Alvarez's warm kitchen filled with the good smells of cooking, and for her certainty in the way life should be lived. Catelina went to bed at nine and rose at five. At five-twenty, the kettle sang and coffee was made. Food brought everyone together in a daily communion. There was no talk of the right or wrong of meat. Meat was god's gift to mankind, a bounty to be gratefully enjoyed, like the fruits and vegetables and all the other goodness from the land. The sin was to be ungrateful, to be critical and shun what was given.

She sat in her office in the diminishing light and thought of such tender memories, of the simplicity of her mind in those days. Good and bad were separated by a wide, unbreachable barrier. Was it only because she was a child? Had it been difficult for Catelina to sustain her confidence in her beliefs, to avoid the undertow of chaos? Did she fight against trends away from it? She did. She had often railed against the direction society was taking. She got on her soapbox on plenty of occasions, the subject anything from the deplorable state of supermarket produce to the downfall of manners in the general public and the naïve dependence on modern medicine. Sunny picked up the phone and dialed the Santa Rosa number. Catelina answered immediately. "*Cara menina!*" she said in her ancient, delighted voice. "I knew it would be you. Tell me about your life."

27

Andre canceled their dinner date before she could think of a graceful way of doing so herself. He called to say he was going out with the money people for the second time in as many nights. They wanted to move forward quickly and were already hammering out business plans for a new restaurant. It would probably be a late night, as one of the backers was taking the red-eye to New York and they were hoping to nail down the basics of a deal before he left. They would be delighted if she would join them, but he would understand if she did not feel like making the drive down to San Francisco after work. She did not. He made promises of future nights together, as well as a bright future generally, in which he would open a new restaurant that was truly his from the ground up, designed and run his way. As much as his enthusiasm pleased her, she was tired, and out of sorts, and grateful to be let off the hook. She absolved him of any lingering guilt related to the matter, put down the phone, and welcomed a quiet evening to herself.

She'd brought a bag of Meyer lemons home from the restaurant. She dumped them into a wire vase and placed it on the counter, took one and rolled it between her palms, and breathed in the delicious citrus smell. Meyers were so much more subtle and yet more potent than ordinary lemons. Regular lemons assaulted the nostrils. They were all acid, like a shout. Their rind was rough and more translucent, as though the fruit had less substantive intentions. Meyers had a warm, soft, velvety rind. Their fruit was softer, heavier, and sweeter. And the smell. The smell of them! It was perhaps Sunny's favorite smell. There was the lemon scent of course, but more delicate and complex than the smell of ordinary lemons. The real difference was the hint of pine resin mingled with the citrus. Normal lemons were merely tart. Meyers were complex, with a base note of pine, like the smell of a hot day in the mountains when the pine needles give off their woody musk, and a mid-tone of sweetness and a bell-like chime of citrus high note.

She looked around the kitchen. It was still early. What she really needed was a swim. On another day, she would have driven straight to the gym from work, to dive into the cool water and let the number of each stroke be her only thought, down and back, down and back, counting one to twenty, one to fifty, one to a hundred. Tonight, she had resisted. The subtle disharmony in her body—the tight muscles, stiff joints, the knots in her shoulders—fit the disharmony in her thoughts, which were largely sullen, vaguely hostile, and conflicted. She was indecisive and had stood by the door to her office for ten full minutes, weighing the pros and cons of driving to the gym. In the end, out of apathy more than a real decision, she had driven home.

There was fresh arugula in the refrigerator, so she made a salad and ate it standing up in the kitchen, even though she wasn't hungry. She ate without noticing what she was doing, and only realized she'd been eating when it was gone. The iPod waited on the window sill. She picked it up and turned it on. Nothing. She carried it into the bathroom and held it in front of the blow-dryer, aiming the warm air at each of its orifices in turn. She counted to a hundred, and a hundred again. At the third one hundred, she turned off the blow-dryer and held the iPod ceremoniously with both hands. Still nothing. Whether the mechanisms worked or not, the battery was probably dead. She paced, arriving in the living room with no purpose in mind. There were deep shadows around the furniture and a patch of waning golden light on the floor. A damp chill was settling in.

Beside the hearth stood a neat stack of firewood and a basket of kindling and pinecones. She put a pinecone in the hearth and made a teepee of kindling around it, then crumpled a scrap of newspaper and lit it. When the kindling blazed up to its peak of intensity, she put a medium-sized log across it and another on top. The flames licked the dry logs hungrily. She set the iPod on the mantle. A cross, sour mind such as possessed her tonight was no good for thinking well or talking, no good for creating or appreciating anything. She was trapped. With such a mind, only dull, rote chores were appropriate. This was a mind best suited to paying bills and cleaning the toilet. She went numbly around the house picking up stray items, returning jackets and shoes to their proper places, and fluffing up disheveled pillows, then sat back down in front of the fire. The orange flames, the occasional pop of resin, and the familiar smoky smell enveloped her, replacing the scattered thoughts with the flickering dance of flame.

Stationed on the couch in the deepening twilight, she eyed the stack of mail across the room. On top of it was the DVD Andre had dropped off yesterday. If watching it was to be bitter medicine, now was the time to take it.

She set up her laptop on the coffee table and put the movie in. Classical music played to the opening credits run over stylized animation of a woman trapped in a spider's web while sinister male faces laughed and jeered around her. The story began at a manor house in the countryside, where a fresh-faced new maid was coming to work. The Japanese dialogue was translated in subtitles, unnecessarily. The animation reminded her of *Speed Racer*, with minimal detail, curt movements, and exaggerated expressions. Soon, and predictably, despite the well-meaning efforts of the other maids to safeguard her, the innocent falls into the evil clutches of the master of the house, who imprisons her in the basement and initiates her into the rites of the bondage cult that obsesses him.

In a state of trancelike immobility, she watched the movie from beginning to end, including the scenes that echoed the nightmare discovery of Heidi Romero's body, those in which the little maid was tied as Heidi had been tied and hung from a bracket high on the wall much as Heidi had been hung from the branch of the oak tree. When it was over, she ejected the DVD, put it back in the case, and left it by the door, where it could be removed from the house as quickly as possible. She began to wish Andre hadn't canceled dinner, that they were squeezed into one of the tiny tables at La Poste right now, laughing and eating artichoke salad and drinking a bottle of French Pinot. They had a hard enough time getting together. He worked nights and weekends, she worked days. Monday and Tuesday nights were their only chance to see each other at a reasonable hour, and they'd missed them both. Now it would be days before she would spend more than a few late-night hours with him.

Gripped by a strange mixture of sorrow, disgust, and arousal that immobilized her in a state of despondency, she lay on the floor and felt the heat of the fire against her face. Her mind was held in thrall to the terrible images of the little maid and she could think of nothing else. They played over and over for what seemed like hours. She thought of every character in the threadbare narrative, relived each scene, went backward and forward and back again to certain moments, watching the movie again and again in her imagination until the sheer repetition of the scenes and emotions it portrayed exhausted her. She walked numbly to the shower and then to bed, eager for sleep to wipe the slate of the day clean so she could start over.

She never knew what woke her. Her eyes opened and she climbed out of bed before she knew what she was doing. In the dark living room, the iPod sat on the mantle where she had left it. The white ashes in the fireplace gave off a faint glow. Sunny stood in front of them, where the floor was warm, and felt the slight heat against her shins. She picked up the iPod. It was warm too. She felt for the button she'd tried a dozen times and pushed it. The tiny screen flickered and lit up, hurting her eyes in the dark. A menu appeared. She sat down where she was and pulled her knees up, turning her back to the ashes and hugging herself to stay warm. She slipped the headphones on and selected the play list. Instead of songs titles, a list of files named by date and time appeared. She selected one called "12Jan6PM."

At first, she couldn't hear anything except a faint hissing. Then she heard the cry of a gull followed by thumping. It was the sound of a houseboat rocking against its mooring. A woman spoke in the distance, offering some kind of condolence to whoever she was talking to. She said, "That's terrible," drawing out the middle of the word in sympathy. She said, "I'm sorry to hear you had a bad day," and then, "What makes you say that?"

Sunny hit pause, then worried about the battery running out and switched the device off. She took off the headphones and turned her face to the ashes of the dying fire. The woman was definitely young and the background noises fit the houseboat. It was Heidi, she was sure of it, either talking on the phone or talking to someone beyond the reach of the recorder. Why would she record a phone conversation? And if the conversation was important enough to record, why not use the answering machine and get both sides of the conversation. Sunny tried to remember if she saw one at Heidi's place. Maybe she used one of the dial-in services, in which case she wouldn't be able to record it. Maybe the iPod was all she had. Sunny shivered in the dark room. That had to be Heidi's voice. As eager as she'd been to free Heidi Romero from the events that ended her life, she had failed to do so. Hearing her talk so casually, Sunny realized that Heidi still lived in her imagination in a perpetual state of torment and suffering at the hands of her killer. This voice was the real Heidi. There was no fear in it, no dread, no urgency. She was just a young woman talking on the phone as if she had all the time in the world.

Sunny took the iPod and went into the bathroom. She closed and locked the door, checked that the window was locked, and sat down on the bathmat. She pulled two towels down from the rack, arranged one over the tub, and put the other around her legs. Then she settled back and put the headphones on. The first recording picked up in the middle of a conversation about a ski trip. Heidi described her abilities, modestly, Sunny suspected. The person on the other end of the line was presumably Mark

Weisman. They talked about various options. Heidi said in theory she preferred the mountains at Whistler or Snowbird, but Tahoe was reporting the best conditions. They talked about skiing Rocky Mountain powder versus the hardpack typical of the Sierras. Heidi's voice was light and full of laughter. The idea of a ski trip with her new romance was obviously exciting. Judging by the sound of Heidi's voice and the occasional cry of a gull, she was sitting on the deck. Near the end of the conversation, someone with a deep voice and much closer to the microphone than Heidi cleared his throat.

The file ended and she skipped down to the next. It was another telephone conversation between, presumably, Heidi and Mark Weisman. They seemed to be talking about Mark's work schedule and when he would be in town next. Sunny listened for a few minutes, then skipped down to the next file. There were several innocuous sentences, then Heidi said, somewhat snidely, "Is your wife going to be there?" She backed off, her voice gentler. "I was just asking. . . . No, no, I love *Vedana*. You know that. I always have a great time. . . . Honey, *Vedana* is the best, but it's your wife's, too. . . . I have some stuff to do in the morning. I can meet you there at noon." Mark must have said something that irritated her again, because her next words sounded edgy. "And whose fault is that? I have all weekend free, but that doesn't do us any . . ." Her voice trailed off and Sunny heard the French doors being forced closed.

She scrolled through the rest of the menu, but there was nothing else in the memory. There were over a dozen of Heidi's phone conversations recorded, all of them, it seemed, with Mark Weisman.

She went into her bedroom and set the iPod up to record, then left it on her nightstand with the microphone angled toward the door and walked out to the living room. The front door was the farthest point from the microphone and she stood in front of it and said, "Good evening, ladies and gentlemen, this is a test of the Association of Culinary Professionals Specializing in Crime Scene Evidence Recovery. This is only a test."

The recording was not as clear as the ones of Heidi, but it was comparable. It stood to reason that the microphone might have been damaged or clogged with mud, which would naturally degrade the quality of the recording. Sunny wrapped the iPod in a tea towel and put it on the bottom of a drawer full of kitchen towels.

She knew the woman speaking was Heidi because she mentioned working at the sporting goods shop, among other details, and even though Heidi never said his name, she knew the person on the other end of the line had to be Mark Weisman, for lots of reasons, but especially because of the reference to the *Vedana*. The person who had cleared his throat had made recordings of Heidi talking on the phone to her lover. It was therefore someone who lived very near her. A neighbor, or at most two boats over. Sunny thought of the woman playing the piano, and how the screech of the parrot named Chopin and the ringing of the woman's telephone both had sounded loud and close enough to be in the same room with them. Standing in the kitchen, her eyes widened with fearful comprehension as she remembered Ronald Fetcher leaning over the wooden railing of the dock, watching her from above while she fished the iPod out of the mud. *The tide reveals all kinds of interesting things. What did you find down there?*

He had an iPod with him then. He'd been wearing one when she first met him. Ronald Fetcher lived two boats down from Heidi, in the place owned by the people who were away. It was then that a memory came back to her. She hadn't thought of it since it happened. She and Rivka and Joel Hyder had been in the canoe, going back under the dock so they could go up and around the other side. They glided between the houseboats. The boat skimmed along level with the downstairs windows. Not intending to, she had spied on Ronald Fetcher watching cartoons in the daytime. She had thought it sad that a grown man would be indoors in the middle of a beautiful day watching cartoons. But he wasn't watching cartoons. She could see the television screen, and the close-up of the buxom Japanese girl with the wide, frightened eyes. Ronald Fetcher had been watching anime, wearing his headphones.

With that thought came the final connection between Kimberly Knolls, Vedana Vineyards, Heidi Romero, and Ronald Fetcher. Everything snapped into place at last and she wondered that she hadn't understood days ago. She tried to remember exactly what she had told Ronald Fetcher when she found the iPod, and what Vurleen had said about him in the parking lot. He was moving, but when? She thought of Vurleen standing outside the harbormaster's office, one hand on her hip, the other patting gently at the side of her well-lacquered hair. Something about the Mendels coming back. Ronald had to leave. *Got to. They'll be back before the end of the week.*

Sunny went to her desk and took her cell phone out of its cradle. It was almost four in the morning, but on what day? Tuesday? She checked the date against the calendar. Wednesday. What exactly did "before the end of the week" mean?

Four A.M. There was plenty of time to drive down and back before work. It might not accomplish much, but it would help kill the time between now and the hour it seemed reasonable to telephone Sergeant Harvey. There would be no more sleeping tonight, but she would certainly reap some satisfaction in confirming that Ronald's little beige sports car was still in the parking lot at Pelican Point. She could even note the license plate for Sergeant Harvey's convenience. If she was very lucky, Vurleen or Dean Blodger might be stationed in the harbormaster's office early. If anybody was an early riser, it was Dean Blodger. She could tell just by the tidy look of him. He would be an invaluable resource when it came to keeping an eye on Ronald Fetcher.

28

The solid dark before sunrise meant one of three things to Sunny, all hardwired by repetition in childhood. One was manual labor. Predawn was the time of work boots, work trucks, toolboxes, and thermoses. Three to five in the morning was the time of day owned by males headed outdoors to work. If that wasn't why a person was awake, getting dressed silently in the dark, then it could only be for a skiing or camping trip. If she had grown up in another household in another place, maybe this would be the hour of the stockbroker, the baker, the doctor on call. As it was, early morning held magic and excitement. In her family, they set off on adventures at this hour, driving out into the mountains, watching the night wildlife coming in from their hunts, waiting for the first glow of daylight to reveal the contours of a new landscape.

Sunny laced her work shoes, pulled on her jacket, and tucked a notepad and pencil into her pocket. The truck waited at the curb, a splash of streetlight hitting its root beer–colored hood. She opened the passenger side and propped a thermos full of coffee in the well by the stick shift, set a slab of toast with jelly on a paper towel on the dashboard, and put her duffle bag, knife kit, and purse on the seat. She rolled down the window the way she liked, so the cold morning air would wake her up on the drive. The streetlight went out as she walked around to the driver's side. She always thought of Catelina Alvarez when that happened, and how such incidents amused her. The old Portuguese woman theorized that the inner light in a person did it, shining in some wavelength our eyes could not detect but the light sensors could. It was one of her few indulgences in the mystical. Her conversation with Catelina had made all the difference last night. She was so certain and sane. "Nothing is pure evil or pure good, Sonya. The world is a constant negotiation between the two. Every minute, you create your way. And sometimes you have to fight."

It took just over an hour to drive to Sausalito. A white moon, perfectly placed above the city skyline, shimmered off the San Francisco Bay as she descended the last hill. The timing was perfect. There was just enough time to get the license plate number, speak with the harbormaster or Vurleen if possible, and get back before Rivka started to wonder where she was. Sunny turned off the freeway and drove under the underpass. She stopped at the first light and a pack of bicyclists pedaled by in the other direction, their matching Spandex gear a blaze of neon sponsorship. At the second light, she waited in the left-turn lane. There were no other cars. The lights seemed to be red in all directions. She waited, watching the red left-turn arrow. She was just on the point of turning despite it when the beige sports car pulled out of the Pelican Point parking lot, paused at the light, and turned toward the freeway. As it went by, she caught a glimpse of Ronald Fetcher at the wheel.

Two cars came from the other direction. Sunny waited for them to pass, then did a U-turn against the red, gunning the big engine and cranking the wheel around. Up ahead, Ronald

Fetcher cruised through a yellow light and continued under the freeway toward Mill Valley. Sunny looked both ways and blew through the red light after him. She fumbled in her purse for her cell phone. The Mill Valley or Sausalito police were the logical people to call. The difficulty would be explaining why they should pull over the beige sports car. Sergeant Harvey could compel them to action, but by the time she reached him, explained the situation, and waited for him to get the local cops on the move, Fetcher could be long gone. If she was right about what had happened to Heidi, she wouldn't be surprised if the car and the name were borrowed. Ronald Fetcher wouldn't move to Guerneville and list his name and phone number in the local white pages to be looked up at anyone's convenience. Any day now, maybe right now, he would simply vanish. The license plate was one tangible way to track him, at least until he landed another ride. It might even make sense to stay with him until he arrived wherever he was headed. If his business took long enough, she might have time to get Sergeant Harvey on the phone and get the professionals on the scene. That was thinking too far ahead. More important to get that license plate.

Fetcher breezed through another yellow light. Sunny stopped at the red to let a stream of early commuters turn toward the freeway in front of her. She rounded the corner to the next intersection just in time to see the last of Ronald's car head west. They began the climb up Mount Tamalpais. She followed, catching occasional glimpses of the beige car as they ascended the curvy road. Ronald's coupe took the curves appreciably better than the truck. Sunny couldn't be sure exactly what he was driving without a better look, but it looked like some kind of old Jaguar. It was definitely a vintage model, probably from the seventies. Two door, conservative lines. None of the curves of the sexier, earlier models. That would be too flashy for Ronald. He went for the country club classic style. He wasn't flying around the corners in a rush, he was cruising, but it was still good work for Sunny to keep the pace. She leaned forward, as though to urge the truck ahead.

He had chosen an excellent road if his intention was to outpace her. There wasn't a stop sign or traffic light for miles. From here on, the narrow two-lane road twisted up the mountain, switchbacking across steep ravines lined with towering eucalyptus. At the ridgeline, there were various options, some that headed down the other side toward the Pacific in switchbacks just as sharp and steep, some that followed the spine toward the summit. If she didn't get close enough to read his license plate soon, she never would. Her best hope was a bus or traffic to hold him up. At this hour, when the sky was just beginning to lighten from black to navy blue, and headed as they were toward open land and open sea, away from houses and cities, they were less and less likely to run into another car, let alone traffic. She was going to lose him. She realized now she should have called Sergeant Harvey the instant she saw Fetcher driving away from Pelican Point. Maybe it wasn't too late. Maybe Steve could still get somebody to intercept him. She flipped open her phone and watched it search for a signal in vain. They were too far out, wending between too many tall trees and steep hillsides. The name of the game now was to stick with him. If she was lucky and he headed down to Stinson Beach, he would hit stop signs in town. She could jot down the license number, head back over the hill, and still be at work before the day got out of hand.

Where could he be going at this hour? If he had decamped from the Mendels' houseboat and was making his getaway, it was a strange direction to make it. Narrow, winding country roads weren't the fastest route out of town, and it was harder to blend in with fewer cars around. He said he found a place in Guerneville. What if she was wrong about Ronald Fetcher? There was always that possibility. In that case, this drive made more sense. A man who liked Guerneville liked countryside. He could be on any number of errands. Maybe he wanted to see the sunrise from the top of the mountain. One thing was certain, with every mile, she was getting farther away from work.

A deer appeared on the bank. Sunny braked and it jogged across the road, trotting up the other side to a place were it could dip back into the forest. She downshifted, accepting the possibility that she had lost him and wondering what Ronald Fetcher did all day. How had the Mendels met him? How did he come to be staying at their place? Who really knew who Ronald Fetcher was, anyway? The thought chilled her.

The road dipped down sharply and flung itself around a hairpin turn and back up the other side of the ravine. The forest crowded in from either side and shut out the faint blue light of morning, cloaking the road in dense darkness. Sunny rolled down the window and smelled the mossy air. She quit driving so hard and let the truck take the corners at more manageable speeds. She told herself she would turn around at the next opportunity. It was getting too late. She would drive back to where there was a signal and telephone Steve Harvey like she should have done to start with, then leave it to them and go to work. Way out here, the police would be able to track down the beige Jaguar, even if it took time to convince them to do it.

There was nowhere to turn around. The road fell away steeply to one side and was carved into the hillside on the other. As far as Sunny could remember, it climbed another ridge up ahead, then ran along the top for half a mile or so before it dove over the side again. There ought to be a place to turn around up there. It was with this thought in mind, watching for a wide spot in the road more than Ronald Fetcher's bumper, that Sunny accelerated out of a turn and nearly crashed headlong into the beige sports car wedged perpendicular across the road.

29

The wheels locked up and the truck went into a slide. All Sunny could think of was what would happen if the truck went off the edge. There would be nothing to stop the fall but bush lupin and sagebrush. Unless the truck slammed into a boulder, it would roll all the way to the bottom of the canyon. She turned into the slide and remembered she was supposed to ease up on the brakes. There wasn't time. All she could do was hope the wheels didn't go over the edge. Even if she avoided a freefall, she'd still be stuck until a tow truck came to get her out of there.

The truck came to rest within a foot of the beige coupe and nearly parallel to it. Ronald Fetcher was not in the driver's seat. Sunny decided not to hang around to find out what happened to him. It would be tight, but it if took twenty tries she would turn around and get out of there. She put the truck in reverse and looked over her shoulder. She never saw Ronald Fetcher emerge from the edge of the road, open her door, and jerk her out of the truck. The first thing she felt was his arm around her neck, cocked under her chin, dragging her backward.

While he was off balance from pulling her away from the vehicle, she took the opportunity to backpedal toward the bank. They went over in a sickening fall and crashed through the brush, landing hard on the rocks. Sunny's head slammed against the ground and she felt something sharp drive into her scalp. Ronald lost his grip on her with the impact and she scrambled away from him, tearing her fingers and gouging her knees as she scrambled back up the rocky bank. She still hadn't had a good look at Ronald Fetcher, but she soon felt his fingers close around her ankle and pull her back down the slope. Her hands gripped at the crumbling rocks. Ronald whipped her onto her side and lunged forward, gripping her throat between his hands. The sensation overwhelmed her. She had never felt anything so debilitating. It was clear, obvious, that he would suffocate her in a matter of minutes, even seconds. He was crushing her esophagus. Even if he let go, she doubted she would be able to breathe again. Her hands pried at his fingers. For a man, Fetcher wasn't particularly strong. His grip was wiry and desperate. Nevertheless, it was doing the job without trouble. Sunny pulled her knees up and tried to force him off her with her feet. Fetcher responded by lifting her up and slamming her back into the dirt. Her head bounced off the ground and vibrated like a tuning fork. She looked into his pale white face flushed red with the effort of strangling her, the reptilian eyes lined in red, the nose too narrow for the span of flaccid cheeks. He was older than she thought. At a glance she would have guessed forty-five, but from this angle she could see his skin slipping forward away from the bone. He was closer to fifty or fifty-five. What a thought to have while dying, she thought, that Ronald Fetcher could use work.

She struggled against him, and Fetcher leaned into her all the harder, pushing with all his weight on her throat. Soon what little light there was would fade, she would lose consciousness, her body would go limp, and it would be over. She stared at the face, distorted with effort, glowering over her. A thread of blood had run from a gash on his cheek. She blinked slowly, for relief from the sight of him, for a taste of the black peace that would come soon enough.

"So you're the one who found my installation," he said, shaking her, staring at her with a wet smile. Saliva had gathered at the corners of his mouth. "That was some of my best work. How did you like it? She looked beautiful, didn't she? Admit it. You liked it. Otherwise you wouldn't keep coming around." Sunny stared into his eyes. She was curious now, with nothing to fear any longer, what the eyes of a killer revealed. He looked back at her with mud-colored eyes that said nothing. There was no passion, no anger, no fire. It was as if they were disconnected from his words, disconnected even from his thoughts.

"She was perfect," he said, swallowing. "The perfect body, the perfect white skin. Most women are too fat. The flesh bulges out when you tie them. She was like a drawing."

Every few seconds, he sucked back the saliva and swallowed. "I hope Bruce Knolls is crying like a baby. I wish I could have been there to see his face. Of course, you had to blunder in with the police and take all the drama out of it. He never even got to see his little whore strung up in front of his precious winery. You robbed us both of that pleasure."

His words were distracting him and his grip loosened. Sunny let go of his wrist and skimmed her hand over the ground as far as she could reach in search of some kind of weapon.

"I'm glad he's stuck with that bitch Kimberly," he said. "He deserves her. The greedy bastard deserves an ungrateful whore like her."

She stretched her fingers over the rocks, prying at them. Those that came away did so by crumbling into tiny, jagged pieces. She wiggled over to gain new ground, causing him to squeeze her throat with renewed force. More than pain, what she felt was immobility. He had found the place where she was utterly vulnerable. She reached blindly for some rock or stick to use before her breath ran out. Her mind was already beginning to let go. She could feel her will to struggle waning as the last of the oxygen in her blood expired.

"We had all the time in the world," he said coyly. "But you had to rush things. Now look what you've done. You've ruined everything, again. Now I'll have to leave you here to rot. There will be no glory for you. Nothing left behind but a dirty corpse. You could have given yourself to art, but instead the buzzards and the maggots will have you."

She pushed with her feet and wiggled another inch to the right, stretching out her arm. At first, when she felt the cold touch of glass on her fingertips, she almost forgot what it meant. She was slipping away from her circumstances and she registered the coolness without thinking anything beyond the sensation. It took a second for her mind to register *glass, bottle*. She gripped it with her fingers and felt the round open end with her thumb. Gathering the last of her strength, she seized it by the neck and slammed it with everything in her power into Ronald Fetcher's temple.

He let go of her and leaned back, stunned. She rolled away and gasped for air. Her throat burned and she convulsed, gagging. Her head hung between her arms as she tried to breathe for what felt like minutes, hours. At last she could sit up and pull a ragged, painful breath into her chest. Across from her, Fetcher was kneeling, his eyes dazed and staring dully at her. A nasty abrasion oozed a thick stream of blood from his temple where it met his hairline. She turned and climbed up the bank, clawing at the rock face as it slipped away under each attempt to move up it. She fought the burning in her chest and the urge to lie down and surrender to unconsciousness.

At the road, she staggered to her feet and ran for the truck, certain she could hear Fetcher behind her. The way the truck had come to rest, the passenger-side door was closest to her now. There was no time to get in, roll up the window, and lock the door. She flipped open her knife kit and pulled out the knife in the middle, her favorite, the seven-inch, forged steel fillet knife, the one sharp enough to slice through a chicken bone with the most tender of downward thrusts. He would be coming up the bank even now, and he would see the knife and know she was not afraid to use it. Her fingers closed firmly around the base and her mind hardened with resolve as she turned to face her attacker.

He had moved more quickly than she expected. When she turned, he was already lunging toward her. She did nothing but hold the blade steady and feel the soft flesh of the abdomen give way as Ronald Fetcher impaled himself upon it.

He sounded bad. Curled in the ditch at the base of the embankment, his breath came in short gasps thick with saliva and blood. She stood over him. The light had come at last, in the form of diffused pastel pink and gold along both horizons. Blood seeped out from under Fetcher's hand where he clutched at his side. His eyes met hers but he said nothing. Fat beads of sweat had broken out on his forehead. She watched him, deciding how seriously he was hurt. He didn't seem capable of getting up, but she went over to the old Jaguar, leaned in, and removed the keys from the ignition, just in case.

Sunny set the knife on the floor of the truck and got in. The truck had slid partway around when she stopped, but it still took several tries to get it headed in the right direction on the narrow road. No cars had come since they'd stopped. She realized with surprise that their struggle had taken no more than a few minutes.

She drove slowly. Operating the steering wheel and the pedals felt like new, alien tasks she wasn't quite sure how to perform. Her hands shook as she flipped open the cell phone. It found a signal at the top of the ridge.

Once the police were on their way, she left the truck and walked up the hill to where the view opened up facing the sea. Sitting in the truck, she kept imagining him in the window behind her, in the rearview mirror, crouching just out of sight beside the door. It was better to be outside. The grass was lush and scattered with early wildflowers. The first spray of California poppies, a scattering of lupin, a splash of tiny white daisies, and nearby, a lone buttercup. Songbirds announced the sunrise as if nothing had happened. As she stood there, she imagined a deeply reassuring peacefulness untouched by human aggression emanated from the mountain. It was people who where sick, she thought. People who destroyed things and caused each other pain. She studied the distant slopes with their patches of deep green forest and open meadow. Nature gives and grows, humans take and consume. Humanity has abandoned the pursuit of peace. It is no longer even a virtue. Now aggression and greed and power are what matter.

The coming light lifted her spirits even as bitter thoughts drove them downward. Ronald Fetcher's face still loomed over her, her throat still ached with the crushing force of his fingers. She thought of him lying in the ditch by the side of the road, enduring the pain of his injury. She hoped no cars would come. He might still be dangerous. She looked back toward the empty road. As she did so, a movement in the grass caught her eye and she turned with animal alertness. It was a large cat, not thirty feet away. She recognized it from pictures in the wildlife books she read as a kid, though she had never seen one in real life before. It was not a mountain lion, it was a bobcat, with the trademark spots, short tail, and flanged cheeks. It glanced at her, then went back to staring at a spot on the ground directly in front of it with the intensity of those responsible for their own sustenance. It crouched, pulled up on its toes as if about to pounce. Sunny watched for several minutes. The bobcat didn't move. She turned back to staring at the open horizon of the sea.

Some tiny adjustment made her look again, just in time to see the bobcat pounce, coming up with a soft bundle in its mouth. There was no noise and no squirming. The tiny prey lay quietly in the bobcat's jaws. The cat turned immediately and disappeared into the bushes.

Sunny felt a tickle and put a hand to her head. Her fingers came away wet with blood.

30

Wade Skord lifted the paellera from the ground like a man lifting a pot of molten steel from the forge. Monty ducked in and fed the pit fire with dry lavender clippings and oak chips. Lavender-scented smoke rose up, filling the backyard with its ancient smell. Wade lowered the simmering paella back into the pit and backed away, shaking off the heat on his face. Rivka squatted next to the fire and edged the corner of a spatula under the thick stew, revealing a crusty golden-brown layer on the bottom of the pan. She looked up at Wade with obvious pride. "Nice. We've got a perfect layer of *socarrat*."

"That's some kind of Mexican field hockey, right?"

"That would be the layer of rice that sticks to the bottom of the paellera. It's the best part."

Annabelle, Monty Lenstrom's live-in girlfriend and new fiancée, edged closer to the fire and peered at the bubbling expanse of yellow rice and vegetables. "What is this we're going to eat?"

"Paella," said Rivka. "Vegetarian paella, to be precise. It's kind of like Spanish risotto, but less creamy."

"No meat?" said Andre, walking up to the group with a frown. He was wearing a white button-down shirt and had his black hair pushed back in easy waves from his forehead. Sunny looked at him like she hadn't seen him in a month, basking in the sight of him.

"No meat," said Rivka. "We thought we'd give the beasts of the earth a break for the night. Except for the chickens. I had to do in one of our feathered friends for the stock. Vegetarian stock is a crime worse than poultricide."

"What else is in it?" said Annabelle, holding the stem of her wineglass between pale fingers.

"Are you eating again?" asked Rivka, standing up. "Monty said you were on some crazy diet."

"Of course I eat. I just eat less, and I fast more frequently. It's not a diet, it's a lifestyle change. Carrying around large quantities of food in your digestive system all the time is hard on your body. We're not designed to digest constantly."

Rivka studied the willowy Annabelle. "I feel springier when I'm thinner, that's for sure."

"Me too," said Annabelle. "Besides, food tastes better when you're really hungry. Is that a fiddlehead?"

Rivka looked at the paella. "It has fiddleheads, roasted red peppers, eggplant, fava beans from the garden, fresh morels, peas from the garden, rice, tomato, aioli, thyme and baby carrots from the garden, artichoke hearts, a ten-dollar pinch of saffron threads for color, and about a pound of garlic."

"I hope you didn't make it vegi on my account," said Sunny. She took the bottle of Pinot that Monty had just opened. "Anyone?" She filled the empty glasses, then poured one for herself. "I'm over the meat hang-up. I mean, I don't think I'll ever like the smell of raw chicken, but I'm more or less back to normal."

"Just when I was preparing to become a vegetarian cook," said Andre.

"That would be a spectacular transformation."

"I was going to open Napa Valley's first vegetarian raw foods restaurant."

"You laugh now," said Annabelle, "but when we're all eating raw foods and living to be a hundred you'll have to apologize for making fun."

"You guys enjoy it," said Andre. "They can bury me with a duck leg in my hand and a greasy smile on my face."

"Finding a dead body would put anybody off meat," said Monty. "What I want to know is how skewering Ronald Fetcher like a pig on a spit brought you back into the carnivorous fold."

"The great spirit sent me a vision," said Sunny. "I was standing up there on the ridge waiting for the cops to arrive when I saw a bobcat catch a bunny. I saw the whole thing. There was no malice in the bobcat. He was just having his breakfast. I had been enjoying this fantasy that nature was peaceful and only humans were deadly. Then the bobcat put on his carnivore show for me and I remembered the obvious truth. Death is part of life."

"That's what I've always said," said Wade. "These people who think being a vegetarian absolves them of violence haven't taken a good look at a garden. Those carrots don't want to die any more than anybody else, they just can't say so. Look out there." He gestured to the vineyard. "Bud break is like a high note that starts soft and builds. By summer it's a gospel choir shaking the rafters. Those vines are as full of life as any living creature."

"But there's a difference, don't you think?" said Sunny. "If I cut my arm it hurts, but cutting my hair doesn't. Some things feel pain, some don't."

"Anything that strives feels pain when it's thwarted," said Wade. "The vines don't mind being cut back in winter. They don't mind giving up their grapes. But if you pull them up when they're in full leaf, you hear about it."

"By that logic, we should only eat what is willingly given," said Annabelle, flicking her red hair over her shoulder. "That was actually a quite eloquent argument in favor of vegetarianism, from the last source I would ever have imagined could produce it."

"It might be, if I believed life was meant to be or ever could be an entirely painless process, which I don't," said Wade. "We've insulated ourselves so well from the facts that we forget pain and loss are built into the system. Everything grows, peaks, gets old, and dies. Pain and loss are part of that process. And along the way, in order to survive, we have to eat, which is as inherently destructive as it is generative. I must consume another life, whether it's part of a fern or part of a lamb, in order to sustain my own life." He paused to sip his wine and give Sunny a long look. "Besides, if God didn't want us to eat animals, he wouldn't have made them out of meat."

"I'll drink to that," said Monty, lifting his glass. "Now, can I get the lowdown on this whole Ronald Fetcher business, or are you going to keep it secret forever?"

"It's hardly a secret," said Sunny. "The *Napa Register* published everything I knew and more two days ago. What do you want to know?"

"Well, first of all, why on earth did you follow a murderer into the middle of nowhere and nearly get yourself killed? This new tendency of yours is getting chronic."

"I wasn't sure he was a murderer, for one thing, and for another, I couldn't let him get away. Would you really want

Ronald Fetcher running around out there? And besides, I was in the truck. I never imagined he would be so good at getting me out of it before I even knew what happened. I always feel invincible in the truck."

"And why did he kill Heidi Romero?"

"The most tragic reason. A mistake. Not that he probably wasn't going to kill somebody someday, but he chose Heidi based on a misunderstanding. You have to go back to the beginning. Kim Knolls started the ball rolling when she met Ronald at the Flamingo Inn for an afternoon delight. Ronald basically fell for her in his psycho way. When he started hounding her to meet him again, she used her husband as a foil. She told Ronald she couldn't see him anymore because she was married and couldn't betray Bruce. Which was a line, of course. She'd had her fun with the creepy stranger and she was done with him, end of story. As far as I can tell, he started to believe that Bruce Knolls had stolen Kim away from him, or at the very least Bruce stood in the way of his relationship with Kim. Meanwhile, he moves into the Mendels' houseboat on Liberty Dock and voilà, a new obsession presents itself in the form of Heidi Romero, which was natural enough since every man who crossed her path seemed to want her for himself."

She left off. Monty gestured for her to keep going.

"Those houseboats are not very private, especially Heidi's. He could look in her windows if he walked by the dock. He could even catch a glimpse of her taking a shower. From a canoe, he could watch her sunbathe on the back deck. And if the French doors were open or if she was on the back deck, he could hear practically every word of her phone conversations."

"Thus the iPod," said Monty.

"Exactly. He started recording her conversations, presumably for later personal enjoyment. Somewhere along the line he heard her mention something about *Vedana*. That put him over the edge. Here he'd gone to the trouble of finding himself a new obsession, and that bastard Bruce Knolls was messing it up again. Either he never actually heard Mark's name, or he was too far gone to realize his mistake. It was the wrong Vedana too, but he never knew that.

"After that it's pretty much a standard abduction scenario. He chooses a night when she's home alone. He's already established a habit of fiddling around with the trash at odd hours. He either breaks in or gets her to let him in, incapacitates her somehow, and puts her in a big trash bag. Then all he has to do is carry her out to the dock, toss her in the big rubber trash can, and take her back to his place. Later, he just takes the container out to the bins in the parking lot like always."

"Why didn't she scream?" said Rivka.

"Probably he drugged her. Steve Harvey is being mum about the details. He doesn't want to do anything that could mess up the trial."

"Will you have to testify?" said Monty.

"Steve says I'll probably have to. I'm going to have to give testimony at the courthouse with Fetcher staring at me."

"Not fun."

"It's Kim Knolls who's going to have a tough time. That whole scene is going to set every tabloid on fire from here to New Jersey."

"When all that dirt comes out, it's going to destroy their marriage and their business," said Wade. "There's not going to be anything left of Vedana Vineyards but a FOR SALE sign."

"Maybe, maybe not," said Annabelle. "It depends on how they handle their scandal. Kim Knolls could come out of it a pop culture icon. She could become some kind of S&M diva."

Monty stared at the paella. "So he brought the body up here to rub Bruce Knolls's nose in it."

"Right."

"And he used the harbormaster's truck to do it."

"Right. He broke in and took the keys to the truck and Dean Blodger's work shoes. That way, if anybody traced the truck or the footprints, they'd lead to the harbormaster. When he got back, he put the keys and the shoes back, and took some petty cash to make it look like a robbery."

Rivka poked at the paella. "Wade, I think it's time to take this bad boy off the fire."

"Exactly when did you figure all this out?" said Andre.

"Not until it was almost too late. The recordings were the big breakthrough. But I should have figured it out before then. I should have known the day we heard the neighbor playing the piano and I saw Ronald Fetcher watching anime. I was so fixated on Heidi's secret lover, it took me a long time to see the obvious. Then even when I figured it out, I still thought maybe I was wrong. What Fetcher really was didn't sink in until we were up there on the mountain and I realized he was going to kill me. If he hadn't dropped his iPod, he would have gotten away."

"And Dean Blodger would be in hot water," said Wade. "Or Mark Weisman. Some kind of warrant would have been waiting for that guy at the airport."

"Absolutely," said Sunny. "Do you know what Steve Harvey was doing while Fetcher was leaving his blood all over Mount

Tam? He was driving down to Pelican Point to question Dean Blodger for the fourth time."

"I just hope they convict that guy and put him away for good," said Annabelle.

"You're telling me," said Sunny. "I wouldn't sleep too easy if I knew he was out roaming around. People tend to hold a grudge for that kind of experience, even if they brought it on themselves."

"Knife fights do have a way of sowing enmity," said Rivka. "Everyone to the table, it's time to eat before the paella gets too thick."

They sat at benches and upturned sections of logs arranged around the rough table in back of Wade's house, and Rivka filled everyone's bowls while Monty filled their glasses. From his place at the head of the table, Wade raised his glass. "To peace in the valley," he said, "and to bud break."

"To spring," said Sunny.

They stood to chime glasses, then settled in to devour the savory paella. Andre Morales leaned close and placed a warm kiss on Sunny's nape. "My samurai."

Monty turned to Annabelle. "My testa rossa."

31

The board rose up with the cresting green wave, nose pointed skyward, then tipped over the other side. Sunny paddled with single-minded vigor, worried the next wave would break before she made it over the top. She'd already had enough icy salt water forced down the back of her wetsuit and up her nose that morning to encourage her to paddle harder. The next wave was less steep. With a dozen more strokes, the water flattened and she made good progress. When she paused to look around, she saw the others were sitting their boards nearby, gazing toward the horizon. She was outside.

She sat up and caught her breath. Joel Hyder gave her an ear-to-ear grin. Rivka flashed her a smile laced with terror. Rivka's hands were white with cold and gripped the sides of the surf-board as though it was about to be ripped out from under her. Beyond them, a pod of seasoned surfers waited in stern silence for the next set. The water sparkled with a hundred thousand flashes of sunlight on ripple. Sunny looked back toward the shore. The hills to either side framed the sandy beach with lush grasses and wildflowers. Overhead, seagulls cruised a sky blue like a marble. Sunny's feet dangled to either side of the board, snugly wrapped in thick neoprene. She took in the fresh morning, then judiciously scanned the water for fins. A wave rolled toward them, mounting as it neared. It lifted up her board and passed under her. She turned to watch its back swell and finally roll over with a crash. Another ridge followed.

"Get ready," said Joel. "This one's ours. Ready? Turn around now and start paddling."

Sunny and Rivka wiggled their boards around and stretched out flat on them, dipping their arms in the cold water.

"Paddle harder. Harder!" Joel called from farther down the swell. "Paddle!" Sunny felt the wave raise her up, growing under the board. The beach seemed far below. It was like riding at the top of a ladder hurtling toward the sand at reckless speed. "Stand up now. Now!" came Joel's voice.

She put her hands on the rails and held her breath, pulling her feet underneath her in one gesture. Slowly, she stood up. The board held steady as she raced toward the shore. She threw a glance at Rivka and saw her standing on the wide deck of her longboard, braced like a dog on a horse's back. Beyond her, Joel Hyder and his enormous grin egged them on. Rivka rode steady and flashed her a look she'd never seen on her face before. It was the uncalculated, spontaneous expression of pure, wordless delight. No wonder Heidi had loved surfing so much. To be lifted up by a force of such grace and power and carried along for a few exhilarating seconds was pure magic. Sunny had never felt anything like it. She looked at the green valley ahead and the blue sky above, and felt the rush of wave speed. The journey was over. Heidi Romero was free.

Acknowledgments

Quite a number of people contributed to this book in one way or another, whether by reading early drafts, sharing insights and experiences, offering their expertise, or, in the best cases, opening a bottle of something juicy over a good meal and great conversation. These include but certainly are not limited to Rebecca Harrach, Jonathan Waters, Randy Brown, Michal and Iran Venera, Suzanne Groth Jones, Becky Buol, David Tellman, Giulio at Ferrari, Katherine Rochlin, David Pierce, Elise Proulx, Dale C., Randy S., Gary B., Doug and Sue Antonick, Tom and Gretchen Worthington, Norm, Fred Mills, Sue Antonick, Andrew Stern, and David Polinsky. Regardless of whom I may have consulted during the research of this book, any errors in the final text are entirely my own. I would also like to thank the incomparable Mr. Ewers for his steady supply of amusing commentary and inspiration, and Judy Balmain, whose wisdom and companionship make everything possible. Finally, more thanks and gratitude to Jay Schaefer and the staff at Chronicle Books for their ongoing good cheer, intelligence, and generous support.

—NG